ANOTHER YOU

Jane Cable

SAPERE
BOOKS

ANOTHER YOU

Published by Sapere Books.

11 Bank Chambers, Hornsey, London, N8 7NN,
United Kingdom

saperebooks.com

ISBN: 978-1-913028-51-0

In memory of my parents, the six men who died at Studland on 4th April 1944, and a whole generation who sacrificed so much.

ACKNOWLEDGEMENTS

Another You began as a short story and when I showed it to my mother, she told me I had the opening of a novel. Although the manuscript has changed beyond all recognition since then, I am hugely grateful for her insight.

There is a fair amount of history in the book and two people in particular have helped in this respect. The first was John Pearson, the man who restored the Valentine tank referred to in the story and organised the memorial to the six soldiers and the 2004 commemorations. I was lucky enough to meet him — and his tank — on the seventieth anniversary of Exercise Smash. Background on wartime Studland was provided by National Trust warden Stewart Rainbird, who received a lottery grant to research the oral history of the era on the peninsular and was happy to share his findings.

I also needed to know what serving in the army in the Middle East was like at the time of the book, and former Paratrooper Kevin Stokes was generous with his time and his insights into both this and the after-effects of combat. On a lighter note I also needed to research life in a pub, and time spent propping up the bar at The Victory Inn at Towan Cross in Cornwall has proved invaluable. Thank you, Buffy Smith.

A special mention goes to my Texan friend Marsha Smith, who checked the American dialogue. Any errors in this respect are purely my own.

My road to publication started when my first novel, *The Cheesemaker's House*, won the inaugural Words for the Wounded Independent Novel of the Year Award and Margaret Graham, the moving force behind Words for the Wounded, has become my literary godmother. I owe her a huge debt of thanks her encouragement and support.

Having established authors you can turn to for advice is invaluable, and I would like to thank Claire Dyer and Roger Hubank for letting me benefit from their experience. Equally important are the writers in your life you can laugh, cry and scream with. Thank you Carol Thomas, Kitty Wilson, Cassandra Grafton, Susanna Bavin and Kirsten Hesketh.

Amy Durant, the Editorial Director at Sapere, has the patience of a saint and is a very gifted editor. I can honestly say this book would not be the same without her input.

Last but certainly not least, my husband Jim. My rock. My world. Thank you.

PROLOGUE

Sand. It's in his nose, his mouth, his eyes. Flat on his stomach, he burrows into its softness as best he can. Another volley of gunfire bursts overhead and the soldier beside him convulses. He was more than half dead when he dragged him here.

Yesterday — just yesterday — he could not even have imagined this horror. Yesterday is a lifetime ago. Yesterday belongs to a much younger man. Today he's seen death. Caused death. Killed the ones who killed his buddies.

The sky darkens but the salvos of shot continue along the line of dunes. Flashes split the gloom. When it's properly night they should be able to move again. Separate the living from the dead. The sand is in his throat, choking him, stealing his breath. His water bottle is in his pack, flung to one side when he hit the deck. Cautiously he reaches towards it, but a bullet shaves his sleeve. He dare not move again.

Exhaustion takes over and he sleeps. He's on the porch, the fireflies dancing as the citronella scent of the magnolias drifts on the breeze. Through the dusk their white saucers of flowers seem to glow and in his dream he weeps for the beauty of it.

Inside the house she's singing *Don't Sit Under The Apple Tree*. The words reach him across thousands of miles — the hills and cities and oceans that end in this damned sand.

A man screams in the darkness. Another shot, then silence. Even for her, he can't do this anymore. This wasn't what he signed up for. It wasn't meant to be like this. The tanks were meant to protect them, not spew them out to kill and be killed.

"I'm sorry, so sorry." His tears soak the sand. Tears of anger. Tears of fear. Tears of shame.

CHAPTER 1

I am about to turn on the shower when I hear it. Distant at first, almost thunder — but with a definite pulse. I throw open the bathroom window and look to the skies: heavy, low and revealing nothing.

Studland Bay is shrouded in early morning mist, still and silent over the sea. The dampness clings to the folded umbrellas in the pub garden, staining the fabric with dark streaks. With the habit born of years I listen for the sea, but all I can hear is *thrum, thrum, thrum* from above.

The sea is beyond the garden. Figures move along the shoreline, somehow lacking the randomness of dog walkers. Something unfamiliar jars. *Thrum, thrum, thrum.*

The mist makes Studland a strange, enclosed world. On a clear day I can see the cliffs to my right rise to meet the sky at Old Harry rocks, a wall of chalk which dazzles in the sunlight before plummeting into the surf. Now it is as though there is nothing there. I shiver and wrap my towel more closely around me.

As the thrumming fades into the distance my attention is caught by a jeep bumping over the field in the direction of Fort Henry, its concrete mass just visible between the trees to my left. Two men jump out and call to each other, their words indistinct on the breeze. That's it — I remember now — the re-enactment.

Music from Jude's radio alarm reaches me through the wall. Time I was getting on, but a movement in the bay catches my eye. The mist is breaking a little, wisps like candyfloss spiralling past the window. The prevailing wind has changed but there is something else… I sniff the air. The merest hint of cordite.

Shapes shift beyond the thinning curtain: huge, beige, intangible. I lean out further. The men from the jeep are dragging a wooden crate towards the fort. Gears grind in the lane as an army truck negotiates the bend at the bottom of the cliff path. It stops in the dip and soldiers stream out, disappearing down the gully to the beach.

The wind is an unfamiliar visitor to the bay but this morning it sweeps in from the east with a vengeance, whipping the water into angry furrows and peaks. The shapes in the sea edge into view, pitching and tossing in the swell. I can only count three of them, but something makes me think there are more beyond. I strain my eyes — what in heaven's name are they?

There is a tap on the bathroom door. "Just putting the kettle on, Mum. Want some toast?"

"Please." I shake myself and turn on the shower.

But still I am drawn to the window and the sea, gunmetal grey as the shapes emerge from the mist. Steam fills the room behind me as they appear then disappear, never quite reaching the shore.

Jude has the *Bournemouth Echo* spread out in front of him on the kitchen table. I pause at the bottom of the stairs — he's so like his father was when I first met him: tall, blue-eyed and with a smile to melt hearts at fifty paces. All he's inherited from me is my coppery-blonde hair.

"Morning, Mum. Just checking the timings for today."

"The re-enactment?"

"No, that's in a couple of weeks — today's the memorial service for the tank crews."

I sit down next to him and pour myself a mug of tea from the pot. "Are you sure? It's crawling with soldiers out there."

His finger moves across the paper. "Well, there is a bit of historical stuff going on; Bovington Museum's bringing down a tank to drive ashore from a carrier and there'll be an old plane flying over to drop some poppies."

I lean towards him so I can read over his shoulder. It's a big day for Studland; exactly sixty years ago the village stood silent witness to the first of a string of rehearsals for D-Day, which went horribly wrong when the amphibious tanks that were meant to float didn't. The army picked the Studland peninsular because the terrain, with cliffs at one end and sand dunes at the other, was similar to Normandy. And it was secret; the paper says during the war it was almost completely cut off from the world.

Exercise Smash was so hush-hush it's only recently that anyone's heard about it and today a memorial to the men who died will be unveiled. The editorial proclaims that without their sacrifice the story of D-Day might have been very different, but I bet their families didn't think so. There's an interview with the last remaining widow, who says they were told nothing in 1944 and just accepted it. Stiff upper lips and all that. What a time to live.

Jude stands up and stretches. "I'd best go prep the bar. It was busy last night, and if we're opening for coffee we'll need stacks of cups and saucers."

"What time's your father coming in?"

He rolls his eyes. "Who knows? Said he had a date last night, remember?"

Nothing new there.

As Jude clatters down the stairs to the pub the feeling washes over me. Drab, familiar, bleak as the misty dawn. How the hell did the six inches of cold sheet between Stephen and me stretch until it became three miles of chalk headland? And would I change it? No. Not now, anyway.

Jude was conceived in this grey prison of a place, long before the mullions grew bars. Upstairs, on the lumpy mattress of Uncle Ted's spare bed, before we knew it would become our future. Even before we knew we had one. We curled together under the blankets, star-struck by the novelty of a whole weekend together, oblivious to the fact I'd forgotten my pills.

In the morning we walked along the beach, barefoot, my skirt trailing in the sand. Behind the tide, with salt and a bucket we pulled up razor clams. I cooked them for supper, with pork, wine and garlic. Uncle Ted said I should be running the kitchen in his pub. Oh, how we laughed at the idea.

I'll never forget waking here for the first time. We arrived in the dark, not long before closing time. Smoke filled The Smugglers' public bar and Stephen's Uncle Ted, a narrow whippet of a man, was polishing glasses behind it. He grasped my hand.

"Welcome to Studland, Marie." His voice was gentle, his smile slow. I miss him to this day.

The next morning we crept from our bed before he was awake. The sun was already flooding the windows, stamping the pattern of the leads on the wooden floor, and when Stephen took me outside to drink our coffee at a rickety table in the pub garden the view took my breath away.

The sea in front of me was flat, calm and the purest blue. Two sailing boats made slow arcs on their moorings, tucked into the sheltered curve of the bay. Above them the wooded cliffs rose steadily to become sparkling walls of the whitest chalk, topped with green which spilt down in places like a badly iced cake. Stephen put his arm around my shoulders and the world could not have been more perfect.

Abandoning our half-drunk coffee, he led me across the field to the fence on the far side. The grass dropped away and fifteen feet below us were the roofs of a row of beach huts, the tide lapping the shingle in front of them.

"Oh God," I whispered. "Wouldn't it be wonderful — to have a hut here. To be able to close the doors on the world — just the two of us — and still hear the sea."

Three years later Stephen bought me my beach hut.

Away from the cliffs, beyond The Knoll, where the grass gives way to the dunes, is Studland's naturist beach. In the summer of '85, when Jude was a toddler, we'd go there to paddle and play in the sand. For me it was the most normal thing in the world, but Stephen was less than impressed by my all-over tan.

"You're mine, Marie," he said, his fingers trailing across my breasts. "No one else should see you like this — no one."

I wriggled closer to him. "No one does. No one looks; everyone's the same there. You ought to come with me."

His hand ran down my belly and between my legs, caressing me once, twice, before he stopped. "You're not going again." And with that he rolled over and turned out the light.

The beach hut was a peace offering. Or maybe a bribe. But I wasn't so cynical back then.

As eleven o'clock approaches the sky exactly matches the stone mullions that surround The Smugglers' windows. Gradually the hubbub of conversation blows out of the side door as the former servicemen, their families and the sightseers look for the driest way across the road and up the path towards Fort Henry. Now the only sound is the clink of china as Jude and I stack coffee cups onto trays. In about an hour they'll all troop back again for lunch. And Stephen hasn't even shown up yet.

It's not that I want him anywhere near me, but there are times he can be useful. Which almost never match the times he's actually here, lording it over us, like he owns the place. Which he does — well, half of it anyway. He seems to ignore the fact the other half of the pub is mine.

My half is the gleaming kitchen, but I can't leave Jude to clear this mess on his own. I am just imagining what I'll scream at Stephen if he does turn up, when I round the corner of the bar to see an elderly gentleman in a navy blazer sitting alone, his shoulders hunched over his empty cup.

"Not going to the unveiling?"

He looks up. "Too far for me to walk and I'm buggered if I'd let anyone push me. Wouldn't be respectful, anyway, to sit through the service."

"At the Cenotaph —" I start.

"That's different — that's all for show. This is personal."

I pull out a chair and sit down opposite him. "Did you know one of them?"

"Knew all of 'em. Joined up together, we did." He pulls his tie from under his pullover and shows me the crest. "*Quis Separabit.* That's a bloody laugh. The top brass, that's who separated us. Sending us out in those deathtraps."

Poor old soul. "You took part in Exercise Smash?"

"For my sins. I ask you, bloody great tanks and all they had was a bit of canvas skirt blown up with gas and they expected them to float from three miles out. Three miles! It got a bit choppy and we never had a chance."

"So what happened to you?"

"Bloody thing sunk. And once they started, there was sod all you could do to stop 'em. Dropped to the bottom like stones."

He shudders. "D'you know what saved me? Army incompetence. Issued me with the wrong size boots, they did, so I was wearing my own. They were much lighter so I was able to pull free."

"Oh my God — how terrifying. Were you a long way out? Could you swim for the beach?"

He shakes his head. "Broke my arm, but we were far enough into the bay for a destroyer to pick me up. Lucky my Mae West inflated too. But the other poor buggers — trapped, they were. And ours wasn't the only tank to go down — not by a long chalk."

"It's awful to think of it happening here."

"You can't blame the place. I come from Burnley but I met my wife in Bournemouth and stayed. And from that day to this I've never seen it so choppy in that bay."

"It was pretty rough first thing this morning. The wind was coming off the sea."

"Just like sixty years ago. It tipped down then as well."

"Mum?" Jude's voice reaches me from the other side of the bar. "Baz wants to know how many of the caulis you want done."

The old man smiles. "Sounds like you're a bit busy."

"Well, we are fully booked for lunch…"

"Off you go, then."

"Mum?"

I stand up. "On my way, Jude." I turn back to the man. "I'll get him to bring you another coffee."

The Last Post sounds through the gloom and the old soldier struggles to his feet, head bowed. I pick up my tray of crockery and slip away as quietly as I can.

I arrive in the kitchen just as Stephen's car pulls into the yard, accompanied by what sounds like distant thunder.

"Where have you been?" I shoot at him.

He turns to hang his jacket on the peg by the freezer, then peers at his watch, tapping it and shaking his head.

"Looks like only twenty past eleven to me."

"We were open at ten for coffee — it's been manic."

"Good. At two quid a throw it's money for old rope."

I can't think of a suitable retort fast enough and my hands are shaking as I take the marinating chicken breasts out of the fridge to turn them. Flecks of chilli look like spots of blood and my stomach churns.

Jude's hand is on my arm. "He only does it to wind you up. Don't let him — it's not worth it."

I take a deep breath. The thrumming is back, filling my head from the inside out.

I am just about to panic when Baz says, "What's that?"

"It's the flypast," Jude tells him. "They're getting some old plane to drop poppies on the beach. It's going to be a right mess in this rain."

Baz's reply is drowned by the engines overhead and the rattle of the pans on the shelf above the stove. I run to the window but there is nothing to see beyond the blanket of cloud. Nothing except a handful of paper poppies drifting into the corner of the yard.

I pick up a tea towel and shake my head, trying to rid myself of the constant roar and rumble in my ears. The crowds who were here for coffee and lunch have been drawn outside by the improving weather and the fact Sky TV is filming the museum's tank coming ashore. Thank goodness it's Sunday so the kitchen will be closed this evening. I watch Baz disappear across the yard as the sun wins its battle with the clouds.

Sod it. I pull my jacket off the hook in the lobby as I call to Jude. "Just popping out for a breather." I am gone before he can answer.

April. Yes, there is some warmth in the air. As I start to climb the track towards Old Harry the sun gains in confidence, although the damp chalk slips and slides beneath my feet. At the edges of the path the last of the daffodils have been beaten down by the rain, but further up the bank the primroses are taking over, lemon-meringue fresh against the moss.

The sea is hidden from view by hedges and trees topped with a froth of hawthorn. Their dark leaves contrast with the brighter greens of the new growth around them. How many greens are there? Twenty? Thirty? Even Jude would struggle to paint them all.

With the activity centred on the beach I thought I'd be the only person walking on the cliff but coming towards me is a man wearing khaki combats and a white T-shirt, his hair cropped disconcertingly close.

"Good afternoon, ma'am." American.

I smile without breaking my step. "Lovely day."

By the time the path levels out the sweat is pooling on my back beneath my waterproof, but the breeze is a fraction too chill for me to take it off. Clouds skate across the horizon and sheep call from the fields which edge the strip of downland topping the cliffs. One stands patiently in the corner, two lambs at her teats. The pain and joy of motherhood — and for what? For a moment I wonder how I'll ever handle meat again. Imagine telling Stephen I'd become a vegetarian. Imagine the look on his face. Up here I almost feel brave enough to do it.

I settle myself on my favourite bench. After this morning's waves Studland Bay is like glass. A gull swoops below me, sunlight glinting off its wings. I'd like wings. I close my eyes and imagine them stirring under my chef's whites, feathers chafing my skin. Restless to break loose and fly.

"Excuse me, ma'am, but did you drop this?" My head jerks up. Light invades my eyes and I see only the American's silhouette, his arm outstretched. "It's so pretty; I wouldn't have wanted you to lose it."

I hold out my hand and he places something small and cool into it. A tiny silver seahorse, just half an inch long, with a loop attached to its head. I can almost see the chain breaking, the charm sliding off. I look at him, shielding my eyes with my other hand.

"It is pretty — but it's not mine."

A line appears across his brow. He is older than Jude, younger than me. Early thirties perhaps? His face is tanned, his neck muscular, his eyes invisible behind vintage Aviators.

"Should I take it to the police station?" he asks.

I shake my head. "They'll just file it away somewhere. Tell you what, I'll put up notices in the pub and the car park. Whoever lost it is more likely to see them there."

"The owner won't mind?"

"The landlord's my…" Why don't I want to admit to it? "It'll be ok. I work there. In the kitchen."

"Thank you, ma'am."

God, that makes me feel ancient. "It's not ma'am — it's Marie."

He shifts his stance, almost smiles. "So how did an English rose come by a French name?"

I feel the colour rising up my neck. "It's not French, it's just different."

"Well, what do you know? My folks wanted me to be different too so they named me Corbin. Corbin's where my granddaddy Summerhayes had his farm before the town was even built."

"And where's that?"

He all but stands to attention. "Kentucky. In the good old United States of America."

I gaze down at the pendant in my hand. "And do you have seahorses there?"

"Oh my, Marie," he laughs. "We don't even have an ocean to put them in."

"Then I'll take especially good care of this one," I promise as I tuck it into my pocket then set off down the path. As I descend towards the village the thunder in my head begins again.

CHAPTER 2

It's been a very, very long day. Baz and I have been running around like headless chickens preparing for the re-enactment this weekend. Following on from the memorial service a fortnight ago, they're trying to recreate the part of Smash the King and the Prime Minister came to see. Someone's even pretending to be Churchill. And a lot of volunteers are dressing up as GIs and will no doubt have a whale of a time waving toy guns around. Which hopefully will make them very hungry.

I throw my whites into the laundry basket and pull on my pyjamas. Sitting on the edge of the bed I stop and listen. The mutter and mumble of the pub reaches me from two floors below, but there is nothing else. All day my head has been clear of the distant roaring and rumbling but I don't dare be too relieved. It did this last week as well. I thought it had stopped and I was ecstatic. Until it started again. Maybe it's linked to stress, I don't know.

I snuggle under the duvet and pick up my library book — *Far From the Madding Crowd*. I wish I was. But at least I can escape onto the downs with Gabriel Oak's sheep. Their bleating fills my head and takes me ... somewhere ... the man striding towards them is not a shepherd but Corbin with his shaved head. He said his grandfather farmed so maybe he knows what to do? The sheep stray closer to the cliff edge. The weight of the book drops onto my nose.

I wake with a jolt when a car engine bursts into life below my window. Stephen's going now. There was a time it would have broken my heart.

There was no one moment when hurt replaced eagerness, nor one when ambivalence replaced hurt. I can hardly imagine the tingle of my skin beneath his fingers — it happened to someone else, surely? Someone else who was arching and panting for his touch. Someone else does now, that's for sure. Perhaps that's what happened. It really doesn't matter. Not after all this time.

When I told him I was pregnant he was so blessedly clear about our future my misgivings melted away; he wanted me, he wanted our baby and he would provide. Of course we weren't too young; twenty-one and twenty-three were the perfect ages to start a family.

Providing meant The Smugglers. Stephen was always a favourite nephew and before I knew it Uncle Ted had offered us a home. The pub was tiring him, he said; it needed young brains and young legs to breathe new life into its ancient walls. Stephen could manage it, I could cook — a partnership made in heaven.

And for a while, it was. Ted was happy too, sitting at the kitchen table teaching Jude to draw, silently battling the cancer which was eating him away. It won just two weeks after Jude started school. Never had Stephen and I known such grief; it bound us together even closer — an unbreakable bond — or so I thought.

I blamed myself for Stephen's first affair. Too busy, too tired, being a mother and a housewife and a cook. No time for my husband so of course he looked elsewhere. That's what he told me, anyway. But it ended — and he begged me for us to try again, promised me it would be even better. And I was just so happy and relieved that he wanted me back.

Those years, I think, were probably our best. Jude in the village junior school, lots of friends, the pub on an upward curve. Money for staff, money for family treats and time for each other. We even tried for another baby, but I lost it fifteen weeks in. And without any warning at all my world plummeted off the highest of Old Harry's cliffs and down, down, down into a place I did not know.

The emptiness was vast. There was barely room for Jude — certainly no space for Stephen. I drove him away. Again. Or so he said when he ventured back. Was that the second time or the third? Or even the fourth? Jude's teenage years were scattered with the debris of his father's affairs. But what could I do? A boy needs a father and by then I was just too damned knackered to care.

Twenty-two months ago everything changed when, after a period of relative calm, a new woman turned up in Stephen's life. For the first time he brought one to The Smugglers. I peeped out from behind the kitchen curtain; French manicure, brassy hair and acres of cleavage. Jude christened her Pneumatic Nel. I don't think I ever knew her proper name.

Little by little Stephen's CDs went missing from the rack in the living room. Then his wardrobe began to empty, one overnight bag of clothes at a time. Finally his radio alarm and Uncle Ted's watch and then this room became my own. I stretch my fingers and toes to every corner of the bed, the brass posts smooth and cool against my skin. It's over now, him and Nel. Thank the Lord he didn't come back.

As soon as daylight forces through the cracks in the curtain I pull on my dressing gown and escape. Jude's door is ajar and I watch as he bends over his laptop, his hair soft and spikey from sleep.

"Cup of tea?" I whisper.

He turns, smiles, stretches. "That'd be good. I'm just finishing your poster — I'll come down."

"My poster?"

"For this." He holds the silver seahorse on the palm of his hand.

I shake my head. "Sorry — it's early."

"No — it's my fault. I've been busy at uni and I forgot all about it."

He's taken a photograph, laid out on dark fabric, blown up to about four inches across. *Is this yours?* in red above. *Ask at The Smugglers* and the phone number below.

"Should we say where we found it?" I venture.

"No. They have to tell us where they lost it. Otherwise how will we know it's theirs?"

I feel stupid but I laugh. "It really is too early for me."

"Bad night?"

"Not especially. You?"

"The birds woke me. But I'm not complaining. I need to get back into uni this morning to sort out the last few pieces for my degree portfolio. I'll email The Seahorse Trust first though. They had some volunteers handing out conservation leaflets in the car park on the day of the commemoration so it might be one of theirs."

"Do you think there are still seahorses in the bay?"

"Apparently there were thirty-two at the last count. Not that I've seen one for a couple of years."

I take the seahorse down to the kitchen and put it in a little brown wages envelope before opening the safe. Right at the back is my jewellery box, an oblong of pink plush Stephen gave me for my thirtieth birthday. I push up the clasp and flick it open. There isn't much inside: the earrings Jude bought me last Christmas, a coral necklace that was my mother's and my wedding ring. I should get rid of the ring really, but somehow I don't have the heart. I cover it with the envelope and close the lid with a snap.

Before Jude leaves he gives me four posters. In the chill of the pub kitchen I slide two into plastic bags, taping the bottoms shut. Outside, the sea mist flecks my jumper and I hurry down the road to tack the first one to a tree at the bottom of the gully path. I stand, for a moment, looking towards the cliff. Will Corbin see the poster? Will he approve? Will he even care? Yes, of course he'll care. Or he'd never have picked up the seahorse and brought it to me in the first place.

I make a cup of tea and flick through the pile of post on the side. An engine cuts out in the yard below and my Stephenless start to the day is almost over. Bloody hell, he's early. I pull out an art supply catalogue for Jude — everything else is pub business. Except — an official-looking envelope addressed to Mr and Mrs S Johnson. I almost leave it for Stephen. Mrs S Johnson doesn't feel like me.

Paper ripples under my finger as I tear. A single-page letter — sheets of numbers behind.

Dear Mr and Mrs Johnson,

Please find attached your new mortgage repayment schedule following the advance of the additional monies requested. The interest rate is fixed at 8% for twenty-four months and your revised monthly payment is £950.

I would like to remind you that your home is at risk if you fall behind…

The page blurs. *How. Could. He. How. Dare. He.* There's a crack of wood as my chair collides with the kitchen unit.

"Stephen! Stephen!"

He is almost at the top of the staircase anyway. "What the…" He grabs my hand just inches away from his face. "For God's sake, Marie — calm down."

"You bastard — you total and complete bastard!" He has both my wrists now, pinned against my sides. I kick his shins instead, but his tightening grip brings me to my senses and I stop. And there's a moment, like there always is, when his breathing is louder than mine and we know he's won.

He releases my hands. My eyes are closed but I hear a rustle of paper as he picks up the letter, then water gushes into the kettle and he clicks it on.

"Come on, sit down. We'll talk about it."

"It's a bit late for that."

"Trust me, Marie — I've done my sums on this and I needed to extend the mortgage to buy the place in Swanage and do it up. How did you think I was going to fund it?"

To be truthful, I didn't think — but I won't tell him that. "You should have asked me."

He turns away and puts teabags into two mugs. "If I make you one, will you promise not to throw it at me?"

My fingernails dig into my palm. "You condescending shit."

"Flattery will get you everywhere."

We wait in silence while the kettle boils. He pours the water into the mugs then squeezes the teabags, one at a time. It's as he's reaching for the milk I say,

"We struggle to pay the mortgage as it is. How the hell…"

"Shows how much you know about it. Since when have you taken any interest in the books?"

"But you said … back in January when we needed new knives…"

"You needed a new sharpener." He slams the mug on the table in front of me, its contents slopping over the empty envelope.

I ignore the mess. "We needed knives. We still do. But you said … you said … there wasn't any cash to spare. It's Swanage, isn't it? Bloody Swanage!"

He shrugs. "Like I said, how did you think I was funding it?"

"You don't need a palace."

He grabs the front of my whites. "I'm doing it up as an investment. I'm sleeping on a mattress on the floor, while you're living like Lady Muck in our big brass bed."

"It's not our bed. It's my bed — mine. There's no us anymore and good riddance."

I spin from his grip and run for it. My clattering footsteps echo behind me all the way down to the pub kitchen. The mouldings on the door press into my back but he doesn't come. My breathing slows and I make my way across the tiled floor to the fridge. A slab of beef waits, dripping red onto its plate. I transfer it to the chopping board then pull a knife from the drawer. I check it with my thumb. At least the sodding sharpener works. Upstairs, Stephen turns on the radio. I test the blade again; it slides through the meat like butter but there is only one thought in my head. I fling the knife away, mesmerised as it spins across the floor.

Under the circumstances the busy lunchtime service is a godsend. Quite a few people have already arrived to set up for the re-enactment and the bar is packed with burly workmen and volunteers in National Trust sweatshirts. Paninis and burgers fly from the grill and the kitchen is pungent with lemon and crisping batter. I make a note on the chalkboard to order more cod.

I help Baz to wash the pans then take a mug of tea to our upstairs living room and spread the *Purbeck Gazette* across the coffee table. There is no doubt the paper has pulled out all the stops for the re-enactment and the upcoming sixtieth anniversary of D-Day. In between the adverts for Swanage Tyres and Evans & Co solicitors are interviews with everyone they can find who actually remembers the town in the war. One man, who was a nine-year-old boy at the time, speaks fondly of sweets handed out by ever-increasing numbers of GIs.

I discover the Americans began to arrive in October 1943 and were billeted around the town in hotels or private houses. The streets of Swanage apparently filled with jeeps and gun carriers but I find that hard to believe; I thought the build-up of troops was meant to be secret. Perhaps the whole account was embellished by a young child's mind or an old man's imagination.

Another contributor was a dancer in a concert party who entertained the soldiers. Her memories are of polite young men and the wonderful buffet she was invited to at their hotel headquarters. And of the eerie quiet which cloaked the town when they left. "It's not that they were noisy in themselves," she tells the paper. "It was the end of the constant shelling over at Studland while they practised. We'd had almost two months of it with only the weekends off. All of a sudden you could hear the birds sing again."

I put my tea down. For a moment I half recognise what she's saying — it rings the vaguest of bells in the back of my mind, but when I read it again the connection's lost. Maybe there was a similar story in the National Trust leaflet.

Half of the next page is filled with a photograph of twenty or so men outside a house in Burlington Road. I read the words of an American who spent the months before D-Day living, four to a room, in the house in the picture. He's remembered it all; the boredom, the queuing up for the movies, the weekend passes to Bournemouth, the dances in the local halls with rows of mothers sitting on the balcony watching their daughters like hawks.

Then Omaha, bloody Omaha. That's where they went. The first regiment suffered ninety per cent casualties; the second fifty per cent. The man telling the story was in the third to arrive and walked ashore through their bodies. Those poor, poor, boys. Boys just like Jude.

I can stomach no more so I perch on the windowsill to look out over the bay. Beige army tents are being set up in the field between the pub garden and Fort Henry, an American flag fluttering above them. Was it only GIs at this stage of the exercises? Had the other regiments packed up and gone elsewhere? Strange if they had. But the whole thing is strange anyway; disorientating in a way I can't quite work out. I sip my tea as I watch a woman in a frumpy dress stretch blast tape across the windows of the cottage opposite. I hope that doesn't mean the thudding and whizzing is going to start again.

The warmth of the sun reaches me through the window and I rest my head against the glass. Stay here and watch, or grab some fresh air? Friday nights are always hectic. And the weekend will be worse. Best get out while I can.

I leave the hammering and shouts of banter behind me as I stride up the chalky slope. More and more primroses cover the banks beneath the hedge and a tractor clatters and clanks its way over the field breasting the hill. I reach the end of the tunnel of green and the downland spreads in front of me, a wide swathe of grass dotted with gorse.

Now all I can hear is birdsong and the distant murmur of the waves. Up here the hassle of Stephen and The Smugglers feel part of another life. I breathe so deeply my lungs are fit to burst, the freshness of spring replacing the whiff of cordite which seems to fill the bay.

Twenty or so yards away from me towards the cliff a man is lying on his back in the grass. Army issue hair, white T-shirt. The light glints off his sunglasses and I find myself hoping it's Corbin.

I approach him slowly, quietly, picking my way through the scattered gorse. He is motionless, a long blade of grass hanging from the corner of his mouth, hands behind his head, the sleeves of his T-shirt riding up just enough to expose a narrow band of white skin above his tan.

I only speak when he scratches his nose. "Nice place for a snooze, huh?"

He sits up and spins around. "Marie! You really have caught me napping I'm afraid."

"And chewing grass."

He smiles as he scrambles to his feet. "It's what farmer-boy sergeants do."

I nod. "Especially when they should be down at the beach putting up tents."

"I hope you're not saying I'm swinging the lead." His smile is broad, a little lopsided. "I was thinking about a walk to Old Harry and if you're going the same way I sure would appreciate your company."

"That would be lovely."

"Good. I can make sure you don't get too close to the edge."

How sweet; he isn't to know I've been walking here for over twenty years.

The further you go towards Old Harry the cliffs don't only rise but narrow to precipitous points; not just the headland leading to the rocks themselves, but in other places where whirlpools of sea have gouged the chalk into bays over the centuries. On the sheltered Studland side the promontories are cloaked with impenetrable vegetation, but as the headland curves back towards the open sea, the land dives straight down, down, down into the waves, hundreds of feet below.

Corbin sets out across the grass and I fall into step beside him. "So," I ask, "tell me about your farm."

"Well I can't say it's mine — it's Ma and Pa's — like it was his father's before him. The best land in Kentucky is further west but we do pretty good — mainly cattle and fodder for them — hundred and twenty acres."

"And is it very different to here?"

He stops and looks around him. "Yeah, I guess. I mean it's still pretty green — we have some rain most of the year which is why it's good for cattle, but in so many ways… When I wake in the morning at home I look out of the window up towards the mountains and they change with the seasons, but until I left to come here I'd never seen the ocean. And that changes with the hour."

"I know. It's magical."

"Yeah — that's a good word."

The open downland funnels into a narrow tract of scrubby woodland, the slope rising gently to meet the birdsong. If you couldn't hear the sea you wouldn't know it was there, hidden by stunted trees and overgrown gorse. Only the foolhardy brave the perilous tracks to the cliff edge to admire the view.

The trees end abruptly and we emerge onto an open carpet of grass, cropped close by rabbits, which spreads in front of us until it disappears alarmingly into the endless blue of the

English Channel. Ahead the tops of the tallest stacks, No Man's Land and Old Harry himself peep just above the level of the cliffs.

Corbin stops. "Wow — the world just seems to go on forever."

A cloud passes over the sun, taking the shine from Harry's white head as he and his stump of a wife stand guard over the entrance to the bay. Below us seagulls wheel and dive as a motor launch chugs towards the shore. I step forward but there is a tightness in my chest and my head starts to swim. Sweat trickles down my back. I've done this a thousand times — we're not even remotely near the edge…

I cover my panic by looking at my watch. "I'm so sorry," I stutter, "but I really have to go. I … I lost track of the time."

"Some days it's like there is no time up here." He sounds wistful but his eyes are hidden by my reflection in his Aviators. "But if it's ok with you I'll stay a little longer, admire the view."

"Sure, sure. Thank you for your company."

He inclines his head. "The pleasure's all mine, Marie."

I feel like a drunk struggling to walk in a straight line. *Focus, Marie, focus.* I steady myself at the entrance to the wood, turn to wave, but Corbin is nowhere to be seen. It freaks me out for a moment, but he's probably just lying down again, chewing on a piece of grass. Once I am between the trees my vision clears. I stop and breathe deeply, the coconut scent of the early gorse tingling my nose. Panic attack. That's all.

CHAPTER 3

The view from Jude's bedroom is the best in Studland. Long and narrow, squeezed into the eaves next to the bathroom, its row of casement windows means you can see all the way from Old Harry to Fort Henry as it stands guard over Redend Point. I love perching on a stool looking out at the bay while Jude's charcoal scratches and skims over the paper beside me.

This morning we are both riveted by the activity below us. Even though it's early, a couple of khaki jeeps with white stars on their bonnets bump towards Fort Henry. The National Trust's navy blue Land Rover is already parked next to the massive concrete blockhouse, which has been spruced and polished ready for the re-enactment. A couple of GIs are sheltering under the trees having a fag, tin helmets slung over their shoulders and the flag is wrapped damply around its pole. I wonder if I'll be able to spot Corbin?

Jude reads from the National Trust leaflet. "Sixty years ago Smash Three, a set piece rehearsal for D-Day, was witnessed by Churchill, Montgomery, Eisenhower and King George."

I bet that's why the walls of Fort Henry are so thick; you couldn't risk that lot being wiped out by a stray bomb. Luckily none of the ordinary squaddies died either. Not this time. Old photos show soldiers streaming onto the beaches beyond the Knoll from landing craft, and tanks clambering over the sand dunes with varying degrees of success. Today they're going to try to recreate it.

Jude breaks into my thoughts. "I wonder what happened to Smash Two?"

33

"How do you mean?"

"Well, the one when the tanks sunk was Smash One and this one's Smash Three."

"Perhaps it wasn't important."

"Perhaps it was too hush-hush."

I slide from my stool. "Leastways, we're going to be run off our feet."

"Oh I don't know." Jude looks up from the leaflet. "I heard they're going to be giving them powdered egg and spam."

There's a sparkle in his eyes and I laugh. "Exactly. We're going to be busy."

He nods. "I'll just have a quick shower then I'll be down."

"No worries — Baz is coming in early and I expect your father'll turn up at some stage — if only to count the money."

Not in time to help with the coffees though. Soon Jude is running short of cups, so I take a tray and cloth to head out to collect some for the dishwasher.

The veteran in the navy blazer is sitting at the same table, but this time he is not alone. Folded onto the chair next to him is a guy I'd judge to be in his late forties with weather-beaten skin and dark wavy hair greying at the temples. At his feet is a border collie, straining at his leash as I approach.

I drop to my haunches. "Well hello there. You are a gorgeous boy ... or girl..."

The younger man replies. "You were right first time — he's a boy. And he can take any amount of that."

I look up. "He's a handsome devil."

"Shame you can't say the same about his owner."

I laugh. "If you're fishing I'm not rising to the bait." He's not a bad-looking guy though, despite the deep lines etched into his tan beneath his tortoiseshell glasses.

34

He looks down at the dog. "You'd never think he was abandoned, would you?"

"Really?"

"Yes. Somebody chucked him out and I found him at the rescue. Their loss was my gain, wasn't it fella? Lucky old me."

I realise I've been ignoring the old soldier so I stand and shake his hand. "Hello again — come back for a second dose?"

He sighs but there is laughter in his eyes. "You've got me into trouble now — Mark didn't know I came on my own for the commemoration."

"Dad — why didn't you tell me? I'd have brought you."

"You were busy. And anyway, I was all right. They've got time for old folks here — this lovely lady and her son. He's the one who paints the pictures for the pub walls. Shame about some of his subject matter though."

"Don't you like them? He's got a degree in fine art ... well, he nearly has anyway."

"No — they're all very good. Just why he wants to waste his time drawing deathtraps I'll never know."

I smile. "I'd rather he didn't either. But the fact of the matter is they sell. Especially at the moment when there's so much interest in Exercise Smash."

"You can say that again — we'd never have got into the car park if it wasn't for my disabled badge. And with this rain as well. Not sure I can face going out in it again, to be honest. Even to see what a balls-up they make of it. Still — at least the weather's right — it was pissing down in 1944 too."

Mark clears his throat. "My father was here, you know. Met Churchill and the King."

"Met's too strong a word for it, Mark. I was on ceremonial guard duty. Could do bugger all else with my broken arm."

"But the King spoke to you, didn't he?" Wheedling this favourite story out of his father is clearly a well-established routine.

"He did. Your mum was so proud. I'd only just met her as well — had to write it all down for her, bless her heart."

Mark looks up at me. "My mother was deaf. Lost her hearing in a bomb blast and never got it back. Lip reading and sign language are family traits."

"You don't think of those sort of casualties, do you? That's so sad."

"Oh, she was fine, really." I can hear the pride in the old man's voice. "Never let anything get her down, did Eileen."

I bend over the table to pick up their empty cups and a thought strikes me. "This morning, Jude — that's my son — and I were talking about Exercise Smash. We hear a lot about One and Three, but what happened to Two?"

The old soldier laughs. "I guess Two and Four aren't talked about because they just kept rolling on. Weeks and weeks of live ammo practice — they were trying to perfect the creeping barrage. Even when I was in hospital in Bournemouth I could hear it: *whizz, thump, bang* from morning to night. Got you used to it though — you were ready for the real thing when the time came. But I mustn't keep you — you're going to be busy again."

I nod. "Lovely talking to you though. Would you like another coffee?"

"In a bit, maybe — but we won't bother you — Mark will go to the bar like everyone else."

"It's no trouble…"

"You're very kind, Mrs…?" the older man asks.

"It's Marie. Just Marie."

His hand is warm and his skin as fine as crepe paper when I take it. "George," he says. "I'm George."

When Stephen arrives at half past eleven, he unilaterally decides we're going to serve food all day and puts a notice in the bar to that effect. The first I know about it is when Jude slides into the kitchen to tell me.

"He can't do that without asking."

"No he bloody can't," Baz grumbles. "Southampton are playing Man City this afternoon and it's on the box."

"Well I can and I have." Stephen is leaning in the doorway to the bar. "Jude — there are customers waiting to be served. Get back out there while I have a word with our idle kitchen staff."

"Idle? You've got a sodding cheek. We're already up against it because you didn't turn up to help with the coffees again."

He shrugs. "You managed." His voice is calm but there's a vein bulging in his neck and he runs his finger around the collar of his shirt.

"You might want blood from me, but you can't expect Baz to work a twelve-hour shift. Jude will have to help out in the kitchen when he takes his break." That'll stuff him. The afternoon could be the busiest time in the bar.

"It's alright. I asked Gina yesterday if she'd come in early."

"You mean you planned this … you planned this and you didn't tell me? What if I refuse to work this afternoon? What if I have other plans?"

"You won't. You never do." The oven glove just misses his shoulder as he turns to walk back into the bar.

It's been the longest of long days. Even the thudding in my head carried on for hours after the re-enactment finished and there's another bloody lot going on tomorrow. Thankfully that's further along the beach at Knoll. Let the National Trust café take the strain. I sit on the side of the bed and down the brandy I pinched from the bar when Stephen wasn't looking. As an afterthought I swallow a couple of migraine tablets. Today has been too much in so many ways.

I pace the room like a caged tiger. How much longer can I go on working with Stephen like this? The Smugglers ties us together as surely as if we were still a couple and I can't see a way out of it. Who else would employ me? And even when Jude finishes university next month and finds a proper job, where would we live? I open the window and fill my lungs with soft, damp air. The rain has eased to a fine drizzle. I have to get out of here.

I fumble in my drawer for a pair of thick socks and pull them on, together with a fleece. In the lobby I find my wellingtons and anorak and scrabble around in the hallstand for a torch, shining it into my palm to check the battery.

Stephen's laughter from the bar follows me down the road and into the dip where the gully path leads to the beach, but after a while all I can hear is the lap of the waves on the shingle. Not a light escapes from Badgers Cottages on the corner. No cars parked outside either. I could have sworn they were let this weekend but maybe they've gone into Swanage for supper.

The blackness is deeper as the path climbs between the hedges. There is something welcoming about it; something velvety and comforting. I use the torch sparingly to guide my steps. After so much rain a stream tumbles past me, angular flints exposed in its wake. The last thing I need is a twisted ankle. A bird flutters off a branch and when I lift my face, the drizzle cloaks it in a fine, fine mist.

Something is different. Something I can't put my finger on. I turn to look back through the trees towards the village but all is peaceful, all is dark. I am still too. Waiting.

And then I hear it — really hear it. Properly above my head. First a hum and now a throb. A throb of engines. They pass, one after the other, rhythmic and smooth. On and on they go until they fade into the night over the Isle of Wight.

I resume my climb, longing for the space and freedom the clifftop brings. There are times when Bournemouth glitters like a jewel — so much prettier through the darkness — but tonight there'll be nothing but a shimmering glow. The rain is steadier, its pitter-patter on the leaves and the hood of my anorak.

His voice, when it comes, startles me. "Halt — who goes there?" But at least I recognise it.

"Corbin?"

He is nothing but a shape in the dark. "Marie?"

"Yes."

"What in heaven's name are you doing up here?" He is whispering now.

"I just fancied a walk."

"But you can't — it isn't safe."

"Nonsense. I've done it loads of times before."

"But not now, Marie. You can't now."

It dawns on me. "What — because of the exercises?"

"Yes — exactly that. You shouldn't be here. You shouldn't even be out."

"Really?"

"Oh God — yes — really. Please, Marie, just go home."

It's taking re-enactment a bit too far, but perhaps there's a big finale planned for tomorrow or something. But what moves me most is the edge of panic in his voice.

"Of course, Corbin. Of course I will. Thank you."

He exhales. "I'd walk you back if I could, but…"

"I understand. You have to stay here."

"You got it, girl. Now run on home my beautiful English rose and I'll see you around."

Dutifully I turn and make my slow way back down the track. Beautiful — he called me beautiful. Well, I suppose it is dark. But as I laugh at myself I'm still hoping against hope perhaps that wasn't the reason.

CHAPTER 4

The glow from Corbin's words is with me when I wake next morning. Silly, I know, but it's a long time since anyone's called me beautiful. I scrutinise myself in the bathroom mirror and although I look tired and old, my almond shaped eyes are sparkling. And there's even a hint of a smile.

Of course, it isn't to last. Just when I don't want Stephen to be early he strolls into the upstairs kitchen, laptop bag slung over his shoulder.

"What are you doing here?" I snap.

"I thought you wanted me to help with the coffees."

"Not at half past eight." This is my space, my time. But I don't say it.

"I need to cash up from last night first. I was too knackered and Jude said he had to finish writing up a painting or some such crap." He unzips the bag and sets the computer on the table.

"It's only a month until his degree show."

"I know. He asked me if I was going. Told him it was a waste of time."

"You did what?"

He strides towards the fridge and opens it. "Any bread? I fancy some toast."

"Don't change the subject."

He turns and folds his arms, enunciating slowly. "I told him — it was a waste of time."

"Stephen…"

"Well it is, isn't it? From the first of June he'll be working full time here, then what use will a degree be to him? It's been a waste of three years and three grand."

"His three grand. You haven't paid a single penny towards it."

"Exactly. So why should I be interested in his degree show now?"

I slam my empty mug down on the table. "Because Jude's your son, that's why. It's nothing to do with money."

"Everything's to do with money."

The walls of The Smugglers are thick, but not so thick they can disguise an argument. When Jude was a teenager he used to sleep through them. Or pretend he did anyway. Now it's different.

"You're in early, Dad — any tea in the pot?" He bounces down the last step into the kitchen with a forced cheerfulness.

I leap up. "I'll make you some, Jude."

"No, it's fine — I can manage my own. Like another one? Dad?"

"Coffee, please. Instant will do," says Stephen.

I shake my head.

The sound of the kettle boiling fills the kitchen. Stephen's eyes try to meet mine but I refuse to hold his gaze. Jude drums his fingers on the edge of the kitchen unit. Finally he says, "I heard my name mentioned — what have I done?"

"Nothing. What makes you think you have?" Is Stephen really so stupid he thinks he can fob him off?

"Like I said, I heard…"

"You — have done nothing," I snap. "It's this selfish shit; too wrapped up in himself to even go to your final degree show."

"Well I know he's busy… I don't expect…"

"But that's the point — you have every right to expect — he's your father."

"I bet he thinks I'd be more use as a painter and decorator at the moment than an artist, with Project Swanage on the go." Jude laughs but it's too close to the truth to be remotely funny. My eyes fill with red hot tears.

"Don't take his side. I'm trying to fight your corner, make him see what's right and you both gang up on me." I make for the bottom of the stairs.

I am even more angry when I hear Stephen say, "Don't worry, Jude — time of the month and all that. She'll calm down." What the hell would he know about my time of the month? I start to turn, flexing my fingers. I want to gouge his eyes out. But Jude is watching me so instead I pound up the steps as fast as I can.

It's the best part of an hour later when Jude taps on my bedroom door. "It's ok, Mum, he's gone downstairs. And I'm sorry — I was only trying to make a joke — make it better."

"He should be so proud of your work, but all he thinks about is money."

"It doesn't matter; you understand and that's more than enough for me. We both know I'm going to end up running the pub so it'll only ever be a hobby anyway."

"Over my dead body you will. You've got a real talent — you must go to London or somewhere, work properly as an artist. You've got to get away."

It's not the first time we've had this conversation. "We'll see," is all he says, same as he always does. "Come on then, let's have a bacon butty before work, cheer us both up. I'll chef and you make the tea."

Three days later I am still smarting from the argument, although Stephen seems to have completely forgotten it. He's like that at times, and after all these years still I don't know if it's just the way he is or whether he does it to wind me up. The pub is quiet, the re-enactors gone, leaving behind the thudding in my head that fills every daylight hour. That newspaper article said when the real GIs pulled out the village fell silent. Why hasn't it happened now?

I can't think about it. Therein lies the path to madness and I feel as though I'm teetering on the brink as it is. Instead I pull on my fleece, wondering perhaps if there is still just one American who hasn't gone. The air feels soft, gentle on my face as I climb the path to the cliff. There are more lambs in the field now, their bleats filling the hedges and chasing the nesting blackbirds into the sky where they spin and circle and play. Up here my head is clear and I can hear their song.

He is well in the distance when I see him, striding across the down from Old Harry. My fidgeting fingers find a tub of lip balm in my pocket. I turn away from the breeze to open it and inhale synthetic strawberries.

"Good afternoon, Marie. How are you?"

I spin, my sticky fingertip halfway to my lips. I wipe it on the edge of the tub and screw the lid back on. "I'm very well, Corbin. And you?"

"Very well, thank you. Enjoying the English spring while I have the chance."

I laugh. "Me too. I was just trying to count the greens."

"Sea green, grass green, tree green, hedge green..." He stretches a muscular arm across the horizon.

"Hawthorn green, oak green, gorse green, blackthorn green..."

"Rose green." He winks and I feel myself blushing. "More than I'll have time to learn, anyway."

"You're leaving soon?"

"I'll be around a little longer yet, I guess." He starts to walk towards the bench and I follow him. He sits down, pulling his combats up a little around his thighs. "So tell me, Marie, has anyone claimed the seahorse?"

"Not yet. Perhaps it was a day tripper who lost it. But I've put it in the pub safe in case someone comes."

"You said you work in the kitchens?"

"I'm the chef."

"My ma would love to meet you. She's a cook too — for the Parkers — a real old family back home. They've been in Laurel County as long as the railway."

"Laurel green — we forgot that one." Aviator sunglasses green. But I don't say it. Instead I ask about his family.

"Well there's Pa, and Ma, and me and my little sister Ruby. I got a brother-in-law now too; that'll take some getting used to but he's a good, solid guy; works for Ford, making jeeps. But not even a whole jeep, something to be proud of. Just the doggone steering wheels. One after another. Earns good though." He pauses. "Then we got two cats, Jefferson and Monroe and of course the horses."

"Horses?"

"You can't drive cattle without horses, Marie. I mean, we got the tractor now too, but you gotta have horses."

"What, like in the cowboy films?"

He laughs. "Billy the Kid and Hopalong Cassidy sure got something to answer for. No, we just ride quietly around and move the cattle to the next pasture. No guns, no Stetsons — nothing. Sorry to disappoint you."

"Believe me, you haven't. I didn't have you cut out as the Clint Eastwood type anyway."

"Clint Eastwood?"

"You know, the film star."

He shakes his head. "Guess I'm a bit behind the times — I haven't been to the movies for a while. They show them in Swanage, of course, and some of the guys go all the time, but I prefer to be outside."

"You must miss home." I follow his gaze out to sea. Bournemouth opposite is partly hidden by clouds dropping low over its distant tower blocks.

"The people more than the place."

"I guess you would."

"Marie, I'm sorry, I'm completely forgetting my manners, talking about myself when really I want to hear about you, but I'm expected back pretty soon." He stands and brushes his trousers. "Perhaps another time … we can meet again?"

The air is tight in my chest. "Yes."

He is looking down at me, head on one side, waiting.

"I walk most afternoons. I finish work at about half two then I come straight up here. Sometimes even if it's raining."

He nods. "Well, Marie, I'll see you soon. You can count on it." He raises his hand in a mock salute and turns. Somehow, I don't want to watch him go.

My afternoon gets even better when I spy Jude cycling down the lane. We turn into the yard at the same time and he leaps off his bike and gives me a hug.

"Been for a walk, Mum? Lovely to see you with some colour in your cheeks."

"It's beautiful up on the down — you can really taste the spring." I tuck my arm into his. "Anyway, how was your day?"

46

"Not too bad. My thesis has been accepted anyway, so that's a box ticked."

"Good for you. Did they say what grade…"

He shakes his head. "Not yet. Come on, let's have a cuppa."

In the kitchen he pulls out his sketchpad and I can feel him watching me as I move from tap to work surface to fridge and back again. I tuck my hair behind my ear. If he's surprised I'm wearing the earrings he gave me for Christmas he doesn't say.

I put the mugs on the table and turn back to the cupboard.

"Sit down."

"I'm just getting some biscuits."

"Sit down. I want to draw you."

"Why?"

"Just because, ok?"

Because he feels like drawing? Because I'm wearing the earrings? Because, maybe, I look beautiful. Can I still look that way? Sometimes, in the mirror, I catch a glimpse of the person I was but she's so lost behind the bags under my eyes and the deepening lines around my mouth it's hard to tell.

I don't need old photos to remind me of how I used to be — I know. I turned heads as I walked along the Kings Road — I really did. And it wasn't because I was wearing the latest flares or platform shoes. I never felt the need to follow fashion — it was enough to raid my mother's wardrobe for her cheesecloth blouses and pavement-skimming skirts. I wonder if she missed them — or me — when I decided to stay in Glastonbury so didn't bring them back?

I look across the table at Jude. God — he's like his father was when I first met him. Why doesn't he have a girlfriend? Perhaps the fighting has put him off. I want to say to him — don't let it — not everyone screws up. Today I believe it's true, but that's not always the case — not by a long chalk.

47

It's only when I look at Jude that I remember how good-looking Stephen was. Crazily good-looking, with his fair hair, square jaw and dancing eyes. When he smiled, the whole world smiled with him, and his arrival to manage the high street newsagent in Glastonbury set any number of hearts a-flutter. Not mine though. Not at first. Maybe my repeated refusals made him even more determined.

But then I realised — he didn't just want to get me into bed — he wanted me to be his girlfriend, and in my world that was something of a novelty. He made me feel special in a way no one had before, and once we'd committed to keeping our baby and moved to Studland I allowed myself to fall for him hook, line and sinker.

I look at Jude again, glancing from his sketch pad to me then back again. Surely Jude remembers some of the happy days, or have they been engulfed by the hurt and bitterness that followed? I tried to shield him from it but the older he was, the harder it became. What can I say to him now to make him believe in love?

My train of thought is broken by Stephen's tread on the steps. I stand and dust myself down.

"Right — time to put on my whites and get into that kitchen."

Like the bedroom farce our marriage has become I exit stage right up the stairs just as the door from the pub opens and Stephen walks in.

CHAPTER 5

I don't see Corbin for over a week, then one Sunday when the beginnings of a migraine drive me away from the kitchen during lunch service he is there, on our bench. As I sit down beside him my head is blessedly clear, but even so when he asks me about my life I'm reluctant to tell him about my now. So I start at the beginning and hope to divert him along the way.

"I was born in London…"

"You don't sound like a cockney. Not like the old guy in the hardware store in Swanage."

"If he's a cockney he must be from the East End. I lived in the south west, a place called Parsons Green. I didn't take much to school and my parents didn't make me — they were hippies, you see."

"Hippies?"

"Like in California. Perhaps you have a different name for them over there. You know, 'tune in, drop out', that sort of thing."

He shakes his head. "Kentucky's a long, long way from California, Marie." I picture him on his farm and think perhaps it is.

"It's hard to grasp how big America is. I mean, England is so tiny by comparison. You can get most places in a matter of hours."

"I don't know — I've not seen too much. We arrived at Plymouth and they drove us here overnight. I'd love to see London — I was born in a town called London — but I guess it isn't going to happen now."

"Why not? Are you leaving so soon?" My hand creeps along the bench towards his, but he stands and turns his back on me.

"I'm sorry," I venture.

As he shakes his head the close shave at the back of his neck scrapes along his T-shirt. "No, Marie — it's me. Well, perhaps not even me. But it certainly isn't you."

I wait for him to sit back down, my hands firmly in my pockets, but he just stands there, looking out over the bay.

"You said — you might be leaving?"

"You know very well I will be. You're so British sometimes — you live in the village, you can't turn a blind eye — or ear — to what's going on. You know — you know I know — but you act like you don't."

I shake my head. "I'm sorry, you've lost me."

There is a long moment when I watch his shoulders rise and fall. A fishing boat is making its way towards Poole Harbour, followed by a string of gulls. A skylark trills above us.

When he turns he is trying to smile. "Perhaps you're right. Perhaps ... there's just this thin slice of time, with you and me on the cliff. Perhaps nothing else matters."

"Will I see you before you go?"

"I hope so, but best make it soon." He frowns. "Maybe even tomorrow. Yes, tomorrow should be good, but maybe a little later in the day."

"About four?"

"That will be perfect."

Instead of taking the main path to the road I turn right down the track to the beach. As I descend through the arches of hawthorn, the hiss of the waves on the shingle rises to meet me. The bay is sheltered in the early afternoon sun and I shrug off my fleece, draping it around my shoulders. I roll up the legs of my whites, letting the coolness of the water tickle my toes through my crocs.

I know I should go back to the pub but I can't. Not yet, anyway. I need to fathom this out, make sense of what Corbin said. His words slide in and out of my mind with the rhythm of the waves, constantly shape-shifting just beyond my grasp.

The tide is creeping up, licking at my ankles, making them numb. I turn away from the bay and crunch across the shingle bar onto the sand. If only I had the keys to the beach hut. If only I had the energy to stride out along the dunes. If only the thunder in my ears would stop.

With feet like lead I haul myself up the wooden steps and make my way across the grass towards Fort Henry. I haven't been here since they unveiled the memorial. The flowers are dying and the red of the poppy wreaths is smudged with pink where the rain has washed the colour away. The plaque itself is low to the ground, an elegant piece of slate with a view towards the Solent. Six men, six names: Gould, Hartley, Kirby, Park, Petty, Townson. I say them over and over like a mantra as I turn inland towards The Smugglers.

When I sneak back into the kitchen Jude is helping Baz with the last of the pots.

"How are you feeling now?" he asks.

"Better thanks. The fresh air cleared my head."

"That's good, because George is out front and he'd like to see you."

"George?"

"You remember — the old boy who got injured during Smash."

I can't say no — he's probably lonely, poor soul, with only his too-busy son for company.

As I slip behind the bar Stephen is there, chatting to our barmaid Gina. He turns and looks at me. "Couldn't make me a beef sandwich, could you?"

"You're right. I couldn't." I pick up a pint glass and fill it with soda water from the pump, then join George at his table.

Actually, he isn't alone — his son is with him, and tucked under their table is the border collie. He thumps his tail against my legs as I sit down.

"I didn't mean to pull you out of the kitchen," George starts, "I just wanted to let you know what a good lunch we had."

"No, that's fine — it's nice to see you. Especially on a day when we're not quite so busy."

"That wasn't busy?" He draws an arc with his hand, taking in the tables strewn with empty glasses and dessert bowls. "There must be an army of you back there."

I take a draught of my drink. "No, just me and my kitchen porter. We manage. Over the years you get organised and you get used to it."

"Best bit of roast pork I've had in ages," Mark says. "Dad and I have lunch out every Sunday and we'll definitely be coming here again. Don't have to leave the dog in the car either."

"Did he enjoy the pork too?"

Mark shakes his head. "Oh, I never feed him from the table — don't want to get him into bad habits."

George snorts. "He wouldn't want to eat what's generally on your table." He turns to me. "Mark lives off those bloody microwave meals. Don't see why he can't cook properly — I manage it."

"I don't have time, Dad, you know that." Mr Busy again.

The dogs turns under the table, his fur soft against my bare ankles. I reach to scratch his ears.

52

"What's his name?"

"Troy."

"That's a coincidence — I'm reading *Far From the Madding Crowd* at the moment."

Mark looks blank.

"You know … Thomas Hardy. Sergeant Troy."

He shakes his head slowly. "Oh, not that Troy. He's named after the ancient city. And I have a little yacht called *Helen*. I expect you get the connection," he continues.

"It doesn't matter — he's gorgeous anyway." Out of the corner of my eye I can see Stephen looking daggers at me from behind the bar. He only allows dogs on sufferance because it gives us an advantage with the walkers. I turn back to Mark. "Would he like some scraps?"

"He shouldn't … not really…"

"Oh for goodness sake," George sounds frustrated. "Just once won't hurt. You can walk it off him while I sit in the car having a snooze."

I stand up. "Well, the offer's there. I'll be in the kitchen for another twenty minutes or so. Just pop around the back of the pub if you change your mind." I bend to scratch Troy's ears. "He is giving me a hungry look."

Mark laughs. "He's good at that. Take no notice."

On my way through the bar I make a point of touching as many surfaces as possible with the hand that stroked the dog. I even pick up a towel to flick imaginary hairs off my whites. Stephen follows me into the kitchen.

"What do you think you're playing at?"

I walk straight to the sink and plunge my hands into what's left of the washing up water. "I don't know what you mean."

"Yes you do."

"Are you still pissed off because I wouldn't make you a sandwich? You know where the beef is, and the bread. And last time I looked you still had fully functioning arms and legs."

"You'd have made one for Gina if she'd asked. But that's not why I'm angry and you know it."

"Sorry — being psychic isn't one of my strong points."

"Stroking that dog then handling every last bloody thing on the bar."

I turn away from the sink to face him, drying my hands. "D'you know what, Stephen? I might buy a dog. It'd keep me company once Jude goes away."

That stops him in his tracks. "Where's Jude going? He's said nothing to me."

I put the towel down and shrug.

"Marie — tell me." He's at least six inches taller than me and several stone heavier. Gina's in the bar, Baz has gone home — Jude's nowhere to be seen.

"Tell me." He is inches away from me, the armpits of his shirt dark with sweat. If he feels me shaking he'll know he has the advantage. *Marie — come on — he won't hit you — he never has before. He's a bully, a cowardly bully.*

There is a knock on the kitchen door. Stephen looks up, away from me, through the window.

"And you can piss off and all!" he yells. "You and your filthy dog!"

It's my chance and I squeeze between him and the sink, scampering up two flights of stairs to my bedroom.

It's when I hear the living room door open then slam below me I realise I've made a fundamental mistake. But Stephen's empty wardrobe at least gives me half a chance.

He calls my name as he pounds up the stairs and I fold my knees into my chest and pull the door to. Thank God he's being so noisy or he'd hear my heart crashing through my ribs. Maybe I should have faced up to him — if he finds me cowering it'll be so much worse.

The bedroom door reverberates as it hits the wall. "Marie?" A moment of stillness then the same in the bathroom, the force sending a shampoo bottle thudding to the floor. Please, please — let him think I ran down the lane.

Stephen's footsteps move towards Jude's room and finally I can breathe. The air in the wardrobe is rank and stale, full of Stephen. I reach up to the fabric of his black suit, discarded, unloved. A hint of his deodorant lingers, clawing at my throat. I retch, covering my mouth with my hand.

Suddenly, he is back. I hear my name again, but more of a whisper. Has he worked it out? He pads around the bed but stops at the dressing table. There is a scrape of wood on wood as he picks up something — it can only be the photograph; Jude turning ten, the three of us at afternoon tea in the Haven Hotel. Don't smash it — please — don't let him smash it.

Instead, all is quiet. I hold my breath, willing him to go away. The bed creaks as he sits down. "Marie," he whispers. "Oh God, Marie. What in heaven's name went wrong?"

The not-quite silence stretches endlessly; it can't be silent when you're this close to another human being and I wonder why he can't hear me. Then it happens — the jagged lines of light split the darkness and ricochet off the wooden walls. Any second now and I'm going to throw up.

I am saved by his phone. "Sorry, Gina — on my way. Just sorting out a few things upstairs." His voice is businesslike and the bed creaks again before his footsteps retreat towards the bar. I make it to the bathroom just in time.

CHAPTER 6

Even two days later the migraine's left me shaken. The pain threatens when I stand, my legs are like a newborn foal's. The thunder and crump in my head has driven me to this. It's been weeks now, with just the odd couple of days of respite. Maybe I'm going mad. Maybe it's best not to know.

But by six o'clock I am stir-crazy to be away from the pub. I jump every time I hear Stephen's voice in the bar below but he won't come near me. He hates sickness in all its forms. Perhaps the weakness of it scares him; the neediness. So just for the moment I feel safe.

Jude walks me to the beach hut. The steep path to the cliffs is beyond me. Tomorrow. I will go tomorrow. I know I promised I'd be there yesterday, but perhaps, if I sit here in the open, Corbin might come to me. As Jude puts a chair on the decking I rummage in the cupboard under the gas ring for the binoculars. So I can watch the wading birds as the tide drops. That's what I tell him and he smiles, leaving me with a mug of tea before going back behind the bar.

I play the conversation with Corbin over in my head but still it makes no sense. He talked about the exercises and I try to remember what he said but it's gone. Sometimes a migraine leaves holes. Just for a little while, anyway.

At first I do look at the birds but my attention is caught by a yacht moored in the surf close to Redend Point. It's a beautiful little wooden boat with a navy blue sail tied in neat bundles. I strain to see the name painted on the front. It's *Helen*. Why does that ring a bell?

I raise the binoculars to the cliff and refocus them. That great, open world reduced to two circles of white and green, fuzzy at first in my inexpert hands then sharpening until I can make out the shapes of trees, the impression of a bench, perhaps a person. I skim along from left to right; a pair of walkers, the blur of a cyclist. No one sitting. No one waiting.

My arms begin to ache but it's hard to look away. Just in case. Then — from nowhere — a scrabble of claws on the decking and a whine.

"Troy — behave!" The dog is straining on the end of an extendable leash clipped tight.

I lower the binoculars. "It's ok, let him come." The lead clicks as he is freed another metre or two, just enough to nuzzle his head into my lap. "Hello, boy," I murmur, stroking the soft fur between his ears.

I turn to Mark. "He's a friendly soul."

"Well, I guess he was worried about you — wanted to check you're ok."

I frown. How… I remember the knock on the kitchen door and I want to sink through the decking with shame.

"It's all right — we're separated but we still work together. Makes for a lot of arguments, that's all."

Mark shifts Troy's lead from one hand to the other. "I didn't mean to … intrude."

"It was just bad timing."

In the end it is Mark who breaks the silence. "What were you looking at, up on the cliffs?"

"The birds. Someone … someone said there were buzzards there but I've never seen them. Only kestrels and skylarks." I hand him the binoculars. "What do you think?"

He takes them, turns towards the cliffs, then back to me, proffering Troy's lead. "Do you mind?"

He removes his glasses and tucks them into his trouser pocket before finally fixing his gaze on the cliffs. Is there anything there? A man, alone, waiting, on a bench? I shift in my deckchair, impatient to have the binoculars back in my grasp.

In the end I have to ask if he can see anything.

He drops them onto my outstretched hand with a rueful shake of his head. "Couldn't even focus them. It's a bit of a struggle when you're short-sighted — I never know whether it's better with or without my glasses. I guess if I want to find out about the buzzards I'll have to take Troy for a walk up there."

At the sound of his name — and probably the word "walk" — the dog raises his head from my lap and thuds his tail on the decking.

"Ok, Troy — but not now. You've had your exercise and I expect you're getting hungry too."

I smile. "For a share of your ready meal?"

"No — for a bowl of his own grub. Don't think he'd be keen on a Weight Watchers chicken curry, somehow."

"Weight Watchers?" I look up and down his skinny frame with disbelief.

"Picked it up by mistake," Mark mumbles. "Anyway — best go and get it eaten."

"Yes. Well … bring George to The Smugglers for Sunday lunch when you fancy a proper meal." I stand up and hand Troy's lead back to him.

With a cheerful "will do" he strolls down the beach and after a few moments I realise he's heading for the yacht called *Helen*. I watch for a moment as he and Troy scramble in then I refocus the binoculars on the cliffs.

The next lunchtime I return to the kitchen. I'm still running on empty but have willpower and anticipation to carry me through my shift. Stephen is back to normal — as though Sunday never happened. If I said to him, "Why did you want to frighten me?" he would look at me blankly, blue eyes full of innocence. I used to think he was messing with my mind. Now it just messes with itself.

It is just after two o'clock when I grill the last panini and dress it with salad. Baz makes me a mug of tea and I sit on the back step to drink it, wriggling my toes in my crocs as the pale sunlight warms them. I can't leave yet — someone might order dessert and although Baz can plate up the ice creams and pies they never seem ... well ... polished enough.

I look at my watch — only quarter past. I sip at my tea but it's still too hot to drink. I lean against the door jamb and close my eyes. Water gurgles in the pipe beside me as Baz empties the sink, mixed with a gust of laughter from the bar. It reminds me ... takes me back ... but I can't quite clutch at the memory.

In the house at Parsons Green the pipes from the sink in my mother's workroom ran down my bedroom wall. I can see myself lying on the floor in a patch of sunlight, trying to fashion my handkerchief into a kaftan for my Sindy doll. Below me in the kitchen my father was holding court: the laughter reaching me, but not the words. Boring, adult stuff.

The water stopped and minutes later there was a creak on the stair. No, two creaks, the second one more pronounced. My mother's voice, soft and low.

"No, Gerald. I love him — not in a can't-keep-my-hands-off-him, spine-tingling sort of way — not now, anyway. More yin and yang — we fit — make a circle — make each other complete."

"Then why do you…?"

A laugh. "You scratch an itch. And you're very good at it."

I am brought back to the present by Stephen bellowing an order for two chocolate brownies with black cherry sorbet. I glance at the kitchen clock as I reach for the icing sugar. Just gone twenty past. The next ten minutes are going to be endless.

As I sit on our bench and wait for Corbin, my mind goes back to my mother's words. Yin and yang — a lovely idea. Jude painted two seahorses once, curled head to toe in a circle. One the azure of the Mediterranean and the other as white as the finest sand. I'd like him to see the Med for himself. His best friend Michael's spending the summer in Greece but there's no way I could persuade Jude to go with him.

Despite the fact my mother and father moved to Greece, I've only seen the Mediterranean once myself. In early autumn, the grass bleached by the sun, the earth cracked beneath it. It must have been so hard for them to dig my parents' grave. They died in a boating accident — stupid, their neighbours said they'd been, reckless — and although I hadn't seen them for years I still felt angry, abandoned, orphaned, even — yes, that's the word. I was twenty-nine. Jude was eight. I stood alone in that churchyard in Gennadi, eyes on the sweep of the bay as they lowered them into their grave, one after the other. I'd cried more tears for Uncle Ted.

The sea below me is a different blue entirely. A breeze travels over the downs, bringing the scent of gorse and whipping up white horses around Old Harry's feet. I turn to look over my shoulder but the path is empty. I don't really know which way Corbin comes; perhaps he walks from Swanage. I look the other way; a group of hikers stretches out along the cliff but he isn't among them.

Yin and yang. Jude made me complete. Not in the way my mother meant, of course. I've never had that. With Stephen, well we could have been yin and yang but we ended as we started, more like chalk and cheese. I knew Stephen wasn't my type. For our first date he took me to dinner at a Berni Inn. Leather-like steak and rubber mushrooms. I told him we'd get up early and go out in the fields to pick our own, and then I'd cook him breakfast. It amused me he tried not to look surprised.

"Well, weren't you going to ask me back to your place for coffee?" I asked.

"Of course. But I didn't for one moment think you'd say yes. Not on a first date, anyway."

"So are you saying you find my morals a little … loose?"

He stretched his hand across the table, covering mine. "You're different to other girls, Marie. I can't compare… No, that's wrong. You're beyond compare."

The moment we were outside the restaurant he kissed me, his tongue forcing into my throat as he pawed my thighs through my skirt. The combination of his looks and apparent inexperience was an unexpected turn-on.

"Come on — let's go," I whispered.

He pulled away. "Your place?" he asked hopefully. "My landlord's a bit…"

I shook my head. "I share with two other girls. You've got a car, though."

The smile spread across his face. "Yeah — I've got a car."

We drove up towards Glastonbury Tor and struggled into the back seat. It wasn't great, to put it mildly, but afterwards we curled into each other's arms and there was a sort of peace.

I jump as a woman with an Ordnance Survey map in a plastic pocket around her neck sits down on the other end of the bench. She apologises for disturbing me then proceeds to talk about the weather. Incessantly. I excuse myself as soon as I reasonably can and make my slow way down the path towards The Smugglers. I couldn't have waited any longer for Corbin anyway.

When I get home Jude is in his bedroom. He's humming to himself as he stretches a canvas over a thick chipboard block.

"Are you hungry?" I ask and he nods. "Shall I make you an omelette?"

He looks up, his hair flopping into his eyes. "Please, Mum — that would be magic. I'll be down in a few minutes — almost finished."

Two pictures are propped against the window to the left of his computer screen. A thick stripe of yellow runs through both of them, two thirds of the way down. In the first, pinpricks of luminosity spread into the blackness above and reflect exactly in the velvet blue below. In the second a woman's naked form worships a bright ball of sun. Although united by the yellow stripe they don't belong together; Bournemouth pier at night and the nudist beach — between them fit Canford Cliffs and Sandbanks. In Jude's hands is the beach below us. My clever, clever boy.

I must have said the words out loud. He laughs. "For once I agree with you. They told me today they're going to hang all five in the degree show — it's unbelievable."

"No it's not — it's what you deserve. You've got so much talent…" I grind to a halt because his eyes can't quite meet mine.

"There's another thing, Mum. They've offered me a part-time job for next year as a technical assistant. I…"

"But it'll stop you going away!"

He turns the block over and reaches for the staple gun. "I hadn't made up my mind one way or the other."

"But, Jude — this place will suck you in. Before you know where you are you'll be trapped here, running the pub…"

"I could do worse." He says it so quietly it's as if he's afraid I'll hear.

"Nonsense. Reach for the stars, Jude. You're not going to find them in Studland. Or Bournemouth."

He doesn't reply. He doesn't understand. And at the moment it seems I have no way of making him.

CHAPTER 7

Time is like a telescope held the wrong way. Perhaps that's the problem. Perhaps distance distorts. The seahorses dance around the rusty metal box and parade along Jude's yellow stripe of sand. If they leave the sea they'll shrivel into silver and I'll have to hang them out to dry.

The migraine lasts more than thirty hours. Not my longest, by any stretch of the imagination. But it happens like this; nothing for blessed pain-free months then a wave of really bad ones. Four since Stephen made me hide in the cupboard. Four in a fortnight. Four since…

At first the only thing I can keep down is yoghurt. Then, finally, I drink a pill. New ones. I don't remember the doctor calling but Jude tells me she did. I didn't think to ask her how I could ever get out of bed again because even though my head is clearing the rest of me is weighted down with lead.

At some point I ask Jude if anyone has claimed the pendant. He tells me not and brings it to me, tiny and cool in my hand. Corbin. To think of him brings an explosion of pain. *Thud, thud, thud.* It's like I'm running in a loop with no way to break it. The chain is missing from the loop. What happened to the chain?

Jude settles on the edge of the bed. "The little seahorse reminds me, I bumped into Pip the other day."

I frown. "It's not hers, is it?"

"No, what made you say that?"

"You said the seahorse reminded you."

He nods slowly. "Oh yes, I do see. Well you know how keen on them she is? Remember last summer she had Michael snorkelling with her just about every day to try to see if there were any left in the bay?"

"I remember," I mumble. "You couldn't go. You were always working."

"Oh, I went once or twice," he smiles. "And I'm going with her this weekend. She says being in the sea helps with the stress of her A-levels. She's really got a bee in her bonnet about the seahorses now. She's just finished a project for her environmental science course on how the boats are responsible for their reduced numbers. Something about their anchor chains dragging in the seagrass."

"She always was a clever girl, just like Michael."

"Must run in the family. When she's finished her exams she's going to start a petition to stop the boats mooring in the bay."

"Wish her luck from me." I like seahorses. Not that I've ever seen one, but I like the idea of them being there, and they're so tiny they do need protecting. Just like the little silver one slipping between my fingers as I fall asleep.

I don't know how much later it is when raised voices from the pub kitchen wake me. Stephen's yelling at Jude. My knees buckle before I reach the bedroom door. I'm a useless, useless mother. He can't break free because I need him too much. Pathetic, pathetic woman. Oh Jude, I'm so sorry. I hate myself so much.

When he brings me a cup of tea and some toast his face is drawn. "Fancy trying this?" he asks, but his cheer rings false.

"What happened?"

"What do you mean?"

"I heard your father shouting at you."

He puts my mug on the bedside table and hands me the plate before perching on the edge of the bed. "I had a run-in with the relief chef and he says he's not coming back."

"What did he do?"

"Used the meat board to chop the tomatoes."

"So you were right."

He can't look at me. "I threw them on the floor. He wouldn't pick them up. It got a bit ... colourful."

"You were still right."

"Oh, Mum — you'd say that even if I wasn't."

"I don't know... You'd never have learnt right from wrong if that was the case."

At last he grins. "No — it was easy — you always told me I was right and Dad always told me I was wrong."

"Oh God — were we really that dysfunctional?"

"No. You stayed together. We always kind of worked as a family — better than a lot of others, anyway."

"It's broken now, though."

"Is that what's making you ill, d'you think? The stress of it all? You've had four bad migraines in just over a fortnight..."

"The new tablets — they're helping."

"So will food. Are you going to eat that toast? There's just a tiny scrape of honey on it."

I look down. The plate seems full to bursting and my stomach churns. "I'm not sure..."

"One slice each?" He's right, you know — there is just one round, cut in half. I shake my head from side to side. No thud, no crump, no whizz. No whizz? Didn't George say "whizz"? Or did I dream it?

"Mum?"

Anything to make him happy. "Go on."

His piece disappears in two bites while I nibble along the soft edge of mine. I pick up my tea and sip it, tannins cutting the caramel sweetness. And Jude tells me he needs to go into college tomorrow because the degree show's this week and I frown, because just yesterday it was an age away. An age away and over the sea. Time's doing its telescope thing again.

The only good thing about being ill is I haven't seen Stephen. But he is there, all the same, when I venture down the stairs for the first time the next day. He must have heard my tentative footsteps — glanced up to see me clutching the bannister, even — but he pays me no attention until I am well into the kitchen.

He looks up from his newspaper. "Feeling better?"

"A bit. I'm thirsty."

"I was just going to put the kettle on. Tea or coffee?"

"Tea, please."

I sift through the pile of post while he makes our drinks.

"Nothing much there," he says over his shoulder. "Bills, mainly. Money's tight at the moment."

"So we can't afford that new mortgage after all?"

"We could if I wasn't having to pay a relief chef."

Yes, of course it's my fault. "If he was no good you don't have to pay him."

Stephen snorts. "And what happens next time we need someone from the agency? I've had to go down on bended knee to them as it is to get someone else for today. I don't suppose you're up to it?"

I shake my head. "Not yet."

"Any idea how long?"

"Jude says it's the stress." Just thinking it fills my eyes with tears.

"Stress? What stress? You don't have any stress. It's me who should be stressed out, but I don't have the time."

I carry my tea over to the fridge and put some more milk in it.

"Not good enough for you?" Stephen sneers. "Not as good as Jude makes? Well, next time you can make your own."

I reach for a yoghurt and a teaspoon and retreat to the living room.

The morning sun is shooting daggers into my eyes so I draw the curtains before I sit down. In the gloom I peel back the lid of the yoghurt and dip my spoon. Synthetic apricot. But it will do. I'm hungry — that's a good sign — and I scrape every last bit from the bottom of the pot. I think about turning on the television but the daily diet of makeovers and antiques is not remotely appealing. And anyway — I want to enjoy the unexpected silence.

On the shelf under the coffee table are two jigsaws, one of Brownsea Island which looks infernally difficult and the other of the cliffs rising up towards Old Harry. I shudder. I don't want to go there — but perhaps, if I do … if I can … then I'll understand it properly. My stomach churns a little but at least my head doesn't thump at the thought.

I move the magazines from the table and tip out the pieces. One falls on the floor and I scrabble as it threatens to disappear under the sofa. Best count them all first. So I stack them into piles of twenty; five stacks in a row, five rows of stacks. Stephen's voice rumbles between the floorboards.

As soon as I've satisfied myself they're all there I crawl up the stairs and into my bed.

Next morning I make it to the pub kitchen early. The glasswasher swishes and hums in the bar but otherwise all is quiet. I open the fridge. There is lamb, but the blood in the bottom of the dish turns my stomach. But there is also a block of feta and yes — in a plastic bag at eye level — some courgettes. I pull them out to inspect them and they just about pass muster.

Rather than risk the electric mixer splitting my head I mix the dough by hand, making it harder than hard before trickling in the oil. I'm sweating and my heart begins to pump but now I've started I'm determined to finish. While the pastry's resting I'll have a cup of tea.

I am rounding the filo into little balls when I sense someone watching me. I glance at the window but there's no one there. Whatever made me think there was?

When the voice comes it is from the direction of the bar and blessedly familiar. "Feeling better, Mum?"

"You're up and about early." I turn to him and smile.

"Yes, well it's the degree show today, isn't it, and I promised Dad I'd get the bar ready for lunchtime before I leave."

I count the filo balls over and over. Today. The show's today.

"I don't suppose… you're well enough to come?"

I take a deep breath, cover the pastry with a tea towel and put it in the fridge.

"Wild horses wouldn't keep me away, you know that."

He gives me a massive hug and I climb slowly back up the stairs to get ready, wondering what the hell I'm going to wear.

Jude turns off the engine as we wait in the queue to cross the entrance of Poole Harbour on the Sandbanks Ferry. The road north from Studland exists for this reason alone; there is nothing beyond the cluster of houses and the Knoll House Hotel but the dunes and a narrow strip of heathland separating the harbour from the sea. If it wasn't for the ferry no one would come here. If it wasn't for the ferry Bournemouth and Poole would be miles and hours away.

We watch from just beyond the slipway as the Bramble Bush Bay clanks along the chains hauling her towards the Studland side. To our left a fishing boat waits to exit the harbour, dwarfed by the backdrop of seafront mansions lining the Sandbanks shore. The narrowest strip of water. A completely different world.

I turn to Jude. "Nervous?"

He shakes his head. "I'm not good enough to win a prize, Mum, so you can get that out of your mind. You'll be amazed at the amount of talent on my course — there are some seriously good people — I'm nothing special."

I have no doubt Jude is right about the amount of talent as we drift along in the crowd viewing the paintings and sculptures which line the high-ceilinged room. But he's up there among the best. He's very smart today in chinos and an open-necked white shirt; he and most of his course mates have the look of four-year-olds dressed by their mothers for a posh birthday party.

We mill around for a while before being asked to take our seats on rows of wooden chairs. The head of department speaks; a bearded man with an overdeveloped sense of his own importance, brave enough to lay it on with a trowel about how much student funding has improved under the current government. Our recently knighted Conservative MP looks far from impressed but nevertheless sticks to his pre-written speech. My eyes close and my chin hits my chest. Jude doesn't even bother to nudge me.

Eventually they cut to the chase. A man of about my own age wearing a striped blazer stands and explains how the prizes were awarded and that there are three golds, four silvers and a bronze.

"That's Ralph, my tutor," Jude whispers and I can see him now, collecting his gold medal. His passport to a better world.

Two girls go up first, one from the row in front of us, her mother's face glistening with tears. I am tensed, ready to share her pride, but the next name called isn't Jude's. Nor the next, nor the next. I swallow hard. Surely … surely… But then I hear it.

"Jude Johnson, silver for 'Sandlines', a series of five gouache on canvas depicting the changing coastline between Bournemouth and Studland Bay. The judges particularly commend the use of colour which unifies the works." The applause thunders in my ears.

After the presentations the students move like a well-oiled machine. Some remove chairs, others sell programmes. Inevitably Jude mans the bar. I follow him and he pours me a glass of Cava.

"Go on, Mum — a little treat — to celebrate."

"It should have been a gold," I mutter, but in truth I am smiling so much it's beginning to hurt and Jude knows it.

There is a laugh behind me. "All parents think that." It's Ralph, and Jude introduces us.

"No, but I really do. Not that silver isn't marvellous," I add quickly.

"Do you want me to show you why it was silver and not gold, or would you rather just glow with pride?" asks Ralph.

"No… I mean yes… I'm really interested."

As he leads me through the crowd he says, "Jude's often told me you're a huge supporter of his work."

"He's always had talent and I was so pleased he chose this degree so he could learn to channel it. He's been selling paintings off the pub walls since he was fourteen but in the last few years he's grown so much — experimented with what he's learnt. I just wish he wanted to go further."

"Who's to say he doesn't?"

"Well… I … whenever I mention it he seems so … undecided?"

"That's what I think too. And although he's a fine artist he's borderline academically so he mightn't get on an MA course anyway. I hope by offering him the technician's job here I've bought him some time to think about what he wants."

"Do … do artists really need MAs?"

"No. But it puts them in the right milieu. So few make it, Marie, in the sense of becoming famous. But a great many earn a reasonable living by selling paintings or through commercial illustration."

"And could Jude do that?"

"He already is, with his pictures in the pub. And he knows what's saleable. So many students haven't a clue and even at the end of the course they're just creating work to please themselves. Like this one."

We are standing in front of a mass of beaten metal. Ugly squares rise, one in front of the other, some gleaming and others ravaged by rust. If you touched it you just know you'd cut your finger, but all the same my hand is drawn closer and closer towards it. I stuff it into my jacket pocket and Ralph laughs.

"Now do you see why it won gold?"

"It's … it's horrible."

"But it provoked a reaction. That's what wins prizes. Think Damien Hirst. Jude's work is very accomplished — and very saleable — but it lacks edge."

"And that's why it only got a silver?"

"*Only* is the wrong word. Think more in terms of it winning a silver and Jude being the student we offered a job to at the end of his course. My hope is it will give him time to mature a little as an artist and then he can decide what to do."

I turn away from the sculpture to look Ralph in the eye. "My fear is he'll decide to stay here. I mean … he almost has already, hasn't he? And he won't even go travelling with his friend this summer because of that wretched pub…"

"Well, if you ask me, I think it's more to do with his charming girlfriend."

I feel my smile begin to freeze but with Ralph watching me I mustn't react. My glass is slippy in my hand and I take a sip while I search for something to say.

"He's always had an eye for a pretty girl … like his father," I stammer. Now I'm sounding like a bitter old fool. "Like most men," I add with a wink.

Ralph's laugh ricochets around my skull.

"Look, I mustn't monopolise you — there must be loads of other parents gagging to talk to you about their talented children. But thank you for explaining it so well."

I try to wade through the crowd without pushing. A sea of faces; some of them young, female. Who is she? Is she here? And why, why, hasn't he told me? Ralph knows. And he thinks she's the reason he's staying. Must be serious. Must be common knowledge on this side of the Sandbanks Ferry. Must have been going on for a while.

I glance towards the bar. There's a girl serving next to him but it can't be her; there's a ring in her squashed up nose and her dyed black hair hangs limply either side of her over-wide face. Maybe his girlfriend's not a student. Charming, Ralph said. Sounds like someone older. Someone married? Someone he's ashamed of?

Bang. The silver streak is like lightning. Not here, not now. I stumble back to Jude and thrust my empty glass into his hand. "I'm tired, Jude — I'm going home." Can't worry him. Not today. Is that relief in his eyes?

"Shall I drive you?"

"No… I'll walk down through the park to the bus stop … you bring the car later, ok?"

I am several paces away before he calls after me. "Mum? Keys?"

I fumble in my bag for them. Stupid, stupid, stupid.

Get me out of this place before I throw up.

The water from the kiosk carries the taint of warm plastic but I force down a couple of tablets before leaning on the rail by the pond to watch the ducks. A harassed-looking grandmother clings to a toddler's hand as he showers the birds with fistfuls of breadcrumbs, laughing and stomping his feet as greedy beaks fill the water in front of him.

Why didn't Jude tell me? I can think better now, the pain receding to a thud behind my eyes. We've never had secrets — not important ones. He's never brought anyone home but I know there've been girls. Just a bit of fun, he's told me. Nothing serious.

Sex is something we've never talked about. Perhaps if I'd had a daughter… When Jude was sixteen Stephen gave him a packet of condoms for his birthday. He looked them up and down and said, "Cheers, Dad — but I prefer the ribbed ones." We laughed so much — even Stephen. A rare thread of family which disappeared completely soon afterwards.

I look up to see a man in a charcoal suit watching me from the path running alongside the causeway. I loosen my grip from the rail and wave.

In a moment Mark is beside me, shaking my hand. "I wasn't sure it was you. You seem a bit … out of context."

"I've been to Jude's graduation show — he won a silver medal."

"That's bloody good going. I was just heading for the café; you don't … er … fancy a cup of tea and a cake or something to celebrate?"

Most of the seating is in an outsized conservatory overlooking the pond. At the self-service counter the cakes are displayed under plastic domes but they claim to be home-made so I choose a slice of Victoria sponge while Mark goes for carrot cake, telling me it's one of his five-a-day. We find a table close to an open window and I pour the tea from a white china pot with a distinctly dodgy spout.

Mark raises his cup. "To Jude!"

"To Jude," I echo as we chink our cups together.

"Funnily enough, I've been at the university too — interviewing engineering graduates — hence the get-up." He indicates the suit and tie. "I'd have probably had more luck with the arty ones. Jude isn't looking for a job by any chance, is he?"

"Actually they've given him part-time work at the uni next year while he makes up his mind what he really wants to do. My biggest fear is he'll end up running The Smugglers and I want so much more for him."

"A pub's hard graft."

"He's not afraid of that. It's just… I want him to get away from here, see the world."

"And you hoped he might take a gap year?"

"Even a gap few months would be good. His best friend's travelling this summer but he won't hear of going too."

Mark picks up his fork. "I wonder why not?"

"I… I don't know." There's no way I'm admitting it to a virtual stranger.

"Did you travel when you finished college, Marie?"

I give a wry smile. "I barely finished school, let alone college."

"Really?"

I turn my plate around, looking for the best angle to attack my cake. Mark has almost finished his. "I suppose you went away to university?" I ask.

"Well, not exactly away — only to Southampton. It was the best for marine engineering."

"Sounds interesting."

His laugh rumbles around me. "Marie — at least say it like you mean it."

"I'm sorry — I didn't mean to be rude. It's just … I don't think I've met an engineer before. Assuming that's what you still do." I'm gabbling now. How embarrassing. He already thinks I'm an idiot because I didn't go to university.

"I'm more of a designer, really. I run my own business but I'm happiest spending time at my drawing board. Trouble is there are other people who can do that for me."

"But if it's your own business, why can't you do what you want?"

"If only it was like that. Sometimes I think about going freelance, but fifteen other people depend on me for their jobs and I can't let them down. But at least I get to decide what they're designing — in general terms, anyway. And it's exciting being at the cutting edge of environmental technology."

I pick up the teapot and refill our cups. "I thought you said you designed boats?"

"No, just the water recycling systems which go into them. Carrying enough fresh water is a big problem at sea, so you need to use the resources available in the best way you can."

"Oh, I see." I don't — and Mark knows I don't — but this time he doesn't tease me about it. Perhaps I'm too dull and I'm boring him.

"So you didn't design your own boat? When I saw her on the beach the other evening I thought she was beautiful — all that lovely wood."

"No, she came from a firm in the Lake District. And she's an absolute classic — they've been built in exactly the same way since 1912 — even had their own class in the Olympics in the 1920s. Now that's what I call great design — getting on for a hundred years and still perfectly functional."

"So is Helen your wife?"

"Lord, no. Helen of Troy — the face that launched a thousand ships."

"Oh, I get it now — what you meant in the pub. I'm sorry, Mark — you must think I'm a total idiot."

A smile crinkles his eyes behind his tortoiseshell glasses. "Not at all."

"It's just… I know nothing about sailing … even after living here for twenty-two years…" For God's sake, Marie — stop gabbling.

"Would you like to try? Come out on *Helen* sometime? She's very friendly — much more than my wife was, anyway," he winks.

"Oh I don't…" But why shouldn't I? "Yes. I'd love to, Mark. It's years since I've done anything new."

"Brilliant. Give me your number and I'll call you to fix a date."

A date as in an appropriate day, or as in…? As we say our goodbyes he gives nothing away.

CHAPTER 8

For a fortnight I've managed to turn back at the threshold but I can longer help myself. Filled with self-loathing I take two paces into Jude's room, then I stop. *Come on, Marie. You can't poke and pry around your son's possessions to find out something he doesn't want to tell you.* I dig my fingernails — what's left of them — into my palms. *No, no, no.*

And yet I stand here, not moving forwards, not going back. The sun is beginning to beat on the glass; I could always say I was opening the window to let in some air. Say to who? I am completely alone in the apartment.

I do open the window and lean out. I cock my ear — silence. It's weeks since I've heard the rush and roar in my ears and I breathe a prayer of thanks. To my right the down rises beyond the trees, stretching its long finger towards Old Harry. Corbin's sure to have left by now, but I might go up there this afternoon, all the same.

I flick through Jude's sketchpad but stop when I realise I'm looking for a female face. There is one, but it's only Pip, sitting on the shoreline pulling on her fins. It's wonderful the way he's captured the movement of her body, the wind catching her hair as it frames her face, but then he has known her most of his life. The picture's recognisably Studland, too, with the Redend pillbox behind her. It'll sell in days.

As I make my way to the pub kitchen Stephen's car pulls into the yard. The fish wholesaler arrives at the same time so I'm caught up in picking the freshest. Just as he is leaving the man asks very politely if he can have a cheque to settle their account. I call to Stephen in the bar but he doesn't come.

"I'm sorry," I laugh. "I have a disappearing husband. Do you know how much we owe you?"

"Not exactly… I could phone the office."

"Yes — get them to email Stephen to remind him. It must have just slipped his mind."

The man raises his eyebrows. "Again."

I can't look at him. "I'm so sorry. He'll sort it out. Honestly."

As I unload the fish into the fridge Stephen magically reappears. "The fish man needs paying. Said to remind you."

"Everyone needs paying," he shoots back.

"Yes, they probably do."

"And what's that supposed to mean?"

A lead cape envelopes my shoulders and sinks towards my chest. I shake my head. "Nothing. Just nothing."

"It's never nothing with you."

I am saved from answering by Baz steaming into the kitchen.

"Morning, Mar. Morning, Stephen. Lovely day out there."

"Yes … yes it is. We're going to be busy, I think."

"We'd better be." Stephen slams the door as he heads upstairs.

"What's got into him?"

I shrug. "As long as he leaves me alone I don't care."

Baz turns from hanging his jacket on its peg. "Sounds like you need a coffee to get you going."

"Good idea. I'll make them." In the quiet of the bar I check my phone as I wait for the espresso machine to warm up. Nothing from Mark. My toes curl in my crocs at the thought of him taking my number just to be polite. Did I have "desperate" stamped across my forehead or something? I reach for a glass and shove it under the brandy optic. The liquid burns my throat but my hands are steady as I carry the coffee back to the kitchen.

Baz and I work through one of the busiest shifts I've experienced, sweating as we grapple with piles of chips and endless oceans of cod and prawn pie. I fall into bed exhausted and I wake with the same ache behind my eyes as I went to sleep with; no threat of lightning, just the glowering pressure which may or may not break into a storm. The clock on my phone says 6 June 2004. There's a half-empty bottle of brandy on the floor.

Birdsong reaches through my open window; that and the gentle wash of the waves, high on the shingle. I swing my feet onto the boards and tuck the brandy into the old suitcase gathering dust beneath the bed. I'll never use it for anything else. Where would I go?

It's cooler this morning and I wrap my dressing gown around me as I creep past Jude's bedroom and pad down the stairs to the kitchen. My head feels heavy and light at the same time. As I wait for the kettle to boil I open the safe; the silver seahorse is still in my jewellery box, curled into the corner of its envelope. Poor little thing. It's been abandoned, along with my wedding ring. Maybe it once meant something to someone too.

I return the seahorse to its paper prison and push the box to the back of the safe. I make my tea then pop some paracetamol into a glass to dissolve. They'll be enough this morning. *Come on, Marie, admit it: the only thing wrong with you is a hangover.*

I can hear the radio from Jude's room so it's time for me to have a shower. I feel so much fresher afterwards I am even considering scrambling a few eggs when Jude comes down the stairs.

"Like some breakfast?" I ask.

"Later, I think. I'm off to the beach."

I smile. "That's a great idea — I was wondering about going for a walk myself. Fancy some company?"

"Well, yes ... of course ... but I'm meeting Pip. We're thinking of going swimming."

"Isn't it a bit cold this early?"

"Not in our wetsuits. She's still stressed out with revising and she says it makes her feel better. But ... come along anyway. You can always walk while we swim."

"Or make you both breakfast in the beach hut."

He rubs his hands together. "Now you're talking."

We load bread, butter, bacon, ketchup, some plates and a small frying pan into a cardboard box. He's laughing, chatting, more animated than I've seen him in a while. It makes me realise perhaps something has been amiss. Perhaps something he wants to tell me and hasn't dared.

There's just a tiny bit of warmth in the sun. Pip is waiting by the stile at the top of the path, her wetsuit hanging over her shoulder.

"Hello, Auntie Marie. Coming for a swim?"

"Not on your life. But I fancied getting out for a while and Jude's persuaded me to cook you some bacon butties to warm you up afterwards."

"What a fab treat. Thanks ever so much."

"You'll have your walk though, Mum, won't you?"

"Oh, don't worry — I'll stretch my legs."

Although it's early we are not alone on the beach. Way to our right, almost as far as the cliffs, a figure is crouching at the edge of the waves. I lean on the rail of the hut as Jude and Pip haul on their wetsuits, but he's too far away for me to see what he's doing. Once they've gone I'll get the binoculars and have a proper look.

It takes me a while but I focus them just in time to see the man stand and stretch. His shoulders are broad beneath a white T-shirt and a mere scrape of hair covers his head. I swallow hard. But even with his back to me he is all too familiar. I glance down the beach — Jude and Pip have stopped, ankle-deep in water, having a fairly animated debate. I don't care if they go in or not; I need to talk to Corbin. I need to know.

I lock the beach hut behind me and stride towards the cliffs. The man hasn't moved; he is gazing out into the bay, arms straight beside him as though standing to attention.

The dog is on me in a flash, jumping up and barking as though I'm a long lost friend. It wrong foots me and I lose my balance, tumbling sideways onto the soft sand.

"Troy! Troy! Bad dog." Mark sounds angry and he isn't the only one. I ignore the hand he's offering and lever myself into a standing position, desperate to see past him.

"Are you all right?" he asks.

"Yes, fine — just in a bit of a hurry — seen a friend at the other end of the beach — want to catch up with them."

"Oh, yes, of course…" As he steps to one side he turns and we both find ourselves staring at a stretch of empty sand.

It takes a long time for one of us to break the silence.

"They … they've gone." I stutter. "I have to say I wasn't a hundred percent sure anyway…"

"I'm sorry if you missed them because of Troy. He's a bad dog." He glares down at him, trying to sound firm and in other circumstances it would make me want to laugh. Instead I crouch and stroke the soft fur between Troy's ears. Anything not to have to look Mark in the eye.

"He won't learn he's done wrong if you do that."

"No, well … it doesn't matter. It's time I got back to the beach hut. Jude's swimming with a friend and I promised them bacon butties when they come out."

"Lucky them."

"I guess it's what mums do." If he's inviting himself I'm ignoring him.

He digs his hands into the pockets of his walking trousers, jangling his keys. "Look, I'm sorry I didn't phone. I've been away — on business — but I should have explained. I just don't know where time goes. Are you … are you still up for a sail on *Helen?*"

I stare past him, down the beach to where Corbin was. There's no one there. Just like when I turned back from the woods near Old Harry. No one.

Mark reaches inside his fleece and pulls out a card. "Look — I'll leave it up to you. Have a think and call me. The offer's there — genuinely."

I take it from him and I nod.

In the dim light at the back of the beach hut my fingers twist uselessly on the lid of the bottle of water, but after a few frantic moments I spot Jude's T-shirt and use it to get a grip. It splashes on the formica counter as I fill the kettle and I force myself to wipe up every single drop.

My fingers feel too fat to fit into the matchbox so I shake a few out onto the side. The gas gushes from the ring while I struggle to strike them, one after the other. I turn it off. Start again. Flame — no gas. Gas — no flame. Then a whoosh under the kettle which leaves me wringing my hand in my armpit. There was nowhere for Corbin to go.

I pull the bloomer from the cardboard box and manage to cut six fairly even slices. The butter has softened a little on its journey so spreads more easily than I expected. Finally, I separate the pieces of bacon and lay them out in the pan.

It will be a while before the kettle boils although it starts to spit and sing as I put the teabags into the pot and the milk into the mugs. This lid feels different to the water bottle, my hands more my own. At last I can venture past the folded deckchairs and old magazines stacked in the corner to lean on the rail and fill my lungs with air.

Jude and Pip are crouching on the sand behind the receding tide. She is drawing something with her fingers — pointing to a spot. His head kicks back with laughter and he sees me and waves. They stand as one and walk up the beach just as the whistle from the kettle tells me I can make the tea.

As they come up the steps I hand them their towels. The bacon is beginning to crackle in the pan and Pip lifts her nose.

"Oh, Auntie Marie, you're really spoiling us. It's just what I need to set me up for a day of revision."

"Is it going all right?"

"First exam tomorrow."

"So what are you going to do next year?"

She wraps the towel around her hair. "Marine biology. At Cardiff."

"Oh, so that's why you're so interested in the seahorses?"

"It's probably more the other way around; I've chosen what to study because of them. I'm going to start a petition after my exams, to stop the boats mooring in the bay so we can save them."

Jude raises his eyebrows. "Well don't ask Dad to keep a copy on the bar. The Smugglers needs those boats."

"Don't worry, Pip, I'll sign it," I promise her.

"If Dad sees your name…"

"What does it matter?"

The bacon is crisping around its edges so I turn off the gas and begin to make the sandwiches, filling the silence by asking Pip if she'd like ketchup.

I am squashing the bread onto the last piece of bacon when Pip tells Jude to show me what they found in the water. He exchanges a damp scrunch of paper for his breakfast.

I take it onto the decking so I can see it better. The red and white stripes are beginning to run into each other but as I prise it apart I realise it's a paper boat, its sail a mass of blue with tiny stars.

Pip's voice reaches me from the depths of the hut. "We think that bloke by the cliffs was putting them into the water. We saw a few float past. Must be something to do with D-Day."

The stars ooze from the gaps between my clenched fingers and burst inside my head. Silver splits the beach in two. There's cordite again, and smoke. I can't breathe. I just can't breathe.

"Mum?" Jude's hand is on my shoulder.

"I have to go — didn't realise the time — need to get the meat in." I all but run down the steps.

"But your sandwich…"

"You eat it."

I scramble up the wooden stairway. The path inland is a tunnel of trees closing tighter and tighter, squeezing together until they are inside my head and the leaves growing out of my nose and ears. Stars and stripes, and stripes and stars. Vomit splatters my shoes. Shit. This is as bad as it's ever been.

The living room curtains are drawn making a safe, dark womb and I curl on the sofa with the washing up bowl on the floor next to me, praying for the tablets to do their work.

Baz finds me first. He doesn't judge, just shifts from foot to foot.

"I'll get the meat in then bring you some tea. It's getting on a bit though … not sure about the chicken."

So I tell him to cut the beef and pork into smaller joints and to wrap them in foil the wrong way around — and how to quarter the chicken and cheat it into a roast with the deep fat fryer. He's out of his comfort zone but all the same he nods.

"The potatoes … don't forget to coat them in semolina and a bit of paprika. People will forgive almost anything if they get a good roastie."

Thank God it's Sunday — he should be able to cope.

It's Jude who brings my tea. He sits on the sofa next to me, squeezes my hand. "Thought as much."

"I didn't want to spoil your morning…"

He nods. "It's ok."

The tea is milky and weak and he's put sugar in it. He knows I can't face my normal builders' brew when I'm like this. He knows everything. Well, not quite everything. This time he doesn't know why. Secrets. If I share mine, will he share his? Or will he just think I'm going mad?

Next to the mug is the remote control. I turn on the TV and reduce the sound almost to nothing. Through half-closed lids I watch old soldiers interviewed on a breezy seafront. Must be France. Then black and white footage of men crawling up beaches, bullets hitting the sand, rolls of barbed wire. Sitting ducks.

I don't know if I am dreaming when I see Corbin's face. Two soldiers drag a wounded comrade into the dunes. His head is bent with the effort, but that profile... I sat on the bench next to him long enough. But how could I? All of a sudden we're back to colour again, rows and rows of graves, brilliant white against the grass.

When I wake the cushion under my head is soaked with tears. The television isn't even on. Below me the chink of glasses from the bar, a rumble of voices. I raise myself onto one elbow but it is too much; my head pitches and tosses as I reach for the washing up bowl. Somewhere inside a tiny voice is telling me to stop this but I'm too drained to listen. A spiral. That's what it is. A spiral down, down, down.

CHAPTER 9

It's almost a week later when I make it back to the kitchen. But Stephen has the weekend off so I feel safe to try. Through the window I watch Baz hurry across the yard, his head bent against the drizzle, and when he sees me, knife poised over a pile of onions, his look is one of pure relief.

"All right, Mar?" he asks as he puts his waterproof to drip on its peg next to the freezer.

"Still feel a bit spaced out but my headache's gone." It's been gone for days, but he doesn't need to know that. Only Jude has realised it's different this time.

"Back to normal?"

I nod. "Pretty much."

"I'll crack on with the potatoes."

"Please. And wash me a bag of couscous — I'm making tagine."

"Not sure we've got much lamb…"

"It's ok — I'm doing a veggie version. I'm struggling with the thought of handling red meat at the moment. Might have to show you how to make the burgers."

He nods, but he doesn't look keen. He's had a week out of his depth too. Stephen said we couldn't afford a relief chef. We probably can't. Not with Project Swanage on the go. But at least it gets him out of my hair — some of the time. If we divorced… No. Let him do it — I need all the energy I can muster just to breathe.

Jude hovers between the kitchen and the bar. He's spent a week hovering. It's no way for a young man to live. No sign of the girlfriend anyway — perhaps it's over. So now I spend twenty minutes beating myself up for feeling pleased.

At about half past one he brings me an order for two fish and chips. "It's for George," he tells me. "The old boy who was here for Smash."

"Tell him I'll save him some apple crumble."

"He said if you've got time to say hello later…"

"We'll see."

It's coming up to three o'clock and the kitchen is almost clear. Jude brings back the last two bowls, scraped clean of custard and I stack them into the dishwasher before releasing my hair from its chignon.

"Come on," Jude says.

"Come where?"

"To see George."

"I…"

"I told him you would. I'll bring you a mocha." Like a child with a treat.

George and Mark are sitting at one of the tables under the window. The sky outside is as grey as the mullion — a real prison of a day.

Mark stands to pull out a chair for me. Automatically I peer under the table.

"No Troy?"

"I left him in the car. Thought I'd just say hello then take him for a walk."

Oh God — was I that rude on the beach? "It's not very nice out there." Statement of the bleeding obvious if ever there was one.

"We don't mind — we're used to it."

Once he goes I am at a loss what to say. Jude brings our coffees but still I struggle. George is sharper.

"What's wrong, Marie?"

"I'm just worried... I bumped into Mark on the beach... I ... I had a migraine starting... I might have come across as a bit rude."

George snorts. "And he thought Troy had upset you. That's why the poor old mutt got left in the car today."

"Oh no ... it wasn't Troy's fault..."

Another silence and then, from nowhere, I find myself asking, "George — were you there on D-Day?"

He nods. "My arm had healed well enough and I was a tank driver — they needed every last one of us."

"I saw some old news reels on TV. It made me wonder ... how did anyone ever get off those beaches?"

"Some beaches were easier than others. We had quite a good ride on our section of Gold. Right up until the afternoon when we got to Le Hamel. Smack bang in the middle of the beach we were, with the Green Howards and Hobart's Funnies. Not saying we walked in, but there weren't too many Germans about."

"Hobart's Funnies? Who were they?"

He laughs. "Not who — what. Specially adapted tanks; some had flails in front to detonate mines, some had cotton reels to roll out road. Amazing. The Americans thought we were nuts but it would have been harder to get off the beaches without them. Particularly further up the coast. The Yanks had a torrid time of it — especially places like Omaha."

I pick up my spoon and use the back of it to sink the tower of cream into my coffee.

"It was the tanks, you see," George continues. "And the terrain, of course. There were cliffs. But on the beaches themselves ... if the tanks had got ashore..."

"Why didn't they?"

"Either they took no notice of Smash or they bloody panicked. Launched their tanks too far out so of course they sank — only three made it. They'd practised enough too; weeks and weeks of coming ashore just along at Knoll, here. God knows what happened on the day itself."

"So did you get much time to practise? Once you were better, I mean."

George curls his fingers around his cup. "Just the last week. And I mean that literally; Monday to Friday the exercises ran. The Yanks used to laugh at us for it being so British but the reality was they had to get the ammo off the ranges some time. So Fridays at five o'clock we all knocked off. And the poor bloody Canadians came in to clear up the mess."

"I never even thought of that. But they still find old bombs in the dunes, don't they?"

"To be honest it's a bloody miracle they don't find more. Seven weeks of shelling makes a lot of mess. They used some dodgy stuff, too, unpredictable. You know, out of date, a bit damaged — well I suppose they were saving the best for the real thing."

"Oh, I see."

George laughs. "No you don't — you practically glazed over part way through what I was saying."

"I was just thinking … about the people … those poor Americans at Omaha…"

"Oh, it was such a shame — nice lads, most of them. Lot of 'em stationed in Swanage. Some chaps were jealous because they seemed to get all the girls but really they were in the same boat as us. Cannon fodder. The brass didn't care."

My heart thuds in my chest. Can I — should I — ask if he knew any of them?

The moment is lost when a blast of damp air blows Troy into the bar, dragging Mark behind him.

George raises his eyebrows. "So much for a long walk."

"Cocked his leg on the nearest car tyre then made a beeline for the pub door."

Troy's tail thuds against the table leg as I fondle his ears. I indicate the window with my spare hand. "Can't say I blame him."

Mark removes his glasses and starts to clean them with a paper serviette. "Especially when he thinks he'll get his head scratched."

"Especially when there might be a few scraps of food."

"Dad! I don't know what's worse — you begging or the dog."

George winks at me. "If you don't ask you don't get."

He's right... "Did you know any of the Americans stationed in Swanage yourself? It's just my mum was evacuated there and she sometimes told me about them. One in particular was kind to her — he was billeted in the house opposite in Burlington Road. Lovely name — Corbin Summerhayes."

Mark laughs. "Not a name you'd forget in a hurry, Dad."

"I can't say I knew any of them that well. I remember a black guy because I don't think I'd ever met one before. He was a real gentle giant. Big Sam they called him. Used to sing in the dance hall in Bournemouth sometimes — had a beautiful voice."

"My mum always used to wonder what happened to the ones she knew." My fingers wind round and round Troy's ears.

"So is that why you came here, because of your mum's connection to the area?" Mark asks.

I look up. "Stephen's uncle owned this pub. Long story — I won't bore you with it. Now, Troy, let me pop into the kitchen and see what I can find you to eat."

I can't say I like serving behind the bar, but without Stephen I have to take my turn. Jude promised to go seahorse hunting with Pip and Gina's finished her shift. We couldn't pay her to work the extra anyway.

At least it's quiet. A table in the corner yet to pay for their Sunday lunch and a retired doctor and his wife from the village enjoying a glass of wine next to the fireplace. The shelf where the bottles of fruit juice live is almost empty so I decide to give it a good clean; everything comes out onto the floor then I wet a cloth in the kitchen sink and get stuck in.

"Good afternoon, ma'am."

My skull cracks on the edge of the woodwork as it jerks up. I half turn before I crash to the floor, sending bottles rolling for cover. Broad shoulders, square jaw, fuzz of hair. *No.*

I curl my head towards my knees and the lights go out. I hear the flap of the bar lift and sense the warmth of someone beside me, the scent of sweat and lemony cologne.

"Say — are you all right?"

If I open my mouth to speak I might throw up and shaking my head is out of the question. Instinct tells me if I stay in this ball the agony might stop. He puts his hand on my shoulder and is still as though he knows it too.

The nausea fades, taking the worst of the pain with it, but as I raise my head my vision blurs. A khaki-clad knee inches away from my face. I have to know. My eyes pass a fuzz of white T-shirt. Something different — something not right. A watch — a chunk of stainless steel on a pale freckled arm.

Doctor Ireland's voice interrupts my progress. "Marie — what have you done?"

The American answers for me. "She hit her head on the shelf, sir. It was my fault — I made her jump."

I look up properly to see a halo of grey hair loom over the edge of the bar. "I think I'll be ok — bit better already."

"It was one heck of a crack," the American adds.

"Did you pass out?" asks the doctor.

"No. Saw a few stars. That's all." I can't disguise the tremble in my voice although I'm trying to smile. My face feels disconnected from my skull.

"I think you should rest for a while, just to make sure you're ok. Come and sit on the sofa with Pamela and me."

The knee in front of me unbends and I feel the weight of his hand on my shoulder release. His voice comes from a long way above me when he says, "Can I help you up?"

"Please."

In a single movement he scoops me from the floor and for a moment we are face to face. Not long enough for my eyes to focus but the shape is right. Why is he acting like a stranger? Why am I?

He looks around the bar. "Can I perhaps get you a drink of something?"

"Hot tea with plenty of sugar would be nearer the mark," says the doctor.

"I'm not sure I'm that good at English tea…"

"It's ok," I tell him. "Coffee will be fine — there's a jug — filter…"

"I'm sure I can manage that, Marie."

Doctor Ireland leads me back to his wife and I sink so far into the sofa I might never get up. She clucks over me while he feels the top of my skull.

"Bit of an egg forming already — it's going to be sore for a few days. Get yourself to A&E pronto if you have any blackouts."

Having brought my coffee the American joins us, sitting with his back to the window. He has a glass in front of him but I can't see what's in it. The shape of him in the chair — why am I not calling him Corbin? There's something … something — the watch. No, something else. A beard? I screw my eyes tight against the light then open them again. Yes, it's something between designer stubble and a beard.

I cradle my cup in my hands as the American and Doctor Ireland make polite conversation. No, he isn't on holiday — he's on temporary assignment with the British army at Bovington. And what about the doctor and his wife? Yes, he loves Studland too — what a great place to retire to. They're very lucky. So is he. A long way from Ohio.

The accent, the voice almost, are Corbin's. But not the words. Watching from beneath half-closed lids I can see it's the same with his face; the jawline, maybe, the nose, the army-issue haircut. But this man has dancing eyes and cheekbones like Johnny Depp. Not Corbin, no. But perhaps because I was looking for him I thought it was. After Uncle Ted died I saw him everywhere.

Pamela pats my hand. "How are you feeling now, my dear?"

"Much better thank you. I should be thinking about getting on."

"I'd give yourself a little longer, just to be sure. Is anyone else about? Jude, perhaps? You really shouldn't be alone overnight either," adds the doctor.

"It's ok, Jude hasn't gone far and I need to…"

I turn my head towards the corner table but it's empty. The American sees my look of alarm.

"It's ok — I took their money." He hands me a roll of notes. "I hope it's right but they seemed honest enough to me."

"Thank you — you've been very kind."

"Not at all. This whole thing is my fault. I'll wait with you until Jude comes back."

"He won't be long."

The doctor stands. "Well, give him my best. Has he decided what to do now he's finished university?"

"Not really, but they've given him a part-time job there while he makes up his mind."

He indicates the pictures on the pub wall with a sweep of his hand. "He's a talented boy."

Once they've gone the American moves to the chair next to the sofa. "He spoke as though Jude's your son but surely you're not old enough…"

"I'm afraid I am."

"I'd have put you at not much over thirty — about my age, in fact."

"The flattery's lovely but rather misplaced, er — I'm afraid I don't even know your name."

"It's Paxton — Paxton Taylor."

"Marie Johnson." But surely he knows I'm Marie already?

"Look, I feel I want to apologise properly for causing your accident. Can I take you out to dinner someplace nice?"

"That's very kind of you, but accidents are accidents — they're not caused by anything…"

"Oh, there's always a cause, always someone at fault." His voice sounds grim for a second but maybe I misread him because now he's laughing. "But if you couldn't bear my company for an evening or you have a partner who…"

"No — it's not that at all. I'd love to. It's just I don't really have any time off — I'm the chef here."

"But surely they can't make you work every night?"

"It's not so much they, it's — well, I guess I make myself work. Me and my ex-husband. Well, not that he's strictly ex but he's moved out although we still run the pub together…" I'm babbling now. How embarrassing. "I don't normally work on Sunday evenings," I offer.

"Perfect," says Paxton. "I'll pick you up next Sunday at six."

With my sore head I am not the best company for Jude. He tells me I shouldn't be working. I ask him what choice I have. Snap. Snap. All evening. Thank goodness Stephen isn't around. I wouldn't want him to see us like this.

I'm still finding it hard to get to sleep at night, so I down a large glass of brandy then struggle on with *Far From the Madding Crowd*, the book drooping onto the duvet as my eyes finally close and drift towards the cliff where Corbin's waiting for me. But it isn't Corbin on the bench, and the closer I get the more indistinct his features become.

It's a little before six when I wake to the racket of seagulls squabbling over the bins in the pub yard. Through the gap in the curtains pale sunlight is already warming the stones of the church, ushering in a scorching day.

I creep past Jude's bedroom but needlessly as it turns out. On the kitchen table is a scribbled note — he's gone for a swim. Bugger. I want to talk to him before the day gets going. I need to apologise — and pluck up the courage to actually ask him about the mystery girlfriend. He gives so little away but I know there's something bothering him. A mother always does.

The pub is buzzing. Jude's shoulders droop throughout his shift. His face is pale, he doesn't eat. Stephen says we're like the walking wounded. He makes me put my bump in the accident book.

"What am I going to do?" I snarl. "Sue myself?"

He shrugs. "With you, Marie, I never know."

In the quiet of the afternoon I make Jude an omelette, fluffy and soft and packed with melted cheese. His bedroom door is ajar. I speak before pushing it open. "Can I come in?"

He has his sketchpad on his lap but the page in front of him is empty.

"I brought you an omelette."

He reaches towards me for the plate and fork. "It smells lovely, but I'm not really hungry…" His voice is shaking and he has to look away.

"Jude — whatever's the matter?"

"Oh, Mum… I'm so sorry," he sniffs and his voice breaks.

I put the plate on his worktable and wrap my arms around him. "Oh, my darling boy — what's wrong?"

"I'm just so sorry," he snuffles.

"What for?"

"For being … for being…"

"A little bit grumpy last night? Come on, Jude, there's more to it than that."

"No, there isn't — well, there is, but…"

"You don't want to tell me?"

He pulls away and wipes his eyes on his sleeve. "I don't think I can."

Oh my God — what is it? Is his girlfriend pregnant? Is she taking him away? I swallow the lump of fear in my throat. "If there's something making you that unhappy I think you should. I'm your mother, remember, and that means unconditional love whatever it is."

"It isn't that bad," he snorts.

"Well, from where I'm standing it doesn't look too good either."

He turns away and gazes out over the bay. I try again. "Jude — no secrets, no subterfuge. Not from me; it'd break my heart." He is trying to stop his shoulders from shaking. Oh God, am I making it worse? I put my arm around his back. "Please, Jude — I can't bear to see you like this."

He takes a deep breath. "It'll pass, Mum — I'll be ok. By tomorrow, probably — I'll be fine." His hand creeps into mine and he gives it a squeeze.

"Is it something I've done? Is it me and your dad fighting all the time?"

He starts to shake his head, then stops. "In part, maybe. It makes me wonder if … you know … love's worth the candle."

"And you're in love?"

The silence stretches before he answers. "Yes."

So now I know. It's true, what Ralph said. And she's going to take him away.

"Is she nice?" I find myself asking. "Apart from now — does she make you happy?"

"She's everything I've ever wanted. My best friend, as well as…"

"Then surrender to it — enjoy it. Grab that happiness while you can." Sometimes I surprise myself.

Jude twists around to look at me. "I didn't expect you to say that."

"Why? D'you think I'm too old to remember what love feels like?"

"No, but you and Dad…"

"We're not the best example, I grant you. But sometimes, Jude, sometimes… I still like to believe love can transcend everything. All right, so it didn't work out that way for me but you've got to try. Jude — if you want her enough you need to work at it, never let it go."

He hugs me tighter than he has in a long time. "Thanks, Mum. That's good advice. But it's not too late for you, either — you're shot of Dad — you'll find someone…"

I laugh. "I'm not sure I'm looking. Come on, eat your omelette before it gets really cold."

CHAPTER 10

By four o'clock on Sunday, I'm like a bloody teenager, still wondering what the hell I'm going to wear. Or say. Or do. If I had Paxton's number I'd call him to cancel; I even consider phoning Bovington Camp but instead I sit in my bedroom, twisting my lipstick up and down, wondering if it's too bright. I put some on. Wipe it off again. He probably won't turn up anyway.

I've told Jude I'm meeting some friends for a drink in Swanage. That's a joke. Somebody's birthday. Somebody's brother is picking me up. So I'll dress for that and hope to God Paxton doesn't arrive in a US army jeep.

It's almost as bad when a dark green Ford Capri pulls up next to the pub and Paxton's head appears from the window. I've been waiting at the private door to our apartment and make a dash for the passenger seat before anyone sees.

Paxton's eyes are sparkling with amusement. "In a hurry to get away?"

"Well, it's such a lovely evening…"

"You're not wrong there. It's gonna be a real treat to sit on the terrace before dinner."

"Terrace? Where are we going?"

"Some place in Corfe called Morton's House. I asked around the base then checked it out on the web — it looks real classy."

Too true it does. Only two AA Rosettes. I look at my Indian cotton skirt. "I'm not sure I'm dressed…"

"Marie — you look gorgeous. C'mon, let's go."

Sitting opposite Paxton at a wooden table surrounded by a fragrant box hedge I even begin to feel just a little bit gorgeous.

The evening sun warms the grey stone of the building behind us but I've turned my back on it. Too much like The Smugglers' big brother with its stone lintels and leaded windows. Emboldened by my second glass of wine I ask if we can eat outside.

I choose an asparagus and broad bean risotto, delicately flavoured with saffron. Paxton has steak, well-cooked. He seems anxious about the food and I ask him why. He tells me it's because I'm a chef. I laugh. "I'm completely self-taught. No airs and graces — just pub grub to please the masses."

"That's not what I've heard — back at the base one of the first places the guys said to go for a meal was The Smugglers. When I said I was taking out the chef they told me I had to up the ante."

I smile across the table. "Well, you certainly have."

"Good. I wanted you to have a real special time — and to be honest I thought I'd goofed up when you first got in the car."

"Why was that?"

"You looked like you didn't want to be there — like you'd have run back inside and bolted the door if you could."

"Oh Lord, did I?" I fumble around for an excuse. "I think perhaps I was surprised by the Capri — you ... er ... don't see many of them around these days."

"No, they're something of a classic, I believe."

"You could say that. It's just, when I was growing up there was a certain sort of guy who drove one."

He laughs, throwing back his head. He looks completely different to Corbin tonight; fairer altogether, light skin beneath his stubble, relaxed in chinos with a sharp crease up the middle and a navy shirt with a button-down collar. "So were you worried about your virtue?"

"To be honest my virtue's something that's never worried me. But tell me, why did you choose that car?"

And so he does. As we make our way through blackberry parfait with a garnish of redcurrant sorbet and on to coffee, he explains that his father worked for Ford. As a young widower putting in long hours to raise his kids with his parents' help, his only selfish pleasure was a different car every year.

"A Capri's something he's never driven. It was so much a European model and Ford never really marketed it at home. When I arrived here I got onto the Auto Trader website to find an old heap and there one was — some guy near Southampton was selling it — and I couldn't resist. Always thought I'd do it up a bit but somehow I've not started yet. Perhaps I won't now." He rubs the side of his nose.

"Why not?"

"I ought to tell you, Marie — I'm just on a six month tour here and I'm almost halfway through already. Could be extended. I'd like it to be — but there's no guarantee…"

"Paxton — there are never any guarantees." There is a lump of fear in my throat as I say it but it's the truth. I want to look into those grey-blue eyes but I somehow can't drag my gaze away from the fingers of my left hand, curled around my tiny coffee cup, my nails bitten and raw.

Silence. Have I got him wrong? Did he feel he had to tell me for another reason? He's so much younger than me and so damn attractive. He's just being polite. Oh God, I'm making such a fool of myself. I'm too far gone, too long in the tooth for this game.

The touch of his fingers is on my arm, sensuous and slow. I am still too scared to look but he sees me smile and gives me a little squeeze. "Come on, let's get the check."

Except when he has to change gear Paxton holds my hand all the way back to Studland. Pink clouds streak the sky over Old Harry and a warm breeze carries the scent of distant broom from the heath. But the garden of The Smugglers is filled with chatter and Stephen's BMW is still in the yard. As Paxton brings the Capri to a halt in the car park he turns to kiss me but I pull away.

"Wait. I'll get the keys to the beach hut."

Side by side we walk between the trees towards the wooden steps to the beach. A parakeet squawks in the branches and I gabble on about how the first pair appeared when Jude was thirteen and how they've lived here ever since. The hum of the pub is replaced by the swell of the sea as it rakes over the shingle bars.

On the decking outside the hut, Paxton kisses me. It's too long since I've tasted the sweetness of another tongue and its magic floods my body with warmth. As I raise my hands to wrap them around his neck he takes the keys from me and pulls me towards the hut. He guesses straight away which one fits and in just a few seconds the door swings open. For a moment the tangle of deckchairs and sun loungers inside is illuminated by the sunset but Paxton pulls the door closed behind us and we are lost in each other and the velvety blackness.

It's early next morning and the apartment is quiet. I slide my back down the cool enamel of the bath, immersing my breasts in the scented foam. Breasts which were completely irrelevant this time yesterday. Irrelevant and forgotten. I watch my hand as it travels over the curve of my hip towards my thigh and thank the lord of little green apples I haven't run to fat over the years.

That doesn't mean a bit of basic maintenance isn't long overdue, but as I pick up my razor there is a gentle tapping on the bathroom door.

"Mum — have you seen the beach hut keys?"

Damn. Damn, damn, damn. "I'm pretty sure they were on the hook yesterday evening. They aren't there now?"

"Well no, if they were I wouldn't be asking." I suppose he's right to sound cross.

"You need them this minute?"

"Yes. I'm going swimming with Pip and my wetsuit's in there."

"Well, I'm sorry, Jude but I can't help you. You could try texting your father?"

"He never goes near the beach hut." This is beginning to sound like a teenage strop.

"He might have needed one of the other keys on the ring."

"He doesn't drive your car, either." I rack my brains for where I put them when I got back last night but nothing comes to mind.

"Mum?"

I stifle a sigh. "Is it really too cold to go in with shorts and a rash vest? It is the longest day, after all."

"Well, if I have to I have to." He stomps along the landing and a tide of guilt surges up the bath. My hand hovers over my razor — am I being selfish? As a door slams below me I raise my left leg out of the water and begin to soap it.

We search for the keys on and off all day. I even race down to the hut while Jude is having his breakfast, but it is locked fast. I hold my hand against the wood for a moment and close my eyes, feeling more alive than I've done in years. If it never happens again it was worth it.

Jude's mood improves as the morning wears on. He has an evening off to look forward to and I've no need to ask what he's doing. Now he's half told me about her he doesn't need to make excuses. Hearing him tell his father in no uncertain terms that he can't cover the bar tonight makes me feel unusually smug.

"What are you smiling at?" Stephen snaps.

"I'm not smiling at anything. I'm just happy."

"Happy? Why?"

I indicate the sunshine slanting into the yard outside. "Oh, what a beautiful morning," I begin to sing and Baz creases up.

Lunch is relatively quiet but the evening shift makes up for it in spades. More in the bar than in the kitchen but all the same I'm relieved when Baz dries the last of the pans and takes off his apron.

"Want a cuppa?" I offer.

"Nah — football on the telly. Getting down to the business end now." I nod. It's the European Cup or something — we're expecting a quiet night on Thursday when England play their next game. All the same I set the kettle to boil and rest on the door jamb, watching the bats swoop around the church tower.

There is a whisper of my name on the breeze. At first I'm not sure so I step into the yard but yes, there it is again. I turn towards the car park to find Paxton leaning against the wall.

"I've been waiting for him to go. I've brought your keys back — ended up in my pocket last night."

I smile. "Jude's been turning the place upside down for them."

"Did you let on?"

I'm laughing now. "No."

"Why not?"

"Walls have ears." I jerk my head in the direction of the pub.

"Sure. C'mon — let's take a walk."

When Paxton hands me the keys to unlock the hut door it's clear it isn't his first visit tonight. The deck chairs are folded away and the centre of the floor is covered with the cushions from the sun loungers. Tea lights flicker in jam jars and a half bottle of champagne rests in a cooler next to two glasses.

I cover my mouth with my hands. "Oh, Paxton, this is just so romantic."

"Well, tonight I thought, you know, we could take our time."

Afterwards I ask him about his life at Bovington.

"Why I'm here? I'm probably not permitted to say. But my normal job is a sergeant in the First Armored Division of the US army." I am touched by the pride in his voice and I tell him so.

"Yeah, well, it's a pretty special thing, being able to serve your country — especially in times of war."

"War?"

"The war against terror, Marie. At home and abroad."

I guess from that he's probably seen active service. It's an uncomfortable thought that his gentle hands might even have killed. Despite myself, I shudder.

"What is it?"

I shake my head. "War — it isn't nice."

"You can say that again. But what is nice is coming to a peaceful part of Dorset on what's quite an easy gig and meeting a beautiful woman. Anyway, I'm not so much a soldier as a technical guy — fixing tanks, making them run better. I told you my dad works for Ford and Grandpop did too so I guess machines are in my blood."

"Tanks? Studland had a brush with tanks you know."

He sits up and reaches for his champagne glass. "Yes — Exercise Smash. I arrived just in time for the re-enactment."

"I missed it — the pub was heaving. Would have been interesting to see it but there you go. Someone was saying they had a tank here just like the ones they used back then."

"Well, if you're really interested I can show you."

"How come?"

"The tank museum opposite the base has borrowed it for a D-Day exhibition. I volunteer in their workshops when I'm off duty and I'd be more than happy to give you a guided tour on Sunday."

I run my hand over the fine hairs on his stomach. "Now that's an offer I can't refuse."

It's all very well having a distraction like Paxton, but in the everyday grind of the pub things are getting worse, not better. Even on the morning of our date the vegetable wholesaler is at the back door asking to be paid. Stephen talks to him quietly, his voice as low as he can manage.

He sees the man off and returns to the kitchen, his shoulders drooping a little.

"Stephen — why haven't we got any money?"

He mutters something about margin pressure and cash flow and turns towards the bar.

"No, don't try to blind me with science. We're as busy as we were last year; we have the same staff; we're charging more for the food. What's gone wrong?"

"Don't start, Marie."

"I want to know."

"It's complicated…"

I grab his wrist. "It's Swanage, isn't it?"

"Well, of course, there's a certain outlay required…"

"And a huge mortgage to pay off. Stephen — we could lose everything."

"It's not that bad…"

"Then prove it. And stop treating me like an idiot."

He twists away and grabs a piece of paper from the message pad next to the phone, bending over it and scribbling hard. "Right — here are the passwords for the computer. The books are bang up to date. If you're so clever you can work it out for yourself."

Not today I won't. It's already going to be something of a scramble to finish service and get ready for Paxton to pick me up at half past three. I toy with the idea of letting Baz in on my secret but a sea mist keeps the visitors away and I am able to slip upstairs with twenty minutes to spare. Not long for a shower and I almost stab myself with my eyeliner when I realise it's already twenty-five past and I'm still wrapped in my towel. But my best underwear is ready and I squeeze into my jeans and a white cheesecloth blouse before racing downstairs.

The Capri is idling in the lane outside The Smugglers.

"Sorry," I gasp as I slide into the passenger seat.

"No problem — you're worth waiting for. Especially in those jeans. The guys are going to be so jealous."

"The guys?"

"In the workshop at the museum. I thought we'd drop in there first then I'll take you to see the DD at closing time. Nice and quiet — a private view." He winks.

"The DD?"

"Full name Valentine Mark 9 Double Duplex. Not that Mark 9s were used in Smash but this is the only surviving one in the UK so we have to make the best of it."

"And it still floats?"

"Apparently. Although from what I could see at the re-enactment the guy who restored it more or less drove it ashore from the landing craft. Looked impressive though and you've got to admire the work he'd done. We got a Sherman DD coming to the museum soon — that's what was actually used on D-Day. American technology."

"George said a lot of the American tanks didn't make it ashore."

"Who's George?" A tiny furrow appears between his brows.

"A veteran who comes into the pub sometimes. Nice old boy."

The tank museum resembles nothing more than a building site. Paxton explains that a huge new display hall is being built but for the moment the tanks are housed in and around a glass-fronted atrium with what looks like a corrugated iron shed tacked onto one side of it. Behind us the wire fences of the army camp do little to hide the jumble of buildings beyond.

"Is that where you're living?" I ask.

He shrugs. "I've been worse places. I'll take you for a cup of tea in the NAAFI afterwards if you're really good."

I tuck my arm into his. "You Americans sure know how to treat a lady."

His breath is hot on the side of my face. "We sure do," he whispers. "Come on — let's meet the guys first."

The barn-like doors of the workshop are open but stepping over the threshold feels like entering another world. Although daylight floods in, industrial scale strip lights hang from the ceiling illuminating three tanks and various scraps of metal strewn across the floor. From behind a screen in one corner comes the fizz and spark of welding and big band music scratches free from a radio hidden somewhere to my right.

A man in navy overalls is lying on the floor in front of us, his arms stretched between the huge metal teeth of a tank's tracks. A sheen of sweat covers his bald head and an acrid chemical smell fills the air around him. Paxton kicks him gently on the leg.

"Hey, John — I brought a visitor."

"Just a moment, lad. Need to get this pushed right back in. Hand me the size three screwdriver, will you?"

Paxton crouches and picks the tool from a row laid out on the floor. A long-fingered hand emerges from between the tracks and takes it from him. I gaze at the top of Paxton's head. Under the fine stubble a faint scar stretches from his crown towards the end of his left eyebrow. I supress the urge to run my finger along it.

As Paxton hunkers next to John, waiting for instructions, a stocky man of about sixty wanders over to introduce himself. His name is Alex, he tells me, and he's the volunteer supervisor. Runs a garage in Dorchester — been here twenty-five years.

"Good to see Paxo settling in," he says with a wink. "He's not bad for a youngster — it's all electronics these days but he still knows which way up to hold a spanner and his soldering's pretty neat too."

Paxton looks up from his lowly position and grins. "He'd never say it to my face, though. Wouldn't want me getting a swelled head. Treats me like dumb muscle most of the time."

"Isn't dumb muscle what the girls want these days, Paxo?" Alex laughs.

"Marie's not just some girl, Alex, I can promise you she's all woman. I'd like to think I can offer her a little bit more than that."

The heat rises up my chest and spreads towards my neck. I have a strong urge to pull the top buttons of my blouse together.

Paxton stands, wiping his hands on his trousers. "There you go, Johnny, there's the size three. I'm going to show Marie the museum."

By the time we walk between the two camouflaged tanks flanking the entrance, an elderly gentleman in a blazer adorned with an impressive row of medals is locking the doors. He stops when he sees us.

"Hello, Paxton. Bit late, aren't you?"

"Sorry, Harold. Marie's a chef and she doesn't get much time off. I was kind of hoping we could have a little look around after hours. She lives in Studland so she's longing to see the Valentine DD."

"Of course, you would be, my dear. Very important piece of Dorset's military history and it's only here for a few months. Well, seeing as it's you, Paxton."

Paxton takes the keys from him. "I'll lock up when we leave and put these in the guardhouse."

"Best lock up after me now. I've left the float in the till ready for tomorrow — don't want anyone wandering in while you're in the exhibition hall."

Paxton grins at me. "We sure don't."

Inside the hangar the exhibits are illuminated by weak sunshine filtering through the skylights. Paxton leads me down a wide red pathway painted on the concrete floor, past more camouflaged and sand-coloured tanks and armoured cars and into a second hall. Above the archway between the two are a

Union Jack, American and Canadian flags and an enormous banner reading *D-Day: 60 Years On.*

The Valentine is almost the first exhibit we reach. It's smaller than I expected, a box-like beige canvas screen rising from just above its tracks and in the water it would have been impossible to tell what it was. Paxton clambers up the side and the top of the screen sways alarmingly as he grasps hold of it. He steadies himself then reaches his hand back to me.

"Come on — it's perfectly safe — and it's the only way you'll see the machine itself."

Incredibly, the canvas screen does hold our combined weight and we gaze down onto the body of the tank. It is freshly painted in dark green with a white horse about a foot square just behind the gun turret. Paxton explains tanks were often given names by their crews.

"What, even deathtraps like these?"

He looks away from me. "Especially deathtraps. Well, all tanks are deathtraps, one way or another. The names are kind of for good luck."

"White Horse must be luckier than most."

He nods. "I guess so."

I want to ask why he chose the tank corps but he jumps down and walks towards the next exhibit. "Come on," he calls over his shoulder. "Let's see the rest of the show." I slide until I'm perching on the ridge of metal above the tracks then lower myself to the floor.

Paxton is silent as we wander about, but after a while his arm slips around my waist and gives me a squeeze. In front of a jeep with a star in a white circle on the bonnet he stops to kiss me, the merest touch of stubble on my lips.

"You ok?" I ask.

"Uh huh. Just pondering the possibilities."

"Possibilities?"

"Hmm." He starts to walk around the jeep, his fingers trailing along its flank. Under them are what look like bullet holes.

"I bet she's seen some action," I say.

A sudden smile lights his face. "I was wondering if she'd like to see some more."

"Whatever do you mean, Sergeant Taylor?" I tease.

He pulls me towards him with such force he almost takes me off my feet. But his arms are gentle as he kisses me again, his tongue exploring the tips of my teeth. "Back seat action," he breathes. And as he presses his body into mine I am giddy with it, with him, and with the me I thought I'd lost half a lifetime ago.

CHAPTER 11

The trouble with floating on air is back down in the real world something always pricks your balloon. Something like a bank statement with the letters O/D all over it. "Paxton, Paxton, take me away," I murmur as I flick the kettle on. But when I hear Jude's tread on the stairs I realise I don't mean it.

Jude's hair is tousled and he is rubbing his eyes. But he is smiling as he asks me what time it is.

"Almost nine. Treated yourself to a lie in?"

"Yes. My swimming buddy's off to London for the day with her mother and it's not much fun on your own."

He picks up the bank statement.

I shake my head. "It's bloody Swanage — it must be. Nothing else has changed as far as I can tell."

"Yes, but once it's finished…"

"You sound just like your father." I ruffle his hair as I put his tea in front of him.

"But it will make us some money. He showed me the figures."

"That's more than he'd do me. Just threw the passwords for the computer at me and told me to look myself."

Jude reaches across the table for the pub laptop. "Well let's see if we can make head or tail of them together."

The simple answer is we can't. Jude knows where the spreadsheet is but once he opens it his face becomes a blank.

"It was so easy when he showed me but now it's just a mass of figures. But somewhere here to the bottom right there's quite a big number so that looks ok."

"But what does it mean? It says £15,350 but when are we going to get it? And are we sure it's coming in not going out?"

"Hell — I don't know. Sorry, Mum." He picks up his mug. "I can show you the takings sheets if you like — I understand those."

Over breakfast we piece together the money coming in every week for the past eighteen months. Jude calls out the numbers and I scribble them on the envelope the bank statement came in next to the date. Apart from April being much higher this year my gut feeling was right — nothing has changed.

We are so engrossed we don't hear Stephen's car in the yard and before we know it he is standing behind us. He takes one look at what we're doing and bursts out laughing.

"The blind leading the blind."

I swivel on my seat. "Well at least Jude's trying to help me work out what's going on. Not that it's rocket science." I pick up the bank statement but he snatches it away and swears.

"Dad — I wanted to show Mum the figures for Swanage but I couldn't really remember…"

"For goodness sake, Jude, sometimes you're so stupid I wonder if you're really mine. How are you ever going to manage this place if you can't get a grip on the finances?"

Jude goes white beneath his tan, his eyes dark balls of fury. "Then perhaps I won't ever manage it — perhaps I'll get a life!" He pushes back his chair and belts down the stairs, slamming the door behind him.

Stephen sighs as he heads for the biscuit barrel. "Now look what you've done."

"Me? I rather think…" But I grind to a halt. "Stephen. Let's just stop this, ok? Whatever sort of mess we're in, even though we're not a couple any more we're in it together. And we need to get out of it together. Get things straight, move on with our lives."

He throws the barrel on the floor with a clatter, crumbs flying in all directions. "And since when did you become so bloody reasonable?"

Clearly a rhetorical question. I open my mouth to speak but he's already thundering downstairs to the bar.

I pick up Jude's chair, sweep the remains of the biscuits away then return to the spreadsheet he's left open on the laptop. But however hard I stare the numbers don't become any clearer.

Even though it's only Tuesday the fine weather brings out a fair number of local pensioners — including George. When the bar quietens after lunch Jude goes to sit with him, and once Baz stacks the last of the pans on the shelf and disappears across the yard I join them.

"I don't know how you look so fresh after a shift in a hot kitchen," George tells me.

I laugh. "I don't usually."

Jude turns. "George is right, you know — there really is a sort of glow about you these days. It's great to see you looking so much better."

"Have you been poorly, Marie?"

"Well a bit, a few weeks back…"

"Mum gets terrible migraines sometimes."

"Ah yes, I remember you saying — you were starting one when you met Mark on the beach and thought you'd upset him."

"Who's Mark?" asks Jude.

"He's my son," George tells him. "Comes here quite a lot to walk his dog."

"The guy with the collie?" He casts me a questioning glance but Stephen comes through the front door carrying a tray of glasses. He stops by the table and puts them down.

"Well, if you've got time to gas, Jude, I'll be off. Put these in the washer will you?"

Jude looks away but gives a brief nod. His shift must have been hell.

I put my hand on his knee. "Ok?"

"Yeah — I best do as he says though."

George watches as he picks up the tray and disappears behind the bar. "Your — er — husband's not in the best of moods?"

Despite myself I smile. "Er-husband is probably the right description for it. We're still married but in name only. He's living somewhere else and I sure as hell don't want him back. Today's been particularly bloody. He and Jude had an almighty fall out."

"Do you mind me asking what about?"

I look at his neatly-trimmed grey hair and the lines around his pale blue eyes and I just know I can trust him. "Money. Or Jude's lack of understanding of it." I hesitate. "No — that's wrong — Jude was trying his best — he was trying to help me find out why we're in such a financial mess all of a sudden but he's not a figures person either. Stephen's always done the books…"

"Financial mess? I'd have thought this place would have been thriving."

"Me too. But there's no money in the bank. Stephen's bought a place in Swanage he's doing up and I think that's the problem but he won't admit it — just told me to prove it. But he knows I can't — I don't even know how to read a spreadsheet."

George steeples his hands together. "Mark could help you with that."

"No — I couldn't possibly ask him."

"Yes you could. He's been running his own business for donkey's years. He knows about these things. Swap a few lessons in finance for a couple of square meals — you'd be doing you both a favour."

I find myself smiling. "Is he really so hopeless in the kitchen? My mum always said if you could read you could cook and obviously Mark can read."

"It's not so much hopeless as not interested. When Carina left him he just moved into that little flat and bought a microwave. Says he's too busy. I suppose he always was more wedded to the business than to her."

"And she got fed up with it?"

"No. She was a nasty piece of work from the start. He almost lost Clear Water over the divorce too…"

"I can't imagine him with someone like that."

"I'd never tell him as much but it broke his mother's heart. I don't think she ever got over it. He's not an only child but he came to us a bit later on and they were very close." His eyes cloud with tears and I put my hand over his.

He clears this throat. "Thank you, my dear. Still, that's enough of my woes. I'd best let you get on. Can you ask the barman to bring me my bill when he's finished with the dishwasher?" And somehow he finds it in himself to wink.

It doesn't take Mark long to phone so a couple of days later I find myself parking outside the industrial unit that is home to Clear Water Marine. My palms are sweating as I pull the laptop bag from the passenger seat. When I took it from the pub I felt like a thief.

I push open the door to the small reception area. In front of me is an entrance marked *Workshop Authorised Personnel Only* and a typed card on a low table instructs me to dial "0" for attention. I am just summoning the courage to pick up the handset when there is a clatter from the staircase above and a pair of navy deck shoes topped with chinos appears at eye level.

"Hello, Marie — you found us all right? Come on up."

At the top of the stairs are two large offices separated by a glass partition. The far one is populated with drawing boards. Anastacia's latest hit squeezes under the door, accompanied by gales of laughter.

"We call it the zoo," Mark tells me. "It's where the designers work. Bloody good they are — just a bit too noisy for us old guys. This is Paul," he nods towards a grey-haired man peering at a computer screen. "And this is Paul." A tanned hand waves at me while the other cradles a phone to his ear. "Keeps things simple."

Mark ushers me into a boardroom. "It'll be quiet in here — and private. Why don't I make us a cuppa while you switch on your laptop?"

At least I can do that much. When I told Jude where I was going he arranged the spreadsheets I'd need as icons on the screen so all I have to do is click on them. The problem is I don't know where to start. But I've brought a notepad so I square it with the corner of the table and put my pencil on top of it.

When Mark comes back he sits next to me so we can see the screen together. The mug of tea he puts in front of me is so milky I don't know how I'm going to be able to drink it. My palms begin to sweat again.

"Dad said the pub's in some sort of financial trouble but you don't know how to find out what's wrong?"

"I don't think it's the pub. Stephen's bought a house in Swanage he's doing up and I think that's what's draining the cash."

"You could well be right. Plumbers and plasterers and the like don't come cheap, you know."

"I didn't imagine they would."

Mark winces. "Sorry. I'm in danger of treating you like an idiot and you're clearly anything but."

"I feel like an idiot. I feel I should be able to look at the figures and understand what they mean."

He sits back in his chair and curls his long fingers around his mug. "There's no reason why you should. Most people running businesses don't. I mean, by and large you set up a company because you're good at what you do. You're a good chef and I've seen Stephen behind that bar and he's a good host. So you run a pub. I'm a good marine designer so that's what I do. We're none of us accountants."

"Yes, but Stephen understands the numbers — and so do you."

"Well, I don't know about Stephen but it took me a long time. It was only really when we hit a rough patch I had to knuckle down and get a grip on what the figures meant. Before that I just looked at the bank statement and it was all hunky dory."

"The bank statement's what's frightened me. That and people asking for money we don't seem to be able to pay."

"What sort of people?"

"The vegetable wholesaler, the fish man…"

"You mean people you have to pay to keep trading?"

I knew it — I knew it really, but Mark saying it out loud brings it home. I close my eyes but a red hot tear still bursts from under my lashes. "I'm so angry with him," I sniff.

"How overdrawn are you?"

"About a thousand pounds. I don't think it's our limit — I'm pretty sure that's two — but the money's coming in the same as it always did, but it's going straight out again I don't know where."

"Are all the takings being banked?"

"I … I didn't think to look. Jude and I checked the spreadsheets against last year and it's about the same but I never thought to check that. Mark, am I being terribly naïve?"

"The main thing is you're not hiding your head in the sand now. Come on, we'll get to the bottom of it. Have you brought the bank statements?"

I shake my head. "Stephen whips them away pronto, but he says the books are up to date and he gave me the passwords. Is there any way we can check?"

Mark takes the scrap of paper and pulls the laptop towards him, scanning the icons. "Good — the accounting software's the same as we use. Should be able to find my way around."

I stand up. "I think I'll just go and wash my face."

He nods without looking up. "And make yourself a fresh cup of tea while you're at it. I guess I was a bit heavy-handed with the milk."

I take my time over my face and again waiting for the kettle to boil. The tiny kitchen has a porthole-shaped window with a distant view of the harbour and the Purbecks beyond. I think of Paxton on the other side of the hills at Bovington. How does he fill his days? Does he think of me at all? Plan our next sexual adventure? The very thought of it brings a smile to my face. Perhaps if the pub did go bust it would force my hand to do something different with my life.

Mark has been quick with his task. He tells me he's checked the last few months' takings sheets to the banking on the computer and they agree. Then he explains without the bank statements he can't be sure, but at least the books look to be in pretty good order. That being the case, the pub is making a healthy profit but large chunks of cash are being drawn from the business. Too much, in his view.

"So I'm right?"

"I can't be certain where the cash is going, but I'd guess it is the house in Swanage. Is that where Stephen's living?"

"I'm not sure."

Mark's eyebrows shoot towards his hairline.

"It does sound odd, but there's probably a girlfriend somewhere — there normally is although the last serious one ended badly. He could be in the house but I just don't know."

"It's not a great feeling, is it? When someone you thought you could trust plays around."

"The first time Jude was only seven and it broke my heart. But he came back — he always came back. Said he was a fool and all that rubbish. But somewhere along the line I stopped caring and eventually I realised I didn't want him."

"He doesn't seem like the ideal choice of husband."

"Your wife didn't sound like a great choice either."

He nods his head. "Touché. I'm hardly qualified to comment on anyone's marriage."

I sip my tea as he bends his head back over the laptop. "There's a payment — £950 a month — started in April."

"That'll be the mortgage. He pulled a bit of a fast one on me and he'd extended it before I knew anything about it. It's secured on the pub and it terrifies me we could lose everything. There's no money behind us — not anymore. The Smugglers and whatever tip he's bought are all we've got."

"What sort of state is the house in? Could you sell it and pay off the bank?"

"I don't know. I've never been there."

"Marie…" His exasperation is audible.

"I've been really stupid, haven't I?"

"You didn't even go and look when Stephen suggested buying it?"

I turn on him. "He didn't suggest — he just went and did it — you don't know what he's like." Mark's look says it all. "Well, ok, perhaps you did get the idea…" I rub my hand over my eyes. "I'm really sorry but I'm starting to get a headache."

"I'm not surprised. Look, give me the address of the property and I'll go around and take a look."

"I can't ask you to do that."

"You're not asking. Troy will be perfectly happy walking around Swanage with all those lampposts and overflowing dustbins."

"No, really…"

"Come on, Marie, I'd be happy to. And you can cook me a meal afterwards for my trouble."

"I want to do something to say thank you for all this anyway. Stock your freezer with home-made ready meals perhaps?"

He laughs. "Sounds like heaven. Come on then, what's the address?"

I'm in a corner now — really in a corner. And then I remember the spreadsheet Jude was struggling with. I think — I'm almost sure — I lean over and take the mouse from Mark to click it open.

"There it is — Ulwell Road."

Mark peers over my shoulder. "Brilliant. If I pop a data stick into your laptop, can I have a copy of this? Do you mind?"

"No, not at all. I can't understand it anyway."

"Next time," he smiles, "I should be able to explain."

CHAPTER 12

Paxton's taking me to Morton's House again on Sunday — only this time he's booked us in for the night. *A four-poster bed, Marie,* he texts. *I've never been in one of those.* He sounds as excited as I am, but all the same it's given me a problem. I'm going to have to tell Jude.

The opportunity presents itself as I am contemplating starting the Old Harry jigsaw and half watching a documentary about the Glastonbury Festival last weekend. It's so different now to when I lived there. The town's probably changed beyond all recognition too and I feel a stab of regret.

The living room door nudges open and Jude comes in carrying two balloons of brandy.

He flops onto the sofa next to me and hands me a glass. "That was well hectic tonight — thought we deserve a treat."

"How did you smuggle those past your father?"

"He knocked off half an hour ago. Left me to cash up but I've just bunged the takings in the safe — I'll do it in the morning."

"Best hold some back to pay the fish man."

"He'll go mental…"

"I don't care. We've got to have fish."

Jude takes a sip of his brandy and leans back into the cushions. "God, that's good."

"It is too." Silence. "Jude — I've got something to tell you."

He opens his eyes. "Go on."

"I'm — I'm seeing someone."

He nods. "What, Mark?"

"No — not Mark. Someone else — an American soldier. We're … we're going away overnight on Sunday."

"Well good for you. About time you got one back on Dad."

"That's not why I'm seeing him. It's fun."

"That's even better." But his voice is flat.

I take another gulp of brandy. "So how's your romance going?"

He picks at his thumbnail, teasing out a quick. A rush of guilt floods through me.

"Jude — are you still unhappy?"

"Sometimes, I'm so happy I don't know what to do with myself. And other times…"

"What?"

"I think I'm just not used to this rollercoaster. I don't want to get off but it's scary all the same."

I touch his hand. "What's she doing to make you so doubtful?"

He shakes his head. "It's not her, Mum, it's me. It just feels so … fragile … so uncertain. Like it could end any second and then what would I do?"

I want to say, *you'd find someone who makes you feel secure, someone worthy of you.* But then I remember — Stephen and I haven't exactly set the best example.

He downs his brandy in a gulp. "Better go to bed. I'm swimming with Pip first thing then I'll have to do that cash pronto before Dad gets here. Going to be an early start."

"Jude…"

As I listen to his footsteps on the stairs, I realise I'm going to have to find another way to help him.

I stretch across the window seat, my feet in Paxton's lap and the scent of roses and damp tarmac drifting up from the garden below. I'm trying my best to make it special but the gloom of the day does little but reflect my mood.

"Oh my God, this is just so English. I can't wait to write my grandma and tell her."

I eye the crumpled sheets under the canopy of the four-poster. "Not everything, I hope."

"No — not everything. She's pretty open-minded but there are limits."

I raise my leg and stroke his cheek with my toes. "You said she more or less brought you up?"

"Yeah. Mom died when I was six and my father had to work so hard just for us to get by. Grandma's an amazing lady."

"In what way?"

"Well, when you're a little kid you feel so lost without your mom. My sister Darlene wasn't too long out of diapers and there was no way Dad could cope with the two of us and work. Grandma and Grandpop had a rickety old house with a big yard just outside Cleveland so we moved in there. Dad rented an apartment near the factory and came home weekends. But Grandma made it so much fun for us; did all the things moms are supposed to, but kind of better."

"What sort of things?"

"Oh, all manner. She let us climb trees, have a dog, bring friends from school back for picnics on the lawn, sat up all night if we were sick. But the biggest thing I guess was she taught us how to be happy. 'Sing yourself cheerful,' she'd say if we were feeling down. Old songs from the movies — she loved old-fashioned musicals — and we'd dance as well. You just couldn't be sad when you were having such a good time."

"She does sound wonderful."

He kisses my toe. "She's my rock. I call her most weeks and write her in between times — she just loves a proper letter. They don't make 'em like her anymore, even in Ohio."

"So that's where you're from?"

"Sure am. My grandparents moved to Cleveland from Louisville in the 1940s, and Dad was born there and so was Mom so I'm pretty much Ohio through and through."

"What made you join the army?"

"That was Grandma. Her brother was posted missing in France just after D-Day and she talked about him so much. His mom spent years waiting on her porch, just in case he came home. I remember visiting her in my uniform just before she died and she totally freaked out. I was nineteen years old and Grandma still tanned my hide after that one."

"I don't suppose you meant to frighten her."

"No. I thought she would be pleased I was following in his footsteps. No one ever told me…"

There's a knock on the door and I swing my feet onto the carpet to allow Paxton to let the waiter in. He lays out our supper on the table in front of the massive stone fireplace and reluctantly I leave the pool of daylight by the window.

It's all very romantic with candles and cushions and silver cutlery but the room closes in on me. Darkness creeps down the chimney and floods the deep red walls. I cut a slice from my tuna steak but I'm not really hungry. I don't want to seem ungrateful so I swallow mouthful after dry mouthful while Paxton tells me about high school in Cleveland. I try to listen but all the time I'm thinking about Jude; worrying for him, wondering how I can stop him from breaking his heart.

At first I don't really know what wakes me. I am so unused to sharing a bed I almost don't know where the muttering is coming from. I open my eyes and in the half-light of dawn see Paxton next to me, his head moving from side to side, his lips a blur of movement as the indistinct words flood out.

I am just turning my back and pulling the duvet over my ears when he cries out, his arm reaching in front of him. I shake his shoulder and whisper his name.

He is on me like a flash, pinning me to the bed, his breathing harsh.

"You can't make me — you can't make me!" he yells as his grip on my upper arms tightens.

"Paxton — stop it!"

His eyes are terrifyingly blank — there is nothing there as he drives my arms further and further into the mattress and away from their sockets.

"Paxton — it's me — Marie — wake up! For God's sake — wake up!"

My scream reaches him. Horror floods those empty eyes and he pulls away. For a moment we gaze at each other, then he buries his face in the pillows.

"I'm sorry, Marie — I am just so sorry." His apology is muffled and I curl next to him, my arm around his shoulder and my leg hooked over the back of his thighs.

"It's ok — you didn't mean it."

"I was back there — you can't understand — not unless — Marie, I am so sorry."

Once he is asleep I climb from the bed and wrap myself in a hotel dressing gown. From the safety of the window seat I close my eyes and listen to the birdsong rising from the garden below. I never thought before; what a soldier sees, what he has to do — how he carries that with him. There's an ominous

131

thud behind my eye, so I creep to the bathroom and pop a couple of migraine tablets out of their plastic before running a bath.

Paxton joins me just as I am climbing out. He holds a towel and wraps me into him. Bruises are beginning to form on the top of my arms but nothing is said.

CHAPTER 13

After a wet weekend the sunshine has brought visitors out in droves. I leave Baz to prepare the vegetables while I set about making some lemon tarts. Pastry means I need to concentrate and at least it takes my mind off worrying about Jude. And about Paxton, if I'm honest with myself. There's been a nagging doubt at the back of my mind all week that I shouldn't be taking on his issues too, but on the other hand maybe a bit of no strings fun is just what he needs to put them behind him. And after all, it's what I need too.

"Auntie Marie?" Pip's wetsuit is making a pool of water around her feet on the kitchen doorstep. She apologises as she thrusts the flippers she's carrying into my hand.

"Jude lent me these when mine broke — can you give them back for me please?"

"Of course — shall I call him?"

She shakes her head. "He must be busy judging by the number of people in the garden and anyway I need to get home — I'm starving."

"I've just made some beef sarnies for Baz and me — fancy one of those to keep you going? Home-made horseradish."

Her green eyes sparkle. "Oh yes, please. It'll give me the energy to get up the hill."

There is a lull in service so we perch on the wall in the yard together.

"Have you been in the water all morning?"

She nods, her mouth full of sandwich. "I'm trying to do a study of the seahorses. Jude and I saw one last week — first time in ages. I have a new theory they might still be in the bay but have just moved away from where the boats moor so I'm trying to prove it."

"Any luck?"

"Not so far. Perhaps they're attracted to Jude, not me."

"Well, they've always been pretty rare."

"Mmm ... like your lovely beef. Mum always cooks it until it's grey. Gross."

"Would you like another one?"

"I'm not nicking Baz's lunch, am I?"

"No — he's been helping himself to the chips all through service anyway. No wonder he's such a fine figure of a man."

Her giggle hasn't changed since she was in junior school. Nor the freckles across her nose. Like her brother in so many ways. The siblings I was never able to give to Jude.

"So are you going out to Greece to join Michael?"

"I'm not sure — I don't think so. I'm happy here to be honest."

The opening's come so easily it takes me by surprise. "I keep trying to persuade Jude to go but he doesn't seem keen. I'm wondering if it's something to do with his girlfriend."

Her "could be" is noncommittal and she takes another bite of her sandwich. I'll have to use a bigger hook.

"I have to say I'm a bit worried about it. He doesn't seem very happy, does he?"

"You don't think so?"

"Well no. And he kind of half tells me why then stops. He seems very loyal to her, but if she's making him miserable I do wonder if it's misplaced."

Pip licks the last crumbs of horseradish off her fingers and stands up. "Not something he's mentioned to me," she says and sets off across the yard. She is almost at the gate before she remembers her manners. "Bye," she calls over her shoulder before running along the path towards the village.

Back in the kitchen I quash my disappointment by turning leftovers into freezer meals for Mark. He's taking Troy for his walk in Swanage this evening but quite how I'll hide his presence from Stephen when he turns up for his supper I do not know. Things have been bad enough since he discovered I'm paying the suppliers in cash. I can still feel the shelves of the fridge digging into my back and his hot spittle on my cheek.

At the end of service he appears. "I'm going to bank the cash before you spend it," he tells me.

"You make it sound as though I'm taking it from the business for myself."

"You might as well be."

"Stephen — no — I'm only paying the people we absolutely have to, to keep going. If you look in the cupboards upstairs you'll see they're practically empty. I don't mind so much but it's not fair on Jude. He's putting in the hours but he's not getting paid. Please — we need to do something. Why won't you let me help?"

He stops by the door, head on one side. After all these years he still has to weigh me up. He looks almost regretful when he says, "No, Marie — this one's down to me. You just keep cooking your fabulous food and we'll be ok. I promise."

I am too stunned to answer. It isn't until he has driven out of the yard I realise that's what he intended.

It's almost nine o'clock when Jude slips into the kitchen to tell me Mark's arrived. Five minutes before last orders for food and with two tickets still to be cooked. I turn the seabass over in the pan, tipping it to drizzle the butter.

135

"Baz," I call over my shoulder, "what's left to do?"

"Two house burgers but I'm doing the garnishes, one tagine and another seabass."

I turn back to Jude. "What does Mark want to eat?"

"He hasn't said. Just ordered a half of bitter I wouldn't let him pay for."

I scan the pots on top of the stove. "Ask him if he'd prefer tagine or chilli. I'll bring it out when I've finished here."

Mark has hidden himself so far into the corner of the pub I have trouble finding him. Troy jumps up when he sees me, letting out a little whine when he realises he's trapped by his lead. Mark fondles his ears.

"It's for your own good, fella — you'd only get yourself into trouble."

I put two plates of tagine on the table and smuggle a few pieces of cold sausage onto the floor. Troy wolfs them down then looks at me expectantly.

Mark shakes his head. "You spoil that dog."

"I don't expect I'm the only one. And anyway, he's earned some supper too."

"Hmm. I'm not sure you're going to like what we've found though. I'm just hoping you don't shoot the messengers."

I put down my fork. "Oh God — it's a total wreck, is it? No roof, no windows…"

"No, no — it's perfectly fine. Quite a handsome Victorian red brick. There's a skip outside full of old kitchen units and pots of paint but that's par for the course. Means there's work going on."

"So what's the problem?"

"You said Stephen pulled a fast one with the mortgage? Well, I think he really has. I checked with the Land Registry — the house in Ulwell Road is only in Stephen's name. And there's nothing secured on it."

A piece of lamb is already in my mouth so I have to swallow it. I know — well I think I know — but I still have to ask the question. "What does that mean?"

"It means if it all goes pear-shaped you lose the pub, which you own together, and Stephen walks away with the house. Of course, a good divorce lawyer would soon sort it all out, but it's not a very nice thing to do."

I stand up. "That thieving bastard. I'll rip his balls off this time…"

Mark puts out a hand to restrain me. "No, Marie. Best to be calm about this."

"Calm! It's all right for you; sitting pretty with your precious business and your boat and everything but this is all I've got — everything I've ever worked for — me and Jude — he's bleeding us dry and now he's stealing our home from under our feet too."

"Marie — people are looking. You clearly care about the reputation of The Smugglers so for God's sake sit down." He clatters his fork onto his empty plate and folds his arms. Like a bloody schoolteacher. But he's right.

He clears his throat. "My ex-wife — she used to say revenge was best served cold. Not a pretty motto but it has a ring of truth about it." He pulls his briefcase from beside his chair and hands me an envelope. "The papers are all in here. And by the way — the financials on that spreadsheet are pretty sound. It's just a shame he didn't do a cash flow forecast to see how it would drain the pub's working capital. But when the house is finished and let it will make money, I don't doubt that. Enough to service the mortgage and a bit more."

"So you're saying I might be better to wait until the work's done before confronting him?"

"That's up to you. All I'm doing is giving you the facts and the paperwork to back them up so you don't get ripped off. Divorce can be a messy business."

I try to laugh. "And an expensive one. I'm not sure we can afford it."

"Perhaps the time isn't right." He leans down to unwind Troy's lead from the table leg. "Talking of time, we'd better be getting on. I don't suppose you've thought any more about coming sailing?"

Luckily his attention is focused on Troy's lead.

"We've just been so busy," I stammer. "If we get a quiet patch I'll let you know."

He stands up and smiles rather stiffly. "Well, it isn't compulsory…"

"It sounded like an excuse, didn't it?"

"It did rather."

"I'm sorry. You've just given me so much to think about this evening it's all I can do to stop myself from wringing Stephen's neck."

He laughs. "Perhaps it's best to concentrate on that. I wouldn't want to have to stand as a character witness in court."

It's all very well for him to joke, but once I've handed Mark his freezer meals through the kitchen door it is almost beyond me to climb the stairs. My legs ache. My arms ache even more. I hold them out in front of me when I take off my whites to inspect the rings of bruises that are only now beginning to fade.

There is something about the smell of the beach hut at the end of a hot day: warm rubber from the wetsuits, the salt tang of the sea. And now, Paxton's aftershave. Or is it cologne? Does designer stubble need shaving? I ask him as I run my fingers around his jawline.

"Why, don't you like it?"

"I was just wondering, that's all."

He closes his eyes. We made love for what feels like hours and the rush is still flooding through me. But Paxton is dozing, his head flung back on the cushions.

There is just enough light from the storm lamp on the counter to see his face. In repose his bone structure is more skeletal, his cheeks empty hollows where the stubble starts. I'm not sure I like it so I drop my gaze towards the easy sculpture of the muscles on his chest. I smile to myself; Stephen would be so jealous. Is Paxton my cold revenge?

His hand is soft on my arm. "Jeez — almost fell asleep there."

I lean over to kiss him. "And why shouldn't you? You looked so very peaceful."

He sits up, away from me. "You know very well why not. Not with you, anyway." He reaches out for his boxer shorts but I restrain his hand.

"Tell me. Tell me how bad it is."

He shakes his head. "Nah — it's fine. When I'm awake, anyway, so no sweat."

"And when you're having sex you forget about it completely?"

He glances at me over his shoulder. "Well you sure don't act like I'm doing anything wrong."

"Paxton — believe me — I have no complaints whatsoever in that department. And I probably shouldn't pry into something I can't understand, but you seem like a great guy and I don't like it that you're hurting."

The waves wash on the shingle outside. His head hangs and some instinct tells me it would be wrong to comfort him. Then, out of the perfect stillness he says, "It's combat, Marie. That's all. Combat."

Still I say nothing but I allow my hand to creep into his and give it a squeeze.

He looks down at me. "In this light I can't see the bruises on your arms but I know I made them. And I've done far worse. Best not go there."

"As a civilian you don't think what soldiers actually have to do. If you did, there mightn't be wars."

"There'll always be wars, Marie. Because there'll always be injustice and evil. It's human nature."

I sigh. "I think it's really sad you believe that."

"Sad? Damn, Marie — it isn't sad — it's the truth. There's good and evil out there and you'd better wise up or you're gonna find yourself on the wrong end of something you don't even see coming."

I scrape the towel from the floor and pull it around me. "What here? In sleepy old Studland?"

"Hell, yes, Marie, even here — six men died — you've seen the memorial. Six men who would have killed or been killed in France anyway. With thousands and thousands of others. Because they were prepared to stand up and fight evil however scared they were — and whatever the cost."

"Men like you, Paxton," I murmur.

"Men like my grandma's brother. At least I got to go home."

Eventually I fill the silence. "Why are you fighting now? Why don't you let yourself cry?"

The lamp flickers, but as he turns to me there is a ghost of a smile on his face. "Because fighting is actually easier." I push myself up from the floor and wrap my arms around him. I don't understand half of what we've been talking about but it feels like there's a new closeness and I tell him so.

In reply he kisses me on the lips. "You almost make me believe that's a good thing."

"It is. It has to be. Doesn't it?"

He kisses me again but he doesn't answer.

I am surprised to see the light in the upstairs kitchen window as I kiss Paxton goodnight. Before going inside, I check the yard for Stephen's car — no — it's gone. Probably just Jude being thoughtful and not wanting me to come home to a dark flat.

As I climb the stairs I hear a chair scrape back from the table and Jude all but blocks the door, his face obscured by shadows.

"What did you say to Pip?"

"What on earth do you mean?"

"You know very well what I mean."

For half a moment I genuinely don't, but then the penny drops. "Jude — I'm too tired for this. Let's talk about it tomorrow, huh?"

"Don't think you can fob me off just because you've been out with your Yank until one in the morning. I want an answer."

I put my hands on my hips. "Well perhaps you're not getting one. Not now or in the morning. Perhaps what I said to Pip is between her and me."

For a moment his shoulders drop. There are dark circles under his eyes; hollows where his cheeks should be.

"Ok, Jude — let's sit down. Talk about this properly."

He shakes his head. "Just tell me, Mum."

I slide past him into the room. "We chatted about lots of things … seahorses … whether she was going to Greece to see Michael…"

"What did you say about me?"

"I can't remember, Jude."

"You're lying! You're bloody lying and you don't care how I feel. Not as long as you're all right with your new boyfriend — you don't give a shit. It's all about you, isn't it? It's always all about you."

His words rob me of my breath and I slump onto a chair. But he's gone; feet beating up the wooden stairs and the slam of his bedroom door shaking the whole pub. I grip the edge of the table. It's ok — really, it's ok. He'll be calmer in the morning — just his father's temper, that's all. He'll be calmer in the morning — and we'll sort it all out.

CHAPTER 14

It isn't seven o'clock when I stumble down the stairs but Jude's bedroom door is open, the first rays of sunlight bouncing off the sheet twisted on top of his futon. There is a stab behind my eye as the reality of how badly I've betrayed Jude's trust hits home.

The greyness of self-loathing seeps into every pore, deeper and deeper as I wait for the kettle to boil. Silence fills the apartment. I think of the pub kitchen below; row of knives, gleaming tiles. I can't do it — not today. I scribble a note — two words — 'sorry' and 'migraine'. Another lie. But perhaps — just perhaps — Jude will understand. I crawl back up the stairs to bed.

Time telescopes in and out. Voices in the kitchen downstairs; Jude — yes — he's back. Thank the Lord. And Stephen — inevitable — grumbling. He won't like this. Good. But who'll pay the vegetable man? He's down there now, ransacking the fridge and taking back his carrots, his broccoli. What will Baz cook for lunch? Empty plates in front of the punters. No one's laughing. Not even Jude. His voice drifts into my nightmare.

"I won't do it, Dad — it's her own stupid fault."

"For the sake of The Smugglers, Jude. You can't imagine the number of times I've had to eat humble pie."

"Then once more won't hurt because I'm sure as hell not going to."

"What on earth's been going on?"

"Mind your own business."

In the end my body wins and I sleep. Dead and almost dreamless, except for Corbin. Tears ooze from behind his

Aviators but when he takes them off his eyes are empty sockets, cheekbones caved in, teeth fixed to nothing more than a skull. Then Jude — he's yelling at me — *it's all about you — always all about you.*

When I open my eyes he's there, asking rather stiffly if I want a glass of water.

"Please."

By the time he comes back I've eased myself up my pillows but I can't look at him. He hands me the glass and I take a sip, washing the fur from my tongue so I can speak.

"Have you forgiven me?" I ask.

He is already at the door, but he turns, his fingers white as they grip the frame. "No."

"I was only trying to help…"

"Help? You told Pip things I hardly knew how to say to you. Things so … personal…"

"I'm sorry, Jude — I didn't think…"

He shakes his head as he spits out the words. "D'you know what, Mum? That makes it even worse."

At least Baz is pleased to see me back in the kitchen, even though he asks if I'm sure I'm all right.

"I'll take it a bit easy this evening. Let's just say it's grill night and leave it at that."

"Good call."

So he washes lettuce and slices tomatoes while I marinate chicken in lime and ginger and rub steaks with olive oil and paprika. Jude is nowhere to be seen so I hand the revised menu to Stephen to write on the board. You could knock me over with a feather when he nods his approval. He is even more delighted when it goes down a storm with the customers.

I am still waiting for Jude when Stephen comes up the stairs with the cash bags and till roll. I ask if he'd like a cup of tea.

"That'd be good. I want to get the takings done before I go."

"Can I help?"

"No — just make me that cuppa and I'll crack on. Be quicker on my own."

I fiddle with the lid of the teapot. "Where was Jude tonight?"

"I gave him the evening off. He was in such a strop at lunchtime there wasn't a lot of point him being there. I was blaming you left, right and centre but then he admits he's had a row with his girlfriend. Didn't even know he had one, but I told him he should go and sort it so he'd come back to work in a better frame of mind."

"And did he?"

Stephen shrugs. "Must be going all right if he's still out."

"Yes, I guess so."

"I gave him some money, too, out of the till. Said he was a bit broke."

"Well you've not been paying him, have you?"

"I've not been paying me, either." He begins to count the pile of notes.

"Well, you have in a way, all that money you're spending on Ulwell Road."

"That's an investment. For all of us."

"There's not an all of us anymore."

He starts tapping at the keyboard. "Except in the business sense."

So there we have it — out in the open. We are not a family. A wave of something sweeps over me: Exhaustion? Nostalgia? It certainly isn't pain. The agony of losing Stephen left me a long time ago. When I found out about his first affair I was so broken … but when he gave her up he put me back together again. Piece by shattered piece. And I loved him all the more and we were happy for the longest time.

There's an echo in this room of a much younger Stephen lying on the floor making Lego houses with Jude, grabbing the hem of my skirt as I walk past, pulling me down for a kiss. Saying I'm beautiful. And I glowed with it, revelled in it. Only for my world to come crashing down again and again until finally it happened so often the hurting stopped.

For a moment I want to ask Stephen why he did it but instead I tell him I'm off to bed.

He reaches into his pocket and pulls out a black glasses case. "Before you go — your mate George was in at lunchtime. Think he left these. There's a phone number inside but I never got around to calling him. Can you do it tomorrow?"

"Yes, sure. Leave them on the table then I'll remember. And Stephen?"

"Mmmm…" His fingers are whirling over the laptop keys.

"Can we try to be like this more often — not always fighting? It wears me down."

He doesn't look up. "Sure, sure."

It takes Stephen precisely thirteen and a half hours to renege on his promise. Baz overcooks a piece of fish and the customer sends it back so Stephen storms into the kitchen ripping away at both of us, calling us wasteful and incompetent. Baz stammers an apology but I tell Stephen to shut up and leave him alone.

Baz crushes some new potatoes with olive oil and parsley while I cook a fresh piece of bream. It's not the easiest of fish and Stephen's attitude will knock a hole in Baz's confidence. I'm still fuming when I call service — even more so when

Stephen tells me to take the fish myself and apologise to the customer.

I let Baz go home early and vent my fury on the pots and pans. Stephen and Jude are laughing in the bar and it's all too much. I rush upstairs to change — I need to get out of here — and seeing George's glasses on the kitchen table gives me an excuse.

The phone number is on a little gold sticker which also gives George's address. I know the road — it isn't too far from the other side of the ferry. I can be there in twenty minutes and if he isn't in perhaps I can squeeze them through his letterbox or leave them with a neighbour. I stuff my whites into the bottom of the laundry basket and shrug a summer dress over my head. As an afterthought I brush my hair and add some lip gloss — shows a bit of respect to the old boy.

Purbeck Court is a semi-circular terrace of houses around a garden scattered with flowerbeds. The roses are in full display, underplanted with blousy petunias and luminous busy lizzies. In front of what appears to be a communal day room are two visitors' parking spaces and I leave my car in one of them before setting off to find number seven.

I can hear George shuffling along the hall and I hope I haven't woken him from an afternoon snooze. But he seems pleased to see me and ushers me into the house.

"You didn't need to come all this way to bring back my glasses — Mark would have picked them up if you'd phoned me."

"I'm sorry — did I disturb you?"

"No — not at all. Nice to have some company, actually. Do you have time for a cup of tea?"

It would be churlish to decline so he shows me into his lounge while he disappears towards the back of the house. The room has a huge picture window looking out over the garden and one wall is completely lined with bookshelves. I walk over to study them; almost all are about history, arranged in order from the ancient Greeks to the First World War. At the furthest end from the window is a small section about the sea and naval warfare in particular.

"Those are Mark's — there's no more room in his bookcase in the flat," George tells me as he puts a tray covered with a lace cloth on a side table. "He's always been interested in that sort of stuff."

"Looks as though he takes after his father."

"Well, it's fascinating, really, what came before. If you understand that, you've at least got a chance of working out what's going on today."

"I hadn't thought of it that way. I got a bit bored with history at school. Well, I got a bit bored at school full stop, really."

"I'm surprised at that — you always struck me as quite a bright young lady."

I laugh. "Then you're wrong on all three counts."

George grunts and turns his attention to the tea. He removes a cosy in the shape of a cat from a pot and pours the thick brown liquid into a pair of bone china mugs. On the edge of the tray is a plate of Penguin biscuits.

"Help yourself."

"Thank you."

To fill the silence I ask why his collection of books stops with the First World War.

"Because I can remember the rest, Marie — I was there."

"It must have been terrifying — landing on those beaches, not knowing what lay ahead."

"Terrifying isn't the word, but you just did it. It was your duty. Anyway our lot had quite an easy ride — not like the poor buggers further along the coast. Think I told you that. Don't want to go repeating myself."

"And I don't expect you ever talk about what it was really like. I know an American soldier who's been in Iraq. He says you can't understand unless you've been there."

"I don't think you can. Perhaps the years give you a bit of perspective but you never really forget the first time you see a man die. Or the first time you kill someone."

I look at George. He's not like Paxton; it's almost impossible to imagine him killing and I tell him so.

"You're quite right — a feeble old beast like me couldn't even lift a gun. But look at this…" He puts down his cup and makes his way over to a bureau half-hidden behind his chair. "I've got some old photos here and you'll see the difference."

The album is a small rectangle about a centimetre thick with a navy blue leather cover. The first page is a studio portrait of a young woman with shingled hair and enormous eyes.

"That's Eileen," he says proudly. "I made her have it done before D-Day. Carried a little print of it all around Europe. Still in my wallet now but in this one, well, you can really see how lovely she was."

I murmur my assent and he turns the page to reveal eight tiny photographs but he doesn't need to see them — he knows them off by heart. "Here we are in the ballroom in Bournemouth — forget what it was called but we had some good times there. That's me on the end with my arm in a sling. Couldn't dance at all when I first met her — it was purgatory watching her with the others — especially the Yanks — didn't know where they'd end up putting their hands. But she always let me walk her home."

"Were the Americans really that bad?"

He laughs. "Only some of them. Like I said before, most were just guys like us but a long way from home. There's a picture somewhere of that Big Sam I told you about, the one who sang." He turns a few pages. "Yes — here it is — he's up on the stage, crooning away. Brilliant, he was. Often wonder what happened to him."

"I guess it was impossible to keep track of everyone."

"More like keep track of anyone. Most of them you'd just have a beer with and move on. Some you'd bump into more than once but it was all very temporary — you knew you'd be fighting within a matter of weeks. Look — here's another one of Sam with his tank crew. He gave the photo to Eileen's friend Josie — I think he was quite sweet on her."

It's only because the picture is bigger than the others I can see the faces. Sam is leaning against a tank and perched on top are two white men, one dark haired and swarthy and the other … I swallow hard. It's just another GI wearing Aviators. I study the image minutely; the swarthy man is holding onto the gun turret and beneath it, to the left, is a white painted seahorse. Paxton already told me … but I need something to excuse my interest.

"Why is there a seahorse on the tank?"

"Oh, we all did that — gave 'em names. Don't know why, really. Just a bit of fun. The brass didn't seem to mind — probably thought we were bonding with them or something. Ours was Vera after Vera Lynn. Expect a lot of them were."

I can't take my eyes off the photo. "My American friend would be interested in this. He's helping out at the tank museum in Bovington while he's over here — he'd probably even know what sort of tank it was."

"I can tell you that — it's a Sherman Double Duplex — the Yanks had 'em first, like they did everything. But you take it, Marie — take the whole album if you like."

"No, I'd be too nervous — what if I lost it? But if I could just ease this photo out?" My nails are prising it from its corners even before he nods. I have to know. Have to have time … I turn it over in my hand and can't help but gasp.

"What is it, Marie?"

"The names — the names written on the back. One of them's Corbin…"

"Like your mother's friend?" He remembers the lie before I do. "Well what are the chances of that?" He slaps his knee with satisfaction.

"Well, I guess there could have been more than one Corbin."

"Not a common name, though."

"No…"

"All the more reason to take the picture. Although I must say you look a bit like you've seen a ghost."

The word rams home. I look at my watch. "I'm sorry, George, I really must be going — I need to get ready for evening service. I don't know when I'm seeing my American friend again — but I'll bring you the picture back just as soon as I've shown him."

"If it is your mother's Corbin maybe you'd better keep it."

I shake my head. "We'll never know for sure, will we? No — it belongs with the others. They're your memories, after all."

Friday afternoon stretches into the emptiness. This has turned out to be just the worst possible week. Jude is conspicuous by his absence and there hasn't even been a text from Paxton — he must have had enough of me too. I pick up my book but fail to concentrate; the characters dancing around each other is beginning to piss me off. I know they'll have to get together in the end, so why prolong the agony? I slam it shut and hide it under a cushion on the sofa.

My instinct is to take to my bed and weep, but I know from bitter experience it won't make me feel any better. Not that I deserve to. And the pain is fierce, fierce. Losing Jude makes losing Stephen matter too — like I've failed them both and I want nothing more than to turn back the clock and try again.

I know the moment I'd go back to. It's the last day of infant school for Jude and Michael. They finish at lunchtime and Michael's mother is working so I offer to have him for the afternoon. I'd promised them the beach but it's raining so we take the bus to Bournemouth and go to the cinema. Teenage Mutant Ninja Turtles. Those little plastic models were everywhere that summer.

Michael's mother joins us afterwards for ice cream. But as we walk along the side of the Lower Gardens, I spot Stephen sitting on a bench with another woman. His hand is on her knee. She's laughing.

Then, he turns and he sees me. And I could have — should have — left the children with Angie and gone up to them and told her to keep her filthy paws off my husband. Instead I just kept on walking, Jude's tiny hand swinging in mine. And in that moment I told Stephen it was ok. Told him I didn't care. I didn't fight for him — that's what I'd change.

Wallowing is no good. I've been here a thousand times before and I know the point it drags me over the edge. I can't let that happen — I have to fight for Jude and I need my wits about me to plan my campaign.

In the meantime — action. Any action. Anything other than just sitting here. I look around me; there are a million small jobs I could be doing in this neglected room but the first one I see is mending the hem of the curtains. I grab my sewing box from the cupboard next to the fireplace and set to work.

The rhythm of stitching is soothing. Not something I do very often so I have to concentrate and that is enough. Pushing the needle in and out in exactly the right places, catching up the faded fabric to its lining again, checking every so often to make sure it's falling straight.

As I work I am aware of people in the lane below me. Footsteps and voices carry as grandparents and toddlers make their way to and from the beach and walkers set out for the down. A horse trots past and I look to see who's riding it; no one I know — must have been hired from the stables — but as I turn away something else catches my eye.

It's no more than a flash of sunlight as someone glances towards the pub. Sunlight on Aviators. Stubbled head — the back of a white T-shirt — tanned arms pumping. Oh. My. God.

I push my feet into my crocs and race down the stairs two at a time. A car is edging along the lane, giving the horse a wide berth, and between them they block my view. But then I catch sight of Corbin as he emerges from the dip in the road and turns towards the cliffs. Taking my life in my hands I dodge between the car and the grassy bank and run after him.

When I turn onto the cliff path there is nobody ahead of me. The track is wide at the bottom but lined with thick hedges. I chase up the slippery chalk, my breath coming in ragged gasps. But there is no one there. No one.

I only stop when the path opens out onto the down. Walkers and cyclists dot the expanse of grass in front of me, but none of them is Corbin. Did he fork left to the beach? Common sense tells me he must have but in my thumping heart I know I should have seen him when I reached the bottom of the track.

Slowly I retrace my steps. It may be too late, but I have to check. The air is cool and damp beneath the hawthorns as the path winds into the bay, the only sound the squabbling of the sparrows in the branches above.

The sand is dotted with family groups but there is no lone man walking among them. I survey the scene from the grassy ledge in front of the beach huts closest to the cliff. There is one person on their own, and that is someone I know. But whether or not to approach them I can't decide.

In the end Pip notices me. I have to pass within yards of where she is sitting with a notepad in her hand.

"Afternoon, Auntie Marie."

"Hi, Pip — what are you up to?"

"Trying to plot the seagrass. It's easier at low tide because you can see it through the water but it's still very sketchy. I've made a start, though."

"Seen any more seahorses?"

She shakes her head. "No. Jude and I have been in a few times but nothing. It's really disappointing."

I laugh but it sounds false. It's a risk — a big risk — but I have nothing left to lose. "I don't think we're meant to talk about Jude. I'm not very popular at home because of what I told you. You talked to him about it, didn't you?"

Red rises up her neck to the tips of her ears. She doesn't look at me. "Not as such," she stammers. "Not deliberately — it just kind of came out."

I sit down next to her. "Oh, Pip — I'm not cross with you or anything. It was my fault for breaching his confidence. It was unforgiveable and I'm not sure he ever will forgive me." Oh God — my voice is cracking. "It's just … you know … he's my son and I didn't want him to be unhappy…" I bury my head on my knees. *Get a grip, Marie — get a grip. Not here. Not now.*

"If I told you that he is happy — she won't hurt him, that she loves him very much and it's all ok? Would that make it any better?"

I think about it. "Yes, yes it would. As long as it was the truth."

"Well that's all right then."

She stands and brushes the sand off her shorts. I wipe my eyes on my sleeve and look up at her. "How do you know?"

She puts her finger to her lips but I can see it in her eyes.

I feel myself smile. "It's ok — I won't tell him I know, I promise. But why the secrecy?"

As she shifts from foot to foot the teenager reappears. "My folks," she mumbles. "I get a bit more freedom if they think we're just friends."

I nod. "Ok, I get it." I stand up next to her. "Come on, I need to get changed before evening service."

CHAPTER 15

I've never believed the tales of the pub being haunted, but now I'm not so sure. Last night every breeze from the window, every creak of the floorboards sounded unfamiliar and panic began to set in. Even in my bedroom with the lights on around me I didn't feel safe. I saw Corbin again. Why, after all this time?

By morning I'm climbing the walls ... if I just had someone to talk to. Just about normal, everyday things. Well, perhaps there is someone. And anyway, what have I got to lose? If I call and he doesn't pick up I'll know for sure he's had enough of me.

The phone rings three times before he answers. "Marie," he breathes my name, rather than saying it.

"I know it's early ... is it ok?"

"Sure it's ok. It's not like I sleep in or anything."

"I wondered ... if you're all right? I haven't heard from you all week."

"I haven't heard from you, either."

My bedside clock ticks. "And you wanted to?"

"Sure as hell I wanted to. I just wondered ... you know ... if things had got a bit too heavy for you."

"Heavy?"

"After last Sunday."

"We've all got scars, Paxton. Yours are still a bit raw right now, that's all. It's cool."

"It's cool." He echoes my words so softly I can hardly hear him. Is it a laugh, or a choke?

Be honest. Be brave. "I'd like to see you."

"I want to see you too. I want you right now but it isn't possible. I'm on guard duty this weekend." He pauses. "Early next week maybe? I'll text you."

"Cool."

"Yeah — everything's cool."

I pad across to the bathroom just as Jude is coming up the stairs with two mugs of tea in his hands. He holds one out towards me. "There you go," he says as he disappears into his room. But he's smiling.

"Thanks, Jude," I whisper.

We're almost at the end of lunchtime service when Jude asks if I'm seeing my American this afternoon.

"No — Paxton's on guard duty this weekend," I tell him.

"That's good. I thought we could go and chill by the beach hut. I bought a bottle of wine — it's in the fridge upstairs. What d'you think?"

My eyes are red hot with tears and I hug him for all he's worth. "I think that's a wonderful idea."

He pats my back. "Yeah, me too, Mum."

And so the story unravels as we gaze across the bay towards Old Harry. How everything changed when he met Pip on a night out in Bournemouth with her friends; how incredible it was it changed for her too — but how much it bothered him she wouldn't let him tell me. And how frightening to feel so strongly for someone when you knew they were going away in October.

"You could go too, you know. I'm sure you could find a job in Cardiff."

"We've talked about it, but no. She's decided she'll go through clearing — try for a place at Southampton. Maybe we'll get a flat there or something — I can catch the train to Bournemouth for work. Maybe they'll even give me some more hours. It's just hard, you know, leaving The Smugglers the way things are at the moment."

"Look, Jude, you've got to put yourself first. Just because your father and I screwed up … and anyway, sometimes he's quite civil to me these days as long as I don't wind him up. We rub along. We'll manage."

"You're not thinking of leaving too? You know, when Paxton goes back to the States?"

I take a sip of wine. "No, Jude — it's not like that. He's a lot younger than me for a start — it's just a bit of fun for both of us. Stops him getting lonely and helps me to get some of my confidence back."

"Confidence? You've always seemed pretty confident to me. Except when … you know…"

"Except when I hit rock bottom, you mean?" We've not spoken of it before but now it's strangely easy.

"Yeah… I guess so."

"I think I'll always be like it, Jude. Sometimes I just can't come up with a good enough reason to get out of bed in the morning. Like this last week, in fact. Makes it worse when I know it's my own stupid fault. And I haven't even apologised to you properly. I must have caused you no end of grief with Pip."

"You can say that again. But I probably should apologise to you as well — I really overreacted and said some awful things. It was a nightmare, Mum, she finished with me — said if she was making me that unhappy…"

He takes a gulp of his wine. "But it came right in the end. It made us more honest with each other; we'd both been scared about the future and hiding it. We had a row and it all came out. In a roundabout way you did us a favour — we're much closer now — it feels more solid. I just wish we had more time to spend together. We even talked about going to Greece but I realise there isn't the money. And she understands."

I've said it before I even know how. "I'll find the money, Jude, if you want to go."

"Oh, Mum, that would be amazing — I can't tell you."

"How much do you think you'll need?"

"We reckon it'd be about £500 each. Pip's folks have said they'll pay for her flight and she's got some money saved." The smile falls from his face. "But it's impossible, Mum — even if we can afford it it's the time off. Dad will go ape."

"It's time your father realised he can't rely on slave labour. He'll have to put in a few more hours himself … and I'll help out too. It'll only be for a couple of weeks."

"A couple of our busiest weeks."

I fold my arms. "We'll manage."

It's almost five o'clock by the time we finish the wine and the day-trippers start to wend their way up the wooden steps and back to the car park. Jude unfolds himself from his deckchair and leans on the rail in front of the hut.

"Mum — isn't that Mark's boat?"

Riding the incoming tide, the *Helen* is nudging towards Redend Point, Mark crouched with one hand on the tiller and the other pulling down her distinctive blue sail.

"Yes. Look — you can see Troy peeping over the front."

"The bow, Mum, the bow."

I shrug. "Whatever."

We're packing away the deckchairs when Mark calls, "Anyone at home?"

"You've just caught us — we've had a lovely afternoon polishing off a bottle of wine."

"Lucky you. I've been working — so now I thought I'd make it up to Troy — and myself."

I kneel on the decking and slap my thighs. "Come on, say hello."

Troy needs no second invitation and I'm rewarded by a huge doggy kiss across my cheek. I ruffle his coat. "Hey fella, how you doing?"

"He's always pleased to see you," Mark laughs.

"Associates Mum with food, that's why," says Jude.

I look up at them. "The way to a dog's heart is through his stomach." As if to agree Troy thumps his tail across my chest.

"He's out of luck," Jude continues. "It's Sunday, old boy — the kitchen's closed."

"Well the pub kitchen might be but mine isn't. Why don't you both drop by for something to eat after your walk?"

"Oh, I couldn't impose on your evening off," says Mark. "I've already had some of your wonderful cooking today — microwaved a couple of your freezer meals for Dad and my lunch. He wasn't really up to going out."

"Is he all right?"

"Yes. Just feels his age sometimes. It's easy to forget he's eighty-three."

"He is pretty switched on," adds Jude.

"Yes — I'm very lucky. I can handle a wheelchair when I have to, but it'd be tough if he lost his marbles."

I haul myself up on the rail, dislodging Troy's head from my lap. "Where are you off to, anyway?"

"Well, it's a bit too hot to be climbing Old Harry so I thought I'd take him over the dunes."

"Past the nudist beach?" I tease.

He shakes his head, laughing. "All that sweaty flesh is definitely not my cup of tea. But I can always take off my glasses if we get too close."

"It's where I go swimming…"

"In which case I might put them back on again," he jokes.

"I can promise you I'll be serving supper fully clothed. Just a bit of cold pork and some home-made coleslaw — I'll be making it for myself so it really won't be any trouble."

"The coleslaw seals the deal," he smiles. "We'll be about ninety minutes, I'd guess."

"That's ok — it won't get cold if you're longer."

"No, I don't suppose it will. Come on, Troy."

As we walk across the pub yard Jude turns to me. "He's a nice man, isn't he? Got a wicked sense of humour."

"Doesn't mind a joke against himself, that's for sure. It's really quite refreshing after your father."

"Getting to like him, are you?" He digs me in the ribs with his elbow.

"Not in that way. He's a bit *too* nice, if you know what I mean."

As well as nice, other words I associate with Mark include "polite" and "reliable". So I'm surprised when six thirty comes and goes — and so does seven. He must have taken me at my word that supper wouldn't get cold. The best thing on TV is Big Brother, so I go back to mending the living room curtains and wondering where I'll find the money for Jude to go to Greece. The bank won't touch me with a bargepole, but maybe I could get a credit card of my own…

I am mulling it over when my phone rings. It's another mobile but I don't know the number. All the same I pick it up.

"Marie — is that you?" The voice is filled with panic but I recognise it straight away.

"Mark — what's wrong?"

"It's Troy — I've lost him in the dunes — can't find him anywhere. I've called and called him but I've got to keep looking…"

"Where are you?"

"Past the car park … kind of at the place where the big paths cross. It's high up here — I thought I might be able to spot him."

"Ok — stay where you are. I'll be with you in about ten minutes."

Although it won't be dark for a while I grab a torch and a jumper before heading for the car. Mark's gone further than I thought so it's quicker to drive to the National Trust car park at Knoll a mile or so along the road.

As I start to walk towards the dunes I give Mark a call. "Are you still there?"

"No — I'm by the pond. I heard barking but it was another dog. There's some people having a barbecue."

"And have they seen Troy?"

"No."

We arrange to meet on the higher ground. I reach the spot first and watch Mark clamber up the shoulder of the dune, breathing hard. "Marie — I don't know where else to look." He runs his hands over his hair and I can see why it's corkscrewing up in spikes.

"Where did you last see Troy?"

"Just a bit further on from here. He must have seen a rabbit or something and he went careering after it. But when I called he didn't come back. He's normally so good… And the tide's coming up."

"Mark, calm down."

"It's all very well for you to say that — he's not your dog."

It is a shock to realise he's close to tears. I wrap my arms around him and he buries his face in my hair, the dampness from his polo shirt oozing onto my cheeks.

"Sorry," he murmurs.

I give him a brisk hug then disengage myself. "Come on — show me the place."

We walk in silence along a wide sandy track which angles towards the sea. Low gorse bushes edge the path to our right and evidence of rabbits is everywhere. How tempting it must have been for the dog.

Mark stops. "This is it."

"Then call him."

He cups his hands around his mouth and shouts Troy's name over and over. There is no movement from the gorse; no bark of recognition, no flurry of paws.

"Right — we'll have to retrace his steps."

"I've already done that."

"Then we'll do it again. If he normally comes back and he hasn't he must be stuck somewhere so we'll just have to check every bush."

"You think I haven't?"

"I think you might have been panicking too much to do it properly."

He casts me a baleful glance and marches off through the scrub.

We walk almost to the sea but there is no sign. My legs are scratched to buggery from the gorse but giving up isn't an option. We still have at least an hour of daylight and I tell Mark to go left and I'll go right towards the car park, and between us we'll look under every bush between the path and the sea.

It's as I'm walking past the first row of beach huts I hear a whine. It's hard, with the wash of the waves, but the more I listen the more certain I am. There's a dog here somewhere. Tentatively I call Troy's name. A bark — muffled. I call again, louder.

I don't expect a man to appear from between the huts and when he does he's as naked as the day he was born.

"Lost your dog?" he asks.

I look up; thankfully he's carrying a lot of weight and his stomach sags almost to his thighs. "My friend has. I think I can hear something." Together we listen and there's another whine.

"It's coming from under the huts," says my companion. "There's a bit of a hole further along where the rabbits have dug the bank away."

I am absolutely sure the dog is Troy but all the same I lower myself onto the ground to peer into the blackness. There is a rustle of movement accompanied by a sharp yelp. I pull the torch out of my shoulder bag and thrust my head into the hole.

Troy is lying on the sand a few yards away, panting. When he sees me he tries to drag himself to his feet but his left foreleg buckles and he yelps again. "It's ok, fella," I tell him. "You stay still — we'll get you out." As I wriggle further into the hole some sand gives way and I land almost on top of him, but at least I'm all in one piece.

"Are you all right?" asks the man.

"Yes, fine. I'll phone my friend — he's looking somewhere else but he's not far away. I just need to keep Troy still until we can move him properly. Is there any chance you can find him some water?"

I lie down alongside the panting dog and call Mark, explaining where we are.

"Look for the naked bloke," I tell him and he doesn't even question it, just rings off. I picture him running towards the beach huts as fast as he can.

It isn't long before I hear voices and Mark slides into the hole next to me. Troy's tail thumps weakly against my thigh.

"I think he's broken a foreleg. We'll need to lift him out."

"Ok — you go first then I'll try to pass him up to you. I can normally carry him but it's a bit tight."

There are sounds of two or three people behind the huts now. "It's ok — we've got some spades — we'll make the gap larger for you — just hold on for a moment."

I turn off the torch and the three of us lie in the gloom. Mark's voice sounds scratchy when he says, "I can't thank you enough."

I stretch my hand along Troy's back to find his. "Hey — that's what friends are for."

It's almost midnight by the time we get back to The Smugglers and Jude is waiting up for us. We troop down to the beach and he and Mark haul the *Helen* beyond the high tide mark and secure her to the hut railings while I hold the torch. Mark wants to go straight home but I make him come in, if only for a hot drink and something to eat.

"How's Troy?" Jude asks as Mark drops onto a chair.

"He dislocated his front leg, but the vet managed to work it back in." It was a sickening moment. Troy was too drugged up to feel it but I thought Mark was going to faint. Given how deeply tanned his skin is he still looks pretty pale.

I bustle around making pork and coleslaw sandwiches while Jude brews the tea. Slowly Mark comes back to himself, telling

Jude how marvellous I've been then asking him what he's been doing on the laptop.

Jude shrugs. "Just browsing, really. There's a possibility my girlfriend and I might be able to get to Greece for a week or so to join her brother, but there aren't many flights to Athens and they're more expensive than I thought."

"When are you thinking of going?"

"We thought early August so we're back before Pip gets her A-level results."

"So right in the run up to the Olympics?"

Jude laughs. "You know, I hadn't even thought of that. Sport's not my thing."

"Well, generally I'd agree, but there's sailing in the Olympics." Mark takes a gulp of his tea and picks up another sandwich. "These are delicious, Marie — and I didn't even know I was hungry."

"It's the shock."

"Yes. Bit embarrassing really, the way I overreacted."

I shrug. "Perfectly normal under the circumstances."

Mark looks away and changes the subject. "So, do you really need to go to Athens?" he asks Jude. "It'll be terribly hot and it's completely chaotic there at the moment. I went to Piraeus about a month ago and the whole place was like a building site."

"Michael's on Skopelos but we thought we could get a ferry from Athens."

"Much easier from Volos."

"Where?"

"Volos. It has a military airport, but a lot of charter flights go there now and it's a major ferry terminal."

"How do you know so much about Greece?" I ask him.

"I do a lot of business there — it's quite a centre for shipping. And Volos is near Pelion — you know, the only place Alexander the Great lost a battle…" He tails off as Jude and I look blank. "Oh dear — I'm being a boring old history geek now," Mark laughs.

"Of course you're not. It's just, well, Jude and my knowledge of the subject is a bit limited."

"But you always seem so interested when Dad talks about the war. He said you even borrowed one of his photos when you called around to take his glasses back — might have been some connection with the GI your mother met when she was evacuated here?"

"It's possible. But the real reason I took it is to show it to Paxton, my American friend. It's got a Sherman Double Duplex in it and he's a tank man himself."

"The difference is," muses Jude, "what happened in Studland just sixty years ago seems relevant. You know, you can almost reach out and touch it."

"I wish we could," I falter. "I wish we could really know … the people, what happened to them."

"Like your mother's friend, Corbin?" Mark asks.

"Mmm." I gaze into the bottom of my mug. "Not possible though, is it, after all this time."

"I didn't know Gran was here during the war."

Oh God, I'm going to trip myself up on this if I'm not careful. "She was evacuated to Swanage — just for a short while."

"Is she in the photo?"

"No. And it's probably too much of a coincidence to be true, but there was a GI living over the road from where she was staying called Corbin Summerhayes and she always remembered him. When George and I looked at the back of the tank photo, it had the names of the three men on and one of them was Corbin."

"Wow — that's unreal."

Jude's words stick with me as I'm cleaning my teeth. That's what the whole Corbin thing is: unreal. Should I even let it bother me? It happened. It's finished. But then I remember Thursday. Why, after all this time? I rinse my toothbrush under the tap and put it back in the holder next to Jude's. Stephen's hasn't been there for a while but the empty space still looks odd. *Too much, Marie, too much.* I take a last look at my reflection and pad across the darkened landing to bed.

CHAPTER 16

"Bloody hell, mate," says Baz, "you made me jump. How did you creep up like that in broad daylight?"

Paxton is leaning against the doorframe. "Sorry, bud — I was just watching the lovely Marie."

So instead of texting in a few days he's just turned up. "I'm not lovely," I laugh as I arrange slices of apple pie on their plates. "I'm hot and sticky and sweaty and I need a shower."

Paxton growls like a tiger. "Sounds good to me."

Poor old Baz doesn't know where to put himself.

Perhaps because Stephen isn't lurking in the bar, I invite Paxton up to the apartment. It's a beautiful afternoon and even with the windows open the air is still.

"D'you know what?" I tell him, "I fancy a swim."

He shakes his head. "Sounds like a great idea but I've got no shorts with me."

"You don't need them — there's a naturist beach not ten minutes from here."

"Naturist?"

"You know … nudist … so you won't need shorts."

He wraps his arms around me and brushes his lips against mine. The stubble on his chin is shorter, harsher somehow and it prickles, but I don't want to pull away.

"I kind of like the idea of you cavorting in the waves in the buff."

We drive the Capri to Knoll car park. As soon as the engine stops, Paxton reaches over and scrabbles in the glove compartment.

"Gonna need my suntan lotion."

169

"We're not really going to be out there very long, Paxton."

"Yes, but my mom died of skin cancer — you can't be too careful."

I nod. He is exceptionally pale — especially for someone who's been in the Middle East — and that would explain it.

Paxton ignores my suggestion we take off our clothes in the relative privacy of the dunes.

"Too much freaking sand," he says and strides towards a patch of marram grass at the edge of the beach.

"I suppose it does get everywhere."

In reply he rolls his eyes, then starts removing his clothes in what can only be described as a businesslike fashion before liberally applying sun cream to his whole body. I sit on my towel, letting the warmth seep into my skin and enjoying the show.

"You've missed a bit," I tell him, and he hands the bottle to me. I scramble to my feet and rub the cream into his shoulders and the back of his neck, but I'm surprised to see it's a rather dirty brown colour.

"You have caught the sun a little."

He shifts from foot to foot. "Must have been guard duty," he mutters.

"Yes — and here," I run my finger around a faint line halfway across his bicep. A thought — a memory — is beginning to stir but he turns and snatches the bottle away from me.

"Stop fooling, Marie." He tucks it under his neatly folded pile of clothes and marches off towards the sea, buttocks white in the sunshine.

It's always a shock how cold the water feels around your ankles, but how blissful its caress once you take the plunge. We turn on our backs and float, watching the wisps of high cloud glide by.

"This feels so real, Marie — amazing," Paxton breathes.

"I know. It's almost as though you're part of the water. I'd love to be part of the water — just drifting around in its endlessness without a care in the world."

"You're so right; it shouldn't be dust to dust — it should be wave to wave. When my time comes I definitely want to be buried at sea."

"Is Ohio by the sea?"

"Of course not. And anyway it won't be in Ohio, Marie. And it won't be in some desert either." He twists over and strikes out for the shore with an impressive front crawl.

He waits for me in the shallows and reaches down to help me from the surf, his lips brushing mine. "You look like some ancient sea goddess," he tells me.

"Less of the ancient," I laugh and thankfully he joins in.

We are halfway back to our clothes when I hear someone calling, "Excuse me." I turn around to see my friend from Sunday night.

"Hello there," he says. "I had you down as a proper textile. I almost didn't recognise you without your clothes."

"I'm not sure I'd recognise you with yours." Paxton's hand tightens around mine.

"I didn't mean to interrupt, I just wanted to ask how your friend's dog is," the man continues.

"Bored, I should imagine. It was a dislocation but the vet fixed it fairly easily. Mark phoned me to say he's having to keep Troy in some sort of cage for the moment but he's going to be all right."

"Well, I am pleased to hear that. Give him my best, won't you?"

"Yes — and thanks again for your help."

Paxton's grip doesn't relax. "Who's Mark?" he asks.

I tug my hand away. "Remember I told you about George, the veteran? Mark's his son."

"You didn't mention a son."

"I had no reason to. Paxton — what's all this about? There's no call to be jealous. How could I look at another man when I'm fortunate enough to have you?"

His head drops. "Aw, Marie — I'm sorry — I'm being a total jerk. Too little sleep over the weekend. Forgive me?"

I wrap my arm around his shoulder. "Nothing to forgive. We all have our moments — it's what makes us human."

He pulls me so close I can taste the flecks of salt sticking to his skin. "You're so wise, Marie — wise and beautiful. I sure am one lucky guy."

I'm drying my hair after washing out the salt and sand when I hear Stephen's strained voice in the yard below. I can see him in my mind's eye, pacing up and down with his phone to his ear, giving some plumber or other hell. It's only when I hear Jude answer him my interest pricks up.

I creep to my bedroom window and peer out but I can't see them — they must be tucked close to the wall, out of the sun. And if they're both out there and not in the bar it must be serious.

Serious is, in fact, one of Stephen's next words. As in *you can't be…*

Jude explodes back. "I most certainly am. I'm going to Greece next week and there's nothing you can do to stop me."

"Yes there is. I don't have to give you holiday at this little notice — especially not at this time of year. I wouldn't for Gina and I won't for you."

"Yes, but as far as I know you actually pay Gina." Jude sounds bitter. Stephen won't like that.

"Well, you must be doing all right if you can afford a holiday — it's more than I can."

"You've got Swanage — that's just one big holiday as far as I can see. It won't matter I'm away if you do your fair share of shifts — and Mum says she'll help out so I don't see what your problem is."

"Oh, so your mother's in on this too, is she? You two and your secrets — the moment my back's turned…"

"It was your choice — you turned your back on us. Not just once but loads of times. You ought to be bloody grateful we're still prepared to go the extra mile for this shit-hole — and the way you behave sometimes it's a miracle we do."

I watch as Jude strides across the churchyard, sweat darkening his shirt. Stephen yells at him to come back but he's wasting his breath.

Jude returns just as I'm on my way down for evening service. He stops on the stairs.

"You heard about the row?"

"I heard it for myself. I was up here and the window was open. So you're definitely going?"

"Yes — you know Mark asked for my email address? He actually got us some flights to Volos for next Monday — something to do with one of his business contacts there. And — get this — they have a villa just down the coast with a guest wing we can use as well. I couldn't turn it down, Mum, even if I'd wanted to — he'd gone to so much trouble. Said he owed you one for finding Troy."

It's me who owes Mark now — big time. "So I guess I need to give him some money."

"He said not to worry — he's put the flights on his credit card so you can sort it out when you next see him."

How, I don't know, but I can't tell Jude. "And I guess you'll need some euros," I smile, but it feels fixed to my face.

"No, that's cool, Mum. I told Pip we'll sort the flights if she brings the spending money and her folks are fine with that. It's so odd," he laughs, "if they knew about us they'd be up in arms, but at the moment I'm the knight in shining armour looking after their daughter on a perilous journey. God knows what they'll say when they do find out."

"I think you'd do well to let them think it started as a holiday romance."

"Mum — you're a genius." As he hugs me the dampness from his shirt sinks into my whites.

"You need to get changed and back in the bar. You don't want your father kicking off again."

"He can kick off all he likes — nothing's going to ruin my holiday," he beams, but all the same he does as he's told.

To my surprise, Stephen says nothing to me about Jude going away until a few days later. In the meantime, things have been relatively calm but I know from experience it's a state of affairs that isn't destined to last.

I'm marinating a batch of lamb when Stephen puts the rota for next week on the table in front of me.

"Ok," he says, "here's Gina, here's me and I've left Jude's shifts blank."

I frown. "Can't Gina do any extra?"

"Only if you're going to pay her, same as you did for his holiday." I wish he wouldn't remind me — I feel sick every time I think of it. I should really have phoned Mark to thank him and to ask how Troy's getting on, but I'm struggling to pluck up the courage. I run my finger over the paper. "Well, I guess we split them between us — you do the ones while I'm in the kitchen and I'll do the ones I'm not."

"That's a lot of extra hours, Marie — and what about when Jude and I were meant to be on together at lunchtimes?"

I shrug. "It's only for a week. We'll manage."

"It'd be all right if it was the last week of September, not the last week in July," he grumbles.

"Jude will be working at the college by then so it's not an option. Stephen, give the lad a break. He works his butt off for you."

"For us."

I take a deep breath. "Yes, all right, for us. If you can call us an us, that is."

He tugs the rota from under my hand. "Oh, don't start, Marie." The lines around his eyes are so deep he hardly looks like Stephen at all. Maybe it's because he knows I'm right. And that's never a good thing.

CHAPTER 17

On my last afternoon of relative freedom, I want to escape from Studland so I drive to Wool to meet Paxton. We stroll by the River Frome hand in hand and feed the ducks before having an early evening roast in The Ship. He tells me about the hours he's spent working on the electrics of an armoured car, newly arrived at the museum, and I pretend I'm interested because it means so much to him.

When he asks about my week I tell him Jude's going away, how strange it will be without him, even though I'll be busy covering his shifts.

"I'd like to go away with you, Marie," he murmurs. "Somewhere beautiful and remote; somewhere there's just you and me."

"Maybe when Jude comes back?" I falter. It would be something to look forward to; something to get me through this awful week.

He shakes his head. "You know it's not possible."

"Because you can't get leave?"

"I could lie to you, tell you that's the reason, but I don't want lies between us. Plus you already know the truth."

I reach across the table. "Paxton — it was a one-off…"

"If only that was true."

I stroke the hairs on the back of his hand. "You can't go your whole life avoiding sleeping with someone. Isn't there anyone you can talk to about this — professionally I mean? You hear so much about post combat stress…"

"Yeah — you on the outside hear about it and us on the inside live with it. It's just part of the deal. There's no point talking about it — if you haven't seen action you can't understand. And at Bovington, well, it's not like my base at Fort Riley — no one there's been where I've been."

"But surely…"

"Aw, Marie — just leave it, ok?"

The beach is deserted at this time of the morning. Above me the sun slants into the bay, its pale light casting a greyish tinge on the cliffs. I unscrew the lid of my flask and lean back against the door of the beach hut.

Today Jude goes away. He's so excited — he's never been abroad before, never flown. There's never really been the money or the time. Now I wish I'd taken him when I went for my parents' funeral, but back then it didn't seem right. I never dreamt there wouldn't be another chance. For either of us.

I'm as trapped here as ever. Paxton and I don't speak of September because we both know. A kiss — or more likely a shag — goodbye, and that will be that. Will I miss him? Hell, yes. Will I be broken-hearted? No. He'll probably be my last wild fling before I'm too old for anyone to want me.

And then what? The drudgery of the kitchen for another twenty years is too much to contemplate. If we didn't owe so much money I'd ask Stephen to sell — or at very least buy me out — then I'd be free to do what I want.

Which is? This whole damn thing would be easier if I knew. Where are your dreams, Marie? What happened to them? Did you ever really have any, or did you just let the tide of Stephen carry you along? You're nothing but a piece of flotsam. The only good thing you've ever managed to do right(ish) is Jude. But even that's over now; he's grown up, in love, moving on.

I close my eyes. The warmth is seeping into the sun. I tell myself it's good to be alive. Well, it should be.

Even Stephen turns up to wave Jude goodbye. As Pip's father's car disappears along the lane he says, "So Pip's the girlfriend?"

I look sideways at him. "Let's just say if she is, her folks don't know."

"Ok — I get it. I won't tell tales. We don't exactly move in the same social circles as them anyway. Although I seem to recall you used to be quite friendly with Angie."

"Yes, when the kids were little. We had more in common then."

He nods.

"Stephen — do you remember — that day I saw you in the park in Bournemouth with that other woman? If I'd said something … done something … would it have made any difference?"

"To what?"

"To your … affairs?"

"I'm sorry, Marie, I don't know what you mean."

He may have stonewalled me but at least he is civil. He goes back to laying the tables in the bar and I return to the kitchen. Baz is full of Jude's holiday and dreaming of one of his own. Some of his mates are going to Germany in October for a beer festival. He might join them. Sounds like a laugh, anyway. His prattle carries me through the shift when all the time my mind is with Jude: first in the car, then at Gatwick and most terrifyingly on the plane. How many hours until they land?

Baz tidies the kitchen while I run upstairs to change so I can go behind the bar. Navy trousers, a fresh white shirt and a smack of lip gloss. That will do. Stephen hates it when I'm front of house in my whites. Once he told me I was a disgrace in front of a bar full of customers. I won't give him the satisfaction again.

He nods his approval as we hand over. Two tables with unpaid bills, everyone else in the garden or back on the beach.

"Are you sure you don't want me to stay?" he asks.

"No — you take a break now — but if you're back by five I can snatch a breather before evening service."

"I might just go upstairs, chill on the sofa."

Let this peace continue. "Good idea."

It's only once he's gone I notice George sitting at his favourite table next to the window. I am immediately flooded with guilt about not texting Mark but I certainly can't ignore his father.

George stands to greet me. "Hello, Marie. On bar duty as well?"

"Yes — Jude's gone on holiday."

"I didn't realise it was so soon. Mark said he'd fixed something with the Simonides for him."

"He's been very kind. How's Troy coming along?"

"Looking balefully out of his cage most of the time. I've had to do quite a bit of dog sitting, but this afternoon's the check-up with the vet and I'm feeling like it's me who's been let off the leash. God knows how Troy must feel."

"Perhaps after today he'll get a bit more freedom."

George shakes his head. "The trouble is Mark lets him jump on everything at home — the sofa, the bed — and it's just what he mustn't do while it heals. But he might be able to walk him a bit more. Both of them seem a bit stir-crazy to be honest."

"And how are you keeping?"

"I'm fine, Marie. And I have to say you're absolutely glowing."

I laugh. "Painted on a posh face for work, that's all."

"You do yourself down, my dear. Tell me, what did your American friend think of the Sherman DD?"

"I haven't had the chance to show him yet but I've got it safe for when I do. It was very generous of you to let me borrow it."

"Well, seeing it again gave me something to talk to Josie about. Since Eileen died, we phone each other on the last Sunday of every month and it can be hard to know what to say."

"How nice, keeping in touch like that."

"When you get to my age there are so few people you can share the past with. Most have either gone or they're completely gaga. Even poor old Josie's a bit scatty but she can reminisce about the old days, all right. I was pretty sure she wouldn't have forgotten Big Sam but she even remembered your mum's Corbin."

My palms are sweating so much I have to wipe them on my trousers. My voice is hardly my own. "So what did she say?"

"That he was a quiet man, thoughtful. The only time she ever saw him get animated was when a couple of guys from another platoon got stuck into Big Sam — there was an awful lot of racism back then. If you think about it, there was still segregation across huge parts of the United States so perhaps it wasn't surprising. These guys had pushed in front of Sam in the food queue and Corbin practically threw them out of the restaurant. Josie said the supervisor gave Corbin an extra portion of jam roly-poly but he shared it around his men. It does sound as if it's the same bloke — someone like that would be kind to little girls too."

"And to think … a few weeks later he might have been dead…" *Don't cry, Marie — not now. Not in front of George.* But I'm rescued by the pub door banging and a harassed-looking young father asking if he can use the baby change.

It's well past eleven when I bolt the pub door behind the last straggler. Stephen is emptying the cash from the till. I'm desperate for a brandy, but not until he's gone. Please God don't let him want to put everything on his spreadsheet tonight.

The bags under his eyes mirror my own. "I'm shattered," he tells me.

I hold out my hands for the money. "I'll put it in the safe. You lock up down here."

"Thanks. See you in the morning."

I'm not even at the top of the stairs when I hear Stephen's car door slam. The engine purrs into life and the headlamps swing back to face the road. As they disappear into the night, I creep back to the bar and pour myself a generous slug of Martell to drink in the bath.

It's the first time I've spent a night in The Smugglers alone. The emptiness around me beckons as I towel myself dry and climb into my pyjamas. I pull my cardigan around my shoulders and clatter downstairs in my crocs.

In the kitchen I nibble a chocolate digestive while I wait for the kettle to boil. I'll make a pot of tea and sit here for hours with my book. Or maybe I'll finally start that Old Harry jigsaw. Is this what it would be like? To live on my own? I stretch my legs under the table and wriggle my toes. I pick up the teapot. Put it down again. Another brandy would be nice.

Moonlight spills into the bar. I can't have another Martell — one too many and Stephen will notice. Instead I ram my glass into the optic; come on, Marie — make it a double. You've earned it. I lean against the shelves, cradling my glass, watching the streaks of silver from the window make their way across the floor.

When we first came to The Smugglers there were two bars: a snug cosied around the great stone fireplace and a public bar — in front of where I'm standing now — its door straight from the road, bringing in the rain and weather when you opened it. The leaded mullions were the same but in the moonlight they've lost their heaviness. I wish I could do the same.

What was it Paxton's grandmother told him — sing yourself happy?

"*We'll meet a*—" Stop it, Marie. You never could sing so it won't work for you. George called his tank after Vera Lynn — I wonder what he'd think of my pathetic warbling?

Did George ever come to The Smugglers back then? Did Corbin? I close my eyes and I can picture him in the public bar with his fellow GIs. How did the locals take that? I see a trio of old boys in the corner, playing dominos. The Americans sit under the window, pint glasses on the table in front of them half empty. Corbin is facing me but he doesn't look in my direction. He's older than the others. He's their sarge. One is very young indeed — younger than Jude — just a child, really.

I want to reach out to them, stop time. The clock on the mantelshelf chimes one. My hand wraps around my glass but they are crowding in on me, demanding to be served. Old men in cloth caps, young men in uniforms — pushing, shoving, and smelling of the sea. Behind them is Corbin. He holds out his hands to me but blood drips from his fingers and onto the floor.

182

I fly through the kitchen. The back door is bolted so I make for the lobby instead. Yale. Easy. Miraculously I have the presence of mind to grab my keys and the door slams behind me, its reverberations following me up the road.

The short slope robs me of my breath so I swerve onto the path to the sea. The moon pierces the tree trunks, striping the track between them with white. A long, long, zebra crossing to safety. A little girl again, skipping across the Kings Road. Choking fumes from buses and taxis.

I collapse onto the decking in front of the hut and fill my lungs time and time again with the crisp, salty air. The wood against my back is safe, comforting. If anyone comes I will see them; I will know what to do.

The lights from the boats moored in the bay help my eyes to focus on the night. The moon glistens on the wet sand and all is still. No rustle from the trees, no wash from the waves. No one following me.

It takes a long while for my legs to stop shaking, but once they do I clamber up and fumble through the keys, at last finding the right one. Jude's wetsuit swings on its hanger, empty and forlorn. I run my finger down its arm, dislodging a scatter of sand. What is he doing now? Drinking in some taverna or fast asleep with Pip's head on his shoulder?

I am tired. Too tired for this. Tired and cold. I pull the cushions from the sun loungers to the floor, and take the huge orange towel from the stack of deckchairs and wrap myself into it before closing the door on the world. The towel smells of Jude and of something else … cologne. *Paxton.* If he was here now I'd feel safe.

CHAPTER 18

There is one thing I'm certain of when I wake on the beach hut floor — I'll struggle to face a night in The Smugglers on my own, never mind a whole week of them. But by the time I've had a shower and eaten some breakfast, I convince myself I'll be fine if I stay in my bedroom. Or drink a lot of brandy. Or both.

I pluck up the courage to ask Stephen if he thinks the pub is haunted. He raises his eyebrows. "Why d'you ask now, after all these years?"

"I just thought I heard a few noises downstairs last night, that's all."

"Probably the kitchen door. Could've sworn I shut it but maybe not. Or perhaps you are right — maybe there was a ghost."

And so he thinks it's hysterically funny to creep up behind me making *woo woo* noises for the rest of the morning.

Pots slam onto gas rings and onions fly from the ends of chopping boards. Even Baz says, "Blimey, Mar, calm down," but I only grunt in reply. So in the end it's inevitable the flashes start behind my eye.

"Oh God," I moan. "Not now."

Baz turns from taking a bowl of coleslaw out of the fridge. "What?"

"Migraine."

"Go to bed."

But I can't. I have to wade through this shift. Baz fetches my tablets and I sit on the wall in the yard to take them. Grass rustles in the churchyard behind me. Birds sing. In the distance

184

I hear Baz call, "Service." He's a good lad. I run the tips of my fingers over the softness of a patch of moss and when I open my eyes I find I can see so I pull my phone from my pocket, aching for a word from Jude. Not that I expect it — he called from a phone box at the airport to say they'd landed safely.

There is, however, a text from Paxton. *How's my crazy seanymph doing?*

I reply: *So-so. I had a bad night last night then a migraine. What are you up to?*

His was a while ago so I don't expect an answer, but my phone vibrates straight away with: *Waiting for a bunch of dumbarse kids to remember what I showed them yesterday. Wish I was with you xx*

I've just sent: *Wish you were too. Come over tonight?* when Stephen calls from the bar.

"Marie — where are you?"

Oh God — here we go. I hear Baz tell Stephen I'm not well and he swears again. I push myself off the wall.

"It's ok — I'm coming."

My phone beeps. *You bet. But just for a while. I'll sit in the bar watching them watching you — turns me on…*

The only man watching me now is Stephen. "You're like a teenager with that phone."

"You're like a teenager full stop. Now get out of my way and back behind your sodding bar."

Baz freezes, spatula poised to lift a burger off the grill. The birds are still singing. A vein throbs in Stephen's neck but all the same he turns and walks away.

Paxton is true to his word. He turns up just before ten o'clock and buys a bottle of Coors before retreating to George's favourite table and watching my every move. He's so obvious even Stephen notices.

"I think that American bloke fancies you," he whispers as we load the glass-washer.

"He does. He's my boyfriend."

"What — has he got a mother complex or something?"

"You're just jealous."

Despite his sniping Stephen is civil when I introduce him to Paxton — too civil, in fact. He talks to him for ages while emptying the till in slow motion and counting the cash twice. I stack the glasses away and wipe every table and still he hasn't finished. I tell Paxton I'm all done and lead him through the kitchen, but Stephen follows us upstairs.

"Don't mind me," he says, opening the laptop. "I'm just going to cash up."

"Stephen — this is ridiculous. Leave it until tomorrow, can't you?"

"Marie, really — you know it has to be done tonight."

"Like it was yesterday?"

"Are you asking me to leave my own home?" It's impossible to tell if he's smiling or growling.

"It's not your home," I hiss. "It's mine — now get going."

"And what if I don't want to?" His eyes have narrowed to dark slits.

Paxton's hand reaches over Stephen's shoulder and smashes down the lid of the laptop. "Then tomorrow morning I'll be helping the lady to change her locks. Sir."

Stephen grabs his wrist. "Don't think you can come here and start throwing your weight around just because you're shagging my wife."

Paxton steps back and folds his arms. "I'm not throwing my weight around. I reckon you'd notice if I was."

Stephen stands to face him, but even he can't fail to notice how poorly matched they are. One swing from Paxton and he'd be out cold. There's a moment I wonder if he's going to chance his luck but he thinks better of it.

"You're not worth the aggro," he mutters, grabs his car keys and stalks down the stairs with as much dignity as he can muster.

Tears of laughter stream down my face. "Oh, Paxton — you were wonderful. But I'm going to be in so much trouble tomorrow."

Paxton is gazing solemnly at me. "If he so much as touches you…"

I put a hand on his arm. "He won't. He's never hit me — it's not his way. Shoved me a few times maybe, but he's too much of a coward for anything else. Come on, let's go to bed."

"Just for a while…"

"Ok — just for a while."

The while lasts until dawn is creeping into the sky. The tenderness of it takes my breath away. It is new, and soft, and different. I ask Paxton why.

"Because it's what you needed."

"What I needed?"

"You were brave with Stephen, but I could tell deep down you were frightened. Like you said to me, Marie — we all have scars — and I think I'm beginning to learn about yours. I don't want him to have that power over you. No other man should have that power over you."

I push my face into the downy smoothness of his chest. "Stay with me, Paxton."

"Maybe … maybe tomorrow. Right now, I gotta go. Catch a few hours' sleep before work."

"You can catch them here."

"C'mon, Marie. Don't spoil it. I did good up 'til now."

I stroke his stubble, my fingers running onto the side of his neck. "You did damn well perfect. Drive safely, Paxton. I'll see you tonight."

Once Paxton leaves, I sleep for so long it's Stephen's car pulling up in the yard that wakes me. But I am singing as I soap myself in the shower, reluctantly washing every last trace of Paxton away. Stephen can say what he likes — I'm impervious.

I'm almost sorry when he doesn't. He doesn't even make a big thing of having to do the cash this morning or of me oversleeping. I make us both a cup of tea and take mine to the pub kitchen to start work.

My phone rings just as I am dicing peppers for my new Mediterranean lattice pies. I twist over my shoulder but I don't know the number — it's a Poole one — could be a supplier — so I gesture to Baz to pick it up for me.

"Yes — hold on — she's just chopping something — won't be a tick."

"Who is it?" I ask as tip the peppers off the board and into a bowl.

"Someone called Mark."

If he couldn't hear everything we're saying I'd tell Baz to get rid of him. He's going to ask for the money. I won't be able to pay him. And to make it worse I haven't even said thank you. *Shit.*

I put on my most cheerful voice. "Hi, Mark — how did Troy get on on Monday? I was going to text you later."

"Not too bad thanks. His leg's healing well and I can start taking him for a few walks as long as the surface is even. I think we're both looking forward to that."

"Your dad did say something about you being stir-crazy."

"You don't realise... I spend almost all of my spare time outdoors in the summer. I don't know what do with myself when I can't," he laughs.

"No, it must be hard."

"Well, it's worse for Troy because he doesn't even understand what's going on. He's so pathetically grateful when I let him out of that damned cage — he must think he's being punished for something."

"Maybe he'll think twice before trying to follow a rabbit into a hole again."

"I doubt it. Anyway, I know you must be busy with Jude away but I thought you'd like to know I've just had an email from Yanni Simonides telling me how charming your son and his friends are."

"Oh bless; they're generally good kids but it's nice of him to say so."

"Yanni's wife and boys have been staying in the villa too and they're all getting on like a house on fire. He's going to take them out on his yacht at the weekend. Sounds like they're having a whale of a time."

"I can't thank you enough for organising this, Mark. I ... I feel so bad I haven't called you but it's just been so busy. We ... we need to sort out the money side of it too. I don't even know how much I owe you for the flights."

"Let's just say flights are cheap compared to vet bills. There's no rush. I know you won't get any time off while Jude is away but perhaps once he's back... I'd like to hear how it all went, anyway."

"Yes — good idea. Nice to talk to you, Mark but I have to get on — a lot to do before service."

"Sure. Well ... see you sometime next week."

Oh God, how am I going to get the money?

Paxton turns up at the kitchen door just as Baz is leaving.

"You're early," I say as he puts down his rucksack and wraps me in his arms.

"Is that a problem?"

"No. It's just I've still got to do my stint in the bar."

"I know. I just reckoned if Stephen didn't think I was here he wouldn't kick up a fuss. How's he been with you today?"

"As if last night never happened. He can be like that."

Paxton releases me. "Probably for the best. Anyway, I'll just sneak upstairs and wait for you. Warm the bed a little."

"You don't know how good that sounds. These next ninety minutes are going to drag like hell."

"I'll be counting every last one of them, Doll."

"Me too."

He traces his hand under the curve of my breast and is gone.

Even now the warmth of the afternoon is trapped in the bay, enticing customers to sit outside for longer and to drink more beer. Stephen allows Gina to stay until closing and it's still hard to serve everyone and collect all the glasses.

Once Stephen calls time I take a tray into the garden. The crew of one of the boats moored off the beach are finishing their drinks and want to chat. I glance up at the windows of the apartment, but all is dark. Paxton must be good to his word, waiting in my bedroom. Every pore of my body wants to be there with him.

Eventually we finish and Stephen lets me take the cash to put in the safe. He downs an espresso and mutters something about cleaning the machine tomorrow morning.

"Take it easy on the road," I tell him.

"Oh, so you do care?"

I shrug. "You look tired, that's all."

"And whose fault is that?"

Once he's gone, I grab a brandy and a Coors for Paxton and race up to the apartment. Even the second staircase doesn't slow me down. I juggle the bottle and glass in my hand to turn the knob on the bedroom door, but as it swings open I stop in my tracks.

Three tea-lights in coloured glass jars flicker on my dressing table, a deep pink glow reflecting off the mirror almost to the edges of the room. The duvet has been stripped from the bed and the sheet covered in rose petals. On the bed is Paxton, totally naked and fast asleep.

I put our drinks on the bedside table as quietly as I can and stand for a moment, drinking in the sculptured muscle of his body. Goosebumps run down my neck. My hands are shaking as I unbutton my blouse and shrug it away before reaching behind my back to unclasp my bra. Clothes drop to the floor and I sink slowly onto the edge of the bed to take off my watch, but it slips from my grasp to land with a clatter on the boards.

Paxton's arm is across my chest, his breath harsh in my ear. "You weren't going to wake me, were you?" he growls.

"I just did."

"You didn't mean to — you were creeping around — you were going to let me sleep."

"No. I was just getting ready to wake you very, very slowly."

"I don't believe you."

"Hey, come on — why would I waste all this? No one's ever done anything like it for me before."

"Except me, in the beach hut."

"Except you — wonderful you." His grip relaxes just enough for me to twist around to face him. "Now you're just going to have to pretend to be asleep so I can wake you like I want."

My knees slot into the gap between his.

"Too late, Doll," he whispers. "I got this all planned out. And you're going to do just exactly what I say."

CHAPTER 19

Once again Paxton leaves me in the dawn. I follow him to the door and watch as he strolls, whistling, to the public car park. Once he is out of sight I go back upstairs and make myself a mug of tea, hugging my dressing gown around me.

In the living room I sit in the window seat as the sun breaks the far horizon over the sea. The parakeets begin to chatter in the trees lining the path to the beach and two sparrows pick at the grit in the lane. On the clifftop towards Old Harry all is still. My tea is cold in the bottom of my mug. Last night was… *Let it go, Marie. It was nothing.*

I need to do something, to concentrate. I kneel on the floor next to the coffee table and pull the jigsaw from under it. The cliffs I've just been gazing at, the bay I know so well. Comfort. Five hundred pieces, mainly white and blue. Enough of a challenge.

I don't bother to count the pieces again. I rake my fingers through the box, taking out the edges and putting them into the upturned lid. I find the top right corner first — pale blue of sky. I shift the back issues of *Radio Times* out of the way and place it on the glass. Likewise the other three. I consult the box again and take the measuring tape out of my sewing box to check the distance between them.

When Jude was tiny he loved jigsaws. A friend of Uncle Ted's used to make them especially for him out of his own pictures. I'll never forget his face when he finished the first one: wonder, pride, and incredulity.

"Can everyone buy my jigsaw, Mum?" he asked me.

"No — it's just for you."

His face crumpled. "Oh. I thought…"

I hugged his tiny body to me. "One day, Jude, one day. When you're grown up. Then they'll all be able to buy your pictures."

I bury my face in my hands. So much is lost.

"What's up with you? Missing lover boy?" How typical of Stephen to pick up on my mood when I don't want him to.

I turn the pastry. "Just a bit tired, that's all."

"Join the club. It's your fault anyway, for letting Jude go away."

"What d'you think's going to happen in the autumn when he goes for good?"

"He's not going anywhere this autumn — that job at the uni's going to make sure he stays put. At least some good's coming out of it."

I slam the rolling pin down on the counter. "He'll go one day. Sooner than you think, probably."

"Want a bet? How's he going to make a living selling his poxy paintings?"

My eyes are red raw with anger and I reach for an onion to cover my tracks. "Sod off, Stephen," I growl. He does, but we both know he's won.

There is no word from Paxton and I don't know whether I'm sorry or not. I glance at my wrist, but there's no need to hide it now Stephen's gone so I roll up the sleeve of my whites, exposing a bruise. It was my own fault, really; I panicked, struggled too much. Afterwards Paxton said he was sorry, caught up in the moment — if it wasn't ok, why hadn't I told him to stop?

The bar is heaving but I need a break. I tell Gina I'll be back in an hour and make a run for it before Stephen can say anything.

The only way to escape the heat pressing down on the bay is to climb. And I know as I set out on the path between the trees that as well as getting away from Stephen, I want to see Corbin again — find out what's really going on. So I can put the whole thing behind me and move on.

A couple of walkers are sitting on our bench so I choose the next one along. The bay below is dotted with boats and the narrow strip of sand has almost disappeared beneath rugs and families and airbeds. But here the breeze is from the west, cooling my back and bringing the sounds of the sheep from the fields. I should have brought my book so I could read while I wait.

Instead, I torture myself. Why didn't I run faster the other day, try harder to catch him? Was I scared? Why am I not scared now? I cover my face with my hands.

I jump about three inches off the bench when an oh-so-familiar voice asks me if I'm ok.

"Yes … no… I mean…"

Mark is standing a couple of yards away, his hands clasped behind his back. "Sorry," he says. "I didn't mean to intrude. I just wondered if you had another migraine or something."

I shake my head. "You wouldn't believe the something."

"Try me."

I shake my head again. "You'll think I'm nuts."

"And would that matter?"

As I weigh the question he lowers himself onto the other end of the bench.

"Where's Troy?" I ask.

"He's not up to a walk like this. I left him with Dad — feel a bit guilty but he said there was no point both me and the dog getting fat and unfit."

"Oh, ok."

"No — what you're meant to say is, 'Mark, you're certainly not fat.' Then I say, 'Yes I am. It's all those wonderful freezer meals of yours I'm eating.' Then you say, 'I'll make you some more when Jude gets back.' And I say, 'Yes please.' "

I can't help but laugh. "I'll make you as many meals as you can eat."

"Yes, but I must pay you for them."

"And I must pay you for Jude's flights."

"Perhaps we can cut a deal." He winks.

"Oh God — would you? It'd be such a weight off my mind."

"That wasn't what you were worrying about, was it?"

I turn to face him. "Well, in part."

"The other part isn't Stephen, is it? He's hasn't been … you know … again…"

"No, really. Look, I must be getting back or he probably will kill me. It's bedlam down there but I just had to get away to breathe."

He stands up. "This is a great place for breathing. Right. I need to be on my way too — I'm going to walk to Swanage and get the bus back."

"Well, enjoy it. I'll drop you a text about the meals next week."

"You do that," he calls over his shoulder.

My phone rests on the shelf in Jude's bedroom while I change his sheets and dust around, ready for his homecoming tomorrow. Time has stretched and stretched and stretched without him. Without Paxton too. Ok, I kicked up a bit of a fuss the other night but if it's made him call time on us, at the very least he ought to tell me.

I'm not due behind the bar until six and it's Sunday — I bet he's at the tank museum. Not safely behind the wire fence of the camp. I'm not sure though… I need a reason to see him — I tap my fingers on the windowsill, gazing at nothing. Then it hits me: George's photo. I dash along the landing to change into my tightest jeans and make up my face, but as I reach into my bedside drawer, the picture isn't there.

I check my handbag but I'm sure I remember taking it out and I'm right. Where else could I have put it? I search the dressing table and even check the living room. But the more I hunt the more certain I am; I put it in the bedside drawer and only one person has been in that room apart from me.

I don't know which is worse: the thought that Paxton went through my things or that the photo is missing. Perhaps … perhaps he just wanted to show it to the guys at the museum? But all the same it's a bloody cheek he didn't ask me.

Even so, when I get to Bovington I find I need to psych myself up. I sit in my car as the visitors come and go, trying not to look at the workshop, trying out different words and phrases in my mind. But I can't prevaricate forever.

Unlike my last visit, all is quiet inside the hanger and Alex is leaning over a workbench near the door, flicking the pages of a newspaper and drinking a mug of tea.

"Excuse me…" I venture. He looks up and after a moment or two recognition appears on his face. "I'm… I'm looking for Paxton."

"He's not here this afternoon, love. In fact, I kind of assumed he was out with you. Didn't say though — never does."

"Oh, it doesn't matter. I was just passing on my way back from a friend's and thought I'd drop by on the off chance."

"Have a cuppa while you're here?"

"I wouldn't want to disturb you."

"You're not. I'm on my own today, just tinkering around. Hard to get motivated with this heat."

"I expect it is."

He straightens up and heads for the back of the workshop, where a kettle stands next to a jar of tea bags.

"Dried milk, I'm afraid — is that ok?"

"Yes — it's fine." My stomach churns even more at the thought of the lumps.

"I have to say, you're making a big difference to young Paxo — seems like he's settling in at last."

"Well, that's good. He's not here for long though, is he?"

"Must be hard on you, being fond of him and knowing he's going away."

I edge past an engine leaking oil onto a thick layer of cardboard on the floor. "It doesn't do to get too serious. A bit of fun — for both of us, really."

"Fun is what that boy needs after what he's been through."

"In Iraq?"

Alex nods as he hands me my tea. "And afterwards. He doesn't know I know, of course, but the welfare officer tipped me the wink so I could keep an eye on him."

"I … I get the impression he doesn't like people knowing."

"Terrible business … terrible…" I watch the specks of milk spin in my mug. "But I guess the worst thing for him is the shame … such a proud man … with his military record … no wonder it's been hard for him to handle."

"Yes. It's been tough." I only wish I knew what on earth he's on about.

Alex puts his hand on my arm. "I'm sorry — it must be upsetting for you as well. Whatever you say you're fond enough of him to see through the damage."

"If I'm helping him then…"

"Well, talk of the devil," Alex booms. "Paxo — I thought you'd gone out."

I turn to see him silhouetted in the doorway, tucking a pair of sunglasses into the pocket of his shirt.

"Hey — Marie — what a great surprise." His voice sounds warm. "I thought you were working all day."

"I'm back on at six — just a spur of the moment thing — thought I'd surprise you."

"Aw, you should've called — I've been to Wool for a walk along the river — we could've met up sooner. I'm on duty in half an hour."

"You? Weekend duty? That'd be a first," Alex snorts.

As Paxton steps into the light, I can see he's in a uniform of beige trousers with a razor-sharp crease down the front and a shirt with three stripes at the top of each arm and "*PS Taylor*" on a label on his right breast.

"Very smart, Sergeant Taylor," I tell him.

"Contrary to what Alex would have you think, I am here on a military posting," he winks. "C'mon — let's pull you away from his clutches and I'll walk you back to your car."

"See you, Paxo," Alex calls.

"Gee — I wish you wouldn't call me that, not in front of the lady, anyway."

"You can't get away from it, mate — it's even on your shirt — Paxo Stuffing Taylor."

Away from Alex's sharp eyes Paxton's kiss feels like a bruise on my lips.

"Why didn't you call?" he snaps.

"It was … you know…"

"So you could talk about me behind my back?"

I pull away. "No, Paxton. And anyway, what made you think we were talking about you?"

"Alex kind of gave the game away when he said 'talk of the devil'." His fingers tighten around the belt loop of my jeans.

"We don't really have anything else in common to talk about, do we? Only you."

"And what was he saying?"

"Just how well you fit in with the team, how it's a shame you're only here for a while."

"And what were you saying?"

My eyes can't meet his. "How much I'll miss you too when you go back."

"Will you, Marie? Will you really?" We're in the shadow of the buildings now and he pulls me against him, his tongue exploring every corner of my mouth, so I don't have to answer. Which rather lets both of us off the hook.

All through evening service on Monday I can't help glancing at the clock. My phone is covered in floury fingerprints from the number of times I've checked for texts but there is only one: *Waiting for our bags — nearly home now.*

When he walks through the kitchen door Jude seems taller and his skin has a deep golden glow. He throws his rucksack under the prep table and hugs me for all he's worth.

"I've missed you, Mum."

"Rubbish. But it's nice of you to say." I pull away to look at him properly and we laugh. "Good time?"

"Oh, Mum — it was amazing. Just amazing. Let me say hello to Dad then I'll come back and tell you all about it."

"Are you hungry?" I call after him.

"You bet. Got any fish and chips on the go?"

I finish the beetroot salad and nestle the dish next to the risotto waiting under the warmer, then batter a piece of haddock. Baz plunges an extra basket of chips into the fryer.

"Put some in for yourself, if you like," I offer and he grabs a huge handful from the bucket.

"I'll never have a body like Jude's," he laughs. "I dunno where he puts it."

"We're all different, Baz — that's what makes the world go around."

When Jude gets back he settles on an old bar stool and between mouthfuls of food paints us a picture of Milina with its morning bustle and afternoon calm; its stone-built villas and olive groves stretching their fat fingers right into the little town; the boardwalk between the tavernas and the narrow strip of sand; the crystal blue sea.

Baz asks him about the price of beer and he says it's cheap as chips. "It's not really a big tourist place, you see, mainly Greeks. It could be a nightmare choosing what to eat from the menus, but luckily Michael's picked up a bit of the lingo while he's been travelling."

"How is Michael?"

"Loving it over there and I can see why. It's just so laid back and everyone's friendly. They don't rush around like we do — I guess running a taverna there is a pretty hand-to-mouth existence but you wouldn't get stressed. And the light … my God, the light."

"Did you paint much?"

"Sketched more like, but I did take my watercolours. And Mum — this is the best bit — Mark's friend Yanni really liked them, so I showed him my online portfolio and he wants to buy my degree show pieces for his office reception. I said I'd give them to him but he told me I must be businesslike and we've agreed a price."

"Oh, Jude — that's amazing — well done. See, you can make a living from your art."

"Mum, calm down," he laughs, putting his plate in the dishwasher. "I've sold five little pictures. But it is a start."

The question I'm burning to ask has to wait until we're alone. By the time I've finished my shift it's gone eleven, but Jude's bedroom door is wide open and he's standing in front of a canvas he's washed turquoise blue.

"I just had to get it down," he says. "While it's still fresh in my mind. To think, I was only gazing at it this morning. Seems light years away already."

"What are you going to paint?"

"I'm not sure. I want to wash three canvasses first and then I'll start. I've got some other colours in my mind too. That dark green of the cypresses. And the way the stone is bleached almost white."

I watch him while he puts his brush in a jar of water and closes the lid of his watercolours. I haven't seen him create a proper work before — not anything like this. It's all been done at college. I hope he doesn't take them away when they're half finished.

I clear my throat. "So, did Pip enjoy her holiday too?"

"It's different, isn't it, when you wake up with someone every day." He's trailing the brush around in the jar, the paint forming greenish-blue clouds in the water.

"Good different or bad different?"

"Good different. Kind of settled and solid. I keep looking at that bed, thinking how empty it's going to feel."

"You told Michael?"

"Yes — as soon as he arrived. We had a night there on our own and met him off the ferry the next morning. We were holding hands on the dockside."

"And what did he say?"

"Nothing then. It was later, when the two of us were having a beer. He wanted to know how serious I was. I think I put his mind at rest."

"So, have you told her parents?"

"She's going to do it tonight. Said she'd text me but I've not heard. I hope they haven't cut up rough about it."

"They've got no reason to — they should be pleased their daughter's got such good taste."

He lets the brush drop into the jar and gives my shoulders a squeeze. "No, but it's more than that, isn't it? It's the effect it'll have on her future. She's not going to Cardiff — she's one hundred per cent decided. She reckons her dad'll be happy she won't be too far away. But they're still going to say she shouldn't change her plans for something as flimsy as love. Only Pip and I know it's not flimsy at all. It's what we want."

"There might have been more of an art world in Cardiff…" I venture.

"Southampton's commutable to London, Mum. And you've always said…"

His phone blares out the first few bars of a song I don't know and he grabs it to read a text.

"What does she say?"

"She fell asleep on the sofa — she'll tell them tomorrow."

"Will you sleep now?"

"Yes. But, Mum — I've got something for you first." He burrows in his bag and pulls out a white plastic box with gold lettering printed on it.

"You shouldn't have wasted your holiday money on me."

"Without you — and Mark — we wouldn't have had this holiday. Go on — open it."

I prise the lid off the box and inside, lying between two layers of pink cotton wool, is a finely worked silver chain necklace.

"Jude — it's beautiful." Oh my God; I could cry with happiness.

"It's for the seahorse. No one's going to claim it now so you might as well wear it."

"I'm not sure…"

"Don't be silly — we chose it specially. Where is it?"

"In the safe still…"

He rushes down the stairs two at a time.

It's a delicate operation opening the loop on the seahorse to fix it to the chain, but with the aid of my tweezers Jude manages it, testing the final result with a sharp tug.

"There you go — try it on."

I turn around so he can fasten it behind my neck and it is warm from his hands as it slides over my skin. I pull it out so we can admire it together before he undoes the clasp and we nestle the whole thing back between the layers of cotton wool.

I give him a hug and say goodnight. As he pads along the landing to the bathroom I sit on the edge of my bed and open the tiny box again. The seahorse glints in the lamplight; it's so lovely. I'll put it back in the safe tomorrow, but for now I open my bedside drawer to put it away and stop in my tracks. There, just under my migraine tablets, is George's photo.

CHAPTER 20

The smudge of concealer beneath my eyes fails to hide the black rings and my eyeliner is a wobbly mess. In the kitchen, with Baz banging pots and Stephen barking orders from the bar, I keep my fear at bay but when my fingers reach into my pocket to check the photo's still there I can feel them trembling. I phoned George first thing this morning to tell him I'd be bringing it back. He's dog sitting so he gave me Mark's address. I was glad to be in the kitchen early, making meals for his freezer.

Mark's freezer is more or less in his living room. His flat is at the end of a modern block about five minutes' drive from his office but without the distant harbour views. Much of the floor space is taken up with an open-plan living area stretched across the back of the building with patio doors giving out onto a small garden. The light streaming in gives it the potential to be truly beautiful, but there are no pictures on the walls and the room is dominated by Troy's cage and two worn Chesterfield-style sofas.

Troy's tail thuds against the metal bars and he whines to be set free. I reach through the side to stroke his ears and he licks my hand again and again, pleading eyes never leaving mine for a moment.

George laughs as he shuffles between the fridge-freezer and the end of the breakfast bar to put the kettle on. "He hasn't learnt — the quicker he pipes down the quicker he'll be let out."

"It's ok. I'll sit on the floor with him so he isn't tempted to jump."

George shakes his head. "You're as bad as Mark, spoiling that dog."

"You've got to feel sorry for him, though."

"Who, Troy or Mark?"

I look around the soulless room. "Both of them really."

George shrugs. "It's men living alone."

"But your house is so homely."

"I spend a lot of time in mine. For Mark, this is just somewhere to sleep."

Once we're settled, with Troy's head in my lap, I open my handbag and pass the photo back over my shoulder to George on the sofa.

"What did your friend think of it?"

"I didn't show it to him in the end."

"You could have kept it, you know."

"I couldn't. I… I almost lost it, you see. I wanted to bring it back." I hope I'm hiding the shake in my voice, but George picks up on it at once and asks what's wrong.

"N-nothing."

"You don't have to tell me if you don't want to, but please don't lie. I brought up my children to tell the truth and I expect the same from you."

I run my hand along Troy's silky flank. Outside the birds sing, closer and sharper than the rumble of traffic. I wasn't brought up like that; I think I understand now. My mother's other men, my father's rather academic hedonism. Perhaps I wasn't brought up at all.

The well of misery overflows. Hot, fat tears scar my cheeks. "I'm sorry, George, I'm so sorry. I've already lied to you… I'm just so sorry."

He rests his palm on my shoulder but says nothing. Troy raises his head to lick my hand and I cry some more. Months and months of tears pushing a grubby tide of mascara down my face. Eventually I scrabble in my handbag for a tissue.

"Tell me, Marie, what did you lie about?"

"Corbin. Corbin Summerhayes. The man in the photo. I couldn't … tell you truth … you'd think I was mad … but it doesn't matter now because you've found out I'm a liar and you'll hate me anyway."

"Hate's a very strong word and much misused. Anyway — one lie does not a liar make," he laughs.

But there isn't just the one lie; there's a whole raft of them. A whole summer of lies and half-truths and things unsaid.

I take a deep breath. "Ok. The lie I told you sounded like the truth. The truth is going to sound like I'm making it up. But here goes anyway." And so it all comes pouring out: about the seahorse necklace, and about meeting Corbin on the cliffs — about some of the strange things he said. And the darker side: chasing up the path to follow him — even seeing him in the bar of The Smugglers on that awful, awful night.

"I was so rattled I slept in the beach hut. It was like a vivid 3D nightmare but it was more than that — truly terrifying. Now I think perhaps I imagined it. I was tired. I'd had a couple of glasses of brandy. Perhaps … it was a sort of hallucinogenic migraine?"

"So you've kept this all to yourself, suffered in silence?"

"Who could I tell?"

George squeezes my shoulder. "Oh, you poor child." But all his kindness does is make me start to cry again.

I calm down more quickly this time, and he asks me if I think the ghost of Corbin hid the photograph.

"Ghost? How can… I … I don't believe in ghosts," I stutter.

"Why not? I do."

I spin around to face him. "Really?"

"Of course. To me, Eileen's never completely gone. And that makes my life bearable."

"In what way?"

"Now, you're going to think it's the ramblings of a senile old man but I can tell you it's not. Sometimes when I've been dozing in my chair and I wake up I can see her, sitting there with her knitting. Perhaps it's half-dreaming, half-hoping, but how do you explain the fact that very often when I go up the stairs I smell her perfume? Lily-of-the-valley, it is. And I never even brought any of it with me when I moved to Purbeck Court. Chucked it all out as soon as she died."

"Does she … does she ever hide stuff?"

He laughs. "I'd like to think so but I fear it really is just my bad memory when I can't find a pen or my keys. Tracked down my wallet to the fridge once — but don't tell Mark."

"I did wonder whether it was my memory when I couldn't find your photo. I hunted high and low. Then I thought Paxton had taken it. It was in my bedside drawer, and after what happened the first night I was on my own in the pub he stayed with me for the next few, so he could have found it when he was looking for something else… But he couldn't have put it back."

"You're sure?"

"Yes, I was thinking about that. I found it last night when I went to put something in the drawer. The last time I opened it before that was Sunday lunchtime. I… I felt a bit heady so I rushed up to take some tablets. I know it wasn't there then."

"And could anyone else have moved it? Stephen or one of the pub staff?"

"The staff never come up to the flat. And pulling a trick like that just isn't Stephen's style."

"Have you mentioned it to him?"

"No. When I asked if he thought the pub was haunted he spent all morning making ghost noises in my ear."

I remove Troy's head from my lap and haul myself up on the sofa. "Is there somewhere I can wash my face? I need to be going soon and I can't drive home looking like this."

The shower room is a narrow tomb-like space on the opposite side of the hall to Mark's bedroom. Through the open door I see a double bed pushed against a teak bookcase crammed with hardbacks. A radio alarm gathers dust on the floor, next to an abandoned mug. Surely living alone can be better than that?

Paxton is waiting under a pool of light in the car park outside the base. Even with the window open all the way from Studland I'm still too hot. I committed to the dance weeks ago so there was no way I could back out. Even on a sodding Thursday night. Even with no more than ten minutes to get out of my whites and into a dress and full make up then foot down over here. I can still feel the sweat balling up with the deodorant under my arms.

"Looking good, Doll," he winks.

"I probably still smell of onions," I grumble.

I haven't seen Paxton in his dress uniform before. As we walk towards the guard hut he swings a dark green jacket from over his shoulder and puts it on. Again his name is on his right breast and on his left is a row of ribbons. I run my fingers along them but he shrugs me off.

"No time, Doll," he tells me and grabs my hand, leading me towards a building blazing with light and big band sounds spilling from the open windows and doors.

It's ten o'clock and the party is in full swing. British soldiers in smart khaki jackets with ribbons like Paxton's prop up the bar, and mainly older men whirl women in tight dresses with flared skirts around the floor to *Straighten Up and Fly Right*. Above them a banner proclaims "*D-Day plus Sixty — let's party!*"

"Wanna dance?" asks Paxton.

"I don't know … it's years… Oh come on, let's give it a try."

Paxton's grandmother taught him well and he knows all the moves. We jive to *Pistol Packin' Mama* and *Don't Sit Under the Apple Tree*, and just as I'm losing my breath the music slows and we melt together in the crush. It's during the opening bars of *As Time Goes By* that Paxton waltzes me to the edge of the crowd, out of the patio doors and into the night.

"Your grandma's one hell of a dance teacher."

"She's one hell of an everything. But never mind that — there's a different type of dancing I've got in mind now."

He takes me by the hand and leads me between two barrack blocks. Lights along the path in front of a row of buildings stretch to my right, but to my left is velvet darkness and the strains of the band mix with the rustle of the trees.

"Wanna see where I live, Doll?" he asks.

I wrap my arm tighter around his waist. "I'd love to. Then I can imagine you there when you text me at night." He squeezes me back.

Paxton's room is a plain oblong with a single bed under the window and a desk against the wall. Behind the door is a built-in wardrobe and there are pictures of local scenes on the walls. All this I see in the glow of a bedside lamp left burning to welcome us. The curtains flutter in the breeze and the duvet is turned down to reveal crisp white sheets.

"It's going to be a bit cramped," he murmurs as he starts to unbutton my dress.

I run my finger along the row of ribbons again. "Tell me what they mean."

"Later." He pulls away and hangs his jacket on the back of the chair. "Now, where was I before you interrupted?"

Tonight is slow and soft, but I guess anything more athletic would have left us banging our elbows against the wall or ending up in a heap on the floor. Afterwards he lies with his face in his pillow while I stretch beside him, stroking his back and feeling his muscles relax one by one.

The crack and bang of the explosion comes from nowhere and Paxton leaps from the bed. I am startled myself, but almost at once a gentle pop and thud tells us what it is.

Paxton drops to his knees. "Fireworks… I hate fireworks," he moans and I clamber past him to close the window.

It deadens the noise but sucks the air out of the room. I crouch next to Paxton and put my arm around his shoulder, saying nothing. His eyes are closed and his chest heaves. What is he hearing? What is he seeing?

"It's not then, it's now," I whisper.

"It's always then."

Once the fireworks stop he stands and stretches.

"I need to take a whiz," he says and the bathroom door slams behind him. I pick up his watch from where it dropped on the floor — almost half past midnight. Time I was going. But something else catches my eye: under the bed, half in and half out of the circle of light. A beige leather glasses case, about six inches long. I pick it up to find its softness comes from genuine age, the gold print of the word "Ray-Ban" barely visible. The metal popper is broken and the lid lifts easily as the toilet flushes. Aviators. Dark green Aviators.

I push them back under the bed and leap up so I'm dressing when Paxton comes back into the room.

211

CHAPTER 21

Sometimes, just before a migraine crashes down with its full force, there is a flash of clarity. Images fit together like the pieces of my jigsaw and suddenly everything makes sense. Trying to capture that moment again is well-nigh impossible.

My hands push the bedclothes away then pull them up again. The window is closed to stop the curtains blowing the light into the room, but still the sounds from the yard drift upwards. I should be down there, cooking, but I cannot even raise my head. My mind is on a permanent loop: Corbin peering over the bar as agony pounds my skull. Corbin becoming Paxton as he crouches on the floor to see if I'm hurt. Corbin — Paxton. Paxton — Corbin. Click. Loop. Click.

I reach in the drawer for George's photo but I know it isn't there. I took it back. But Paxton couldn't have brought it back to me. Couldn't have. Not his fault. Maybe he didn't put the Aviators under his bed either. He likes old cars, old songs. Maybe they're just his. One and one is two, two and two is five, five and five…

Jude wakes me with a fresh glass of water. The old one is still full. "You've got to drink something."

I struggle up and he holds the glass to my lips, dropping sips onto my tongue. I push it away. "Enough."

"It's hardly anything."

"Enough." He is going out of the room when I remember. "Jude — has Pip told her parents yet?"

"No."

"The longer she leaves it…"

"I know."

Jude doesn't tell me then, he tells me later, when I'm feeling more myself. They're already falling out over it, niggling each other. Pip says she can't find the moment — he thinks (and I think) she should make one.

We are sitting together over the barely started jigsaw. I am trying to find the bits with trees on and Jude is turning pieces of sky around and around.

"I'm beginning to wonder if she's changed her mind," he says.

"What about?"

"Me. Or if I'm lucky maybe just about the not going to Cardiff part. But she says not — says the way I'm talking it sounds as though I don't want her any more. It's such a mess."

"I don't want to interfere … especially after last time … but what if I talked to her? I've got an idea about creating the right moment but if she doesn't go for it … well … at least you'll know more where you stand."

Jude presses the heels of his hands into his eyes. "I don't think I could bear to lose her. Not now. It's getting all scary again and just a week ago it was so blissful. Is love always like this?"

"I'm afraid so. You just have to make sure the ups outweigh the downs."

In every possible way I'm better focusing on Jude. When I phone Pip she cries; she's as lost as he is. Is the poor child really that scared of her parents? She grabs at my plan like it's the very last straw. I take a shift in the bar so Jude can finish early. The keys to the beach hut are missing from the rack when I finally climb the stairs to bed, Stephen following with the cash bags. I make him tea while he completes his spreadsheet, yawning all the while.

"Is she keeping you up?" I tease and he grumbles it's none of my business. "Is she special or is she just another woman?" I persist.

"They're all just other women. You ought to know that. Now shut up and let me concentrate."

Cakes are not normally my forte, but this is a special occasion. Or it should be. Nevertheless, my chocolate sponge is understated, filled with whipped cream and raspberries, with just a sprinkling of icing sugar on top. I carry the tin with both hands as Jude and I follow the footpath through the churchyard, cross the main road and walk up Heath Green.

Seeing Pip's father's brand new Mercedes in the drive brings Stephen's comment about the family moving in different circles sharply to mind. The front porch has almost as many pots and hanging baskets as The Smugglers, but the paint is certainly fresher. Still, this is no time to feel like a poor relation and I tell Jude to chill as he shifts from foot to foot beside me.

Angie opens the door dressed in a denim mini-skirt meant for younger legs and air-kisses my cheeks.

"Marie — it's been so long. How lovely to see you. And you've brought one of your marvellous cakes. Greg will be pleased. We're both agog to hear this wonderful surprise the children have for us."

She doesn't draw breath while she runs around the kitchen making tea in a Bodum glass pot. I'm glad to escape outside to where Greg has the Sunday papers spread across a wrought iron table.

"Hi Marie — how's things? I'm just catching up on the sport." He winks. "But don't tell Angie — she thinks I'm reading the business pages."

"Your secret's safe with me." I smile as I fold my skirt to make the metal seat more comfortable.

Greg laughs and passes me a cushion from a pile on the patio. "Style over comfort, these damn chairs."

As I am settling the cushion under me, Angie appears with a tray. "Oh, Philippa, you could have put those out before our guests arrived. Honestly, what have you been doing?"

"I'm afraid she's been listening to me drone on about how hosting the Olympics is going to break the Greek economy. Wow — that's a lovely looking cake. I take it you made it, Marie?"

"I didn't want to come empty-handed. Although I have to say I'm intrigued about why Jude and Pip have asked us today. Stephen sends his apologies, by the way, but it's bedlam at The Smugglers with the lovely weather."

Angie turns to Pip. "Well, honeybunch, what's the news?"

Pip looks across the table at Jude, panic in her eyes. He rescues her. "Pip and I are going out."

Greg is smiling, but Angie looks unsure. It's my turn to gush now.

"Oh, that's so nice — especially as you've known each other nearly forever. Bit of a holiday romance, was it?"

"In a way, Mum. But I think because we've spent so much time together this summer anyway it just kind of grew on us." I'm so pleased he's found a way not to lie.

"And you didn't think to tell us as soon as you got back, Philippa?" Angie asks.

Pip's ready for this — we've talked it through. "We wanted to give it a week to settle. Make sure it felt the same when we got home. And it does."

Jude reaches across and takes her hand.

215

"Well, Jude," says Greg, "I've always wondered what I'd think when Pip brought a serious boyfriend home for the first time and I have to say I'm quite relieved. Much better than someone we don't know, isn't it, darling?"

"The thing is, Dad, it's going to change a lot of things. I… I don't want to go to Cardiff any more. I'm going to try for Southampton through clearing. The course is almost as good and…"

"You shouldn't be settling for 'almost as good'," Angie snaps. "You're very young. You need to stick to your plans — certainly not let a little holiday romance upset your whole future."

"This isn't a little holiday romance," Pip mutters.

"Yes, well, first love and all that. I can just about remember how it feels," Angie simpers. "But it won't seem so important later on when you meet the man you want to spend your life with."

Pip juts out her chin. "I already have."

"I don't think Southampton is such a bad idea," Greg says, and I have to hide a smirk as I realise they're both running almost exactly to the script Pip wrote for them. "Pip will be home every weekend to visit Jude so we'll get to see her too."

"Actually," Jude adds, "we're planning to rent a flat in Southampton because I can commute to Bournemouth on the train. But we will be home a lot because I've told Dad I'll still help in the pub when I can."

"But you won't get any life, Philippa," Angie bursts out. "You'll miss so many opportunities you should have as a student, opportunities to meet other people like yourself — other undergraduates."

"Jude's a graduate, Mum. And I'd love him even if he wasn't."

"Yes, but in art — it's not a proper degree, is it?"

I put out my arm to restrain Jude but it's pointless. He leaps to his feet, the heavy metal chair falling back and smashing onto a ceramic frog. Fragments of green china spray across the patio.

"And what's that got to do with anything? It should be enough I love your daughter, care about her happiness — a lot more than you bloody do anyway."

Pip is halfway out of her seat as his footsteps echo along the side of the house, but one look from me makes her sit back down. With any luck I can still retrieve the situation.

"I'm sorry, Angie," I say, "but you did goad him. He doesn't often lose his temper but Pip is really important to him. And I'm not sure he's such a very terrible catch — although of course I'm biased."

"I think perhaps Angie should apologise to you, Marie," says Greg. "But it's not her style so I'll do it for her."

"You condescending shit! That lout broke my frog."

"Good. It was bloody ugly," Greg mutters as she flounces into the house, a series of doors slamming behind her.

Pip starts to cry. "Oh, Dad — it's going to be awful. I just know it."

"Come on, Pippy, I'm on your side. I've always been fond of Jude and why not give it a go if it's what you want? Southampton's so much nearer than Cardiff — I can even come over to scrounge some supper when your mother's out."

"I'd like that," Pip sniffs.

"And I'm pleased, and I know Stephen will be too, so your mum really is outnumbered. I'm sure she'll come around."

"I'm sure she won't," says Pip.

Angie doesn't reappear and I leave as soon as I can, Pip trailing behind, trying to phone Jude.

"There's no answer," she tells me, eyes filling with tears again.

"He's probably out on his bike, trying to calm down. Text him to tell him you're coming home with me."

Back at The Smugglers we discover the reason for Jude not picking up his mobile: it's on the kitchen table where he put it down to help me lift the cake into the tin. His bike is in the yard too, and the beach hut keys are on their hook. I go into the bar to ask Stephen if he's seen him.

He shakes his head. "I take it it went badly?"

"Only with Angie. Greg was fine. Just what Pip said would happen. Except Jude lost his temper when Angie called a degree in art worthless."

"Well it is — especially compared to Michael's — but that doesn't make Jude a bad person." From Stephen, that scores as a compliment.

I ask Pip if she'd like a drink but she shakes her head, tears welling in her eyes. I put a hand on each of her shoulders.

"Come on, where's your fight?"

"I'm sorry."

Stephen stops polishing glasses. "There's no need to worry, Pip, I bet he'll be back any minute. Got a bit of a temper on him has Jude, but it doesn't last long."

I wonder where he gets that from. The sarcasm is about to drip from my tongue so instead I ask Pip if she'd like to go to look for him.

She nods. "It would be better than doing nothing."

We decide to start on the beach. The tide is almost at its lowest ebb and the glassy blue of the water seems a million miles from the bottom of the steps. I check the beach hut door but it's locked fast.

Pip turns to me. "I did think he might have come here."

I scan the sand, dotted with windbreaks and families with buckets and spades. "Perhaps he wanted somewhere quieter." Like the down, high above us to our right. Or the dunes, straggling invisibly into the distance to our left. In the shallows off Redend Point two dinghies are moored and one of them is the *Helen*.

I pull my phone out of my pocket and search through my contacts. It rings four times before Mark answers.

"Marie — lovely to hear from you."

"Well, it might not be, I'm afraid — I'm after another favour. I've seen the *Helen* on the beach — where are you?"

"Reacquainting Troy with the lower reaches of the dunes. With his lead on, of course. But it's nothing that can't wait."

"No — that's perfect. There's been ... a bit of an argument and Jude's gone AWOL. Pip's a little worried ... can you just keep an eye open for him? We're going to look on the cliffs."

"Sure. What happened?"

"I'll tell you later."

"Fine. Let me know if you find him first."

Pip and I take the path from the beach, blinking as we emerge from the cool tunnel of hawthorns. A straggle of walkers lines the track over the down, stopping every so often to drink from their water bottles and admire the view. We weren't so sensible; we left with nothing but our phones. When mine rings I grab it from my pocket.

"Oh, hello Paxton."

"Hey, Doll, that's not much of a welcome."

"I'm sorry. I was hoping it was Jude — he's gone missing."

"Hell — what's happened?"

"There was a bit of a row with Pip's parents..." I glance at her as she checks her mobile for the millionth time. "Well, just

219

her mother actually … and he stormed off. We've no idea where he is and he's been gone for a couple of hours."

"D'you want me to come and help look for him?"

"Would you? Pip and I are beginning to worry but Stephen doesn't seem too bothered."

"Yeah, well I guess it is too soon to be overly concerned. But hey, you're a mom, and that's always different. I've got a few ideas where to look."

Our search on the cliffs is fruitless and by the time we descend the chalk track back to The Smugglers Pip is close to tears again.

"Oh, Marie, do you think he's all right? It's so not like him…"

I give her a little hug. "No, but by the same token it's not the first time. There's a bit of his father's temper in him, and along the way he's learnt to take himself off until he's calmed down. Chin up — we'll look over towards Knoll, shall we, perhaps link up with Mark? But let's get a drink first."

The afternoon is beginning to cool and the tide is coming up. People are leaving the beach in droves and settling in the pub garden. Gina is taking a break, so I pitch in behind the bar to help Stephen over the worst of the rush while Pip clears a few tables.

"Do her good," Stephen whispers. "Take her mind off Jude."

I turn to him. "Don't tell me you're not just a little bit worried?"

He looks at his watch. "Give it another couple of hours and I will be."

We are just considering whether to search the heath when Paxton texts. *In The Ship in Swanage. Drunk as a skunk. Having a man-to-man then I'll bring him home.*

I try to persuade Pip to make herself scarce but she's adamant she'll stay. She has a point — it may be the first time she sees Jude like this but if they stay the course it won't be the last. From the little I see she handles him magnificently, laughing at his slobbering apology then taking him off to his room with a jug of water and some aspirin.

As soon as they disappear up the stairs I wrap my arms around Paxton. "I can't thank you enough. What made you think to look in the pubs?"

"I'm a guy, he's a guy. I know where I'd be if I was trying to blow off that kind of anger."

"Fancy a beer now?"

"Not if I have to drive back."

"You don't, you know. Not for a while, anyway."

"Then yes, yes I would. How about we take a couple down to the beach hut?"

We are walking up the lane to the stile when I hear a bark. Oh my God — I didn't call Mark to tell him we've found Jude. I disengage my hand from Paxton's and reach for my phone but it's too late.

"Mark, I'm so sorry. Paxton's just found Jude in Swanage and brought him home. Well, poured him home's more like it… I was just about to call you." Troy is straining at his leash to jump up on me but it's clipped too tight.

Mark smiles, looking at Paxton. "Well, as long as he's safe — that's the main thing." He sticks out his hand. "Mark Adams."

"Paxton Taylor. I'm Marie's boyfriend."

"Yes, of course. You're stationed at Bovington, I believe?"

"That's right."

"Well, best get back to my boat before I have to swim out to reach her. Glad Jude's ok, anyway."

Paxton and I watch from the stile until Mark and Troy disappear down the steps to the beach.

"Who is that guy?" Paxton asks.

"Think I mentioned him before. He's George's son, the old veteran."

"Friend of yours?"

"Acquaintance, more like." I bite my lip. "I saw his boat so I called and asked him to keep an eye out for Jude while he was walking his dog."

Paxton sets off down the path but I dawdle behind him. When we reach the end I head towards the Exercise Smash memorial.

"Aren't we going to the beach hut?" Paxton asks.

I stop. "I thought it would be nice to take a look at the memorial first."

"If we must."

"It's ok — we don't have to."

"There's too many memorials in this country, Marie. Every village, every town — there's somewhere. Guys drowned or guys blown to bits."

Below us Mark is wading out to the *Helen*, Troy in his arms. The tide is up to his knees. This is all my fault. I look at Paxton's scowl. Everything's my fault.

CHAPTER 22

I suspect the real reason for Stephen's carping is that I disappeared with Paxton yesterday evening, but the last thing he'll do is admit it.

"Why did you have to interfere?" he rages. "Jude's no use this morning and it's all your fault. If Pip didn't want to tell her folks I don't see the problem."

Even when Jude appears in the pub kitchen he is still looking green. I fetch him a pint of orange juice from the bar while Baz makes him a bacon sandwich.

"Please — no — just the smell's making me want to chuck," he murmurs, but Baz tells him to shut up and get it down his neck. The amount of butter dripping from the bread almost makes me take pity on Jude, but then the fishmonger is at the door with the very bad news he needs to be paid in cash.

I ask him to wait while I run up to the safe but as luck would have it Stephen emptied it last night. My only option is to raid the float in the till. I'm half hoping I can get Jude to do it, but he's nowhere to be seen so I have to brave Stephen and the bar myself.

I peep through the curtain and it's with some relief I see he's serving coffee to a couple in their thirties. They're dressed rather more smartly than the average holidaymaker and the woman is beautifully made-up with subtle lipstick and smoky eyes. I cross my fingers she's sufficiently distracting and creep towards the till.

It isn't so much Stephen who stops me in my tracks but his words. He is smiling at the woman, shaking his head and saying, "Of course I'd consider a serious offer, but my wife would never sell. This place is her whole life."

This place? Working like a slave to live like a pauper? Sneaking around to take my own money out of my own till? "Don't be so sure," I spit as the drawer springs open and I pull out four twenty pound notes.

"What are you doing?" snaps Stephen.

"Paying the fish man. Ever heard of cash on delivery? You know, COD?"

The woman stifles a laugh but I don't wait for Stephen's reply.

It takes quite a few minutes of choosing fish for my heart stop thudding against the wall of my chest. Thick white slabs of halibut almost blow my budget, but spider crabs are cheap at the moment and although Baz hates preparing them I know I can make them sing with fresh tomatoes and a stir of chilli. The fishmonger throws in a bag of mussels with the instruction to use them today and my world is already a calmer, happier place.

I carry the tray of fish inside and put it in the fridge. Baz taps me on the shoulder.

"There's a lady wants to see you — at the kitchen door." And I know before I look it's the woman who was in the bar.

"I hope you don't mind," she smiles, "but I wondered if you were serious about being prepared to sell. We've asked your husband so many times and the answer's always the same. We're desperate for a break, really."

"I honestly don't know. I haven't thought much about it, but in the middle of a frankly rubbish morning it suddenly seemed like a good idea."

"Oh." She looks a bit crestfallen.

"Why do you want The Smugglers so much?"

"It's beautiful and it's got so much potential. We already run two pubs in the New Forest and striking out for the coast feels like the right move. Look — can I give you my card? If you ever feel you want a chat … you know, talk to your husband and…"

I wipe my hands on the tea towel I'm clutching. "He's not my husband. Well, maybe legally speaking but all that ties us together is this place and perhaps that's no longer a good thing. I'd just miss the kitchen."

"We could do a deal — you could stay on as chef — that would be amazing."

"Let me think about it. I will come back to you…" I look down at the card in my hand, "Amy." *Amy Blunt, Hippocampus Inns.*

She's holding out her hand to shake mine. "Thank you. You've given me some hope."

I wonder if that cuts both ways.

By half past two Jude is looking much brighter, and when he announces he's hungry I make him two rounds of beef sandwiches to eat behind the bar. Stephen's buggered off and left him to it, without a word to either of us, but that's probably for the best. If he doesn't turn up this evening, I'm sure we'll cope.

The bar is cool and quiet but the garden is packed with customers. I take a tray around the tables to collect the glasses and by the time I get back Jude has made me an iced mocha, a spiral of fresh cream on top.

"Thought you deserved a treat," he tells me, grinning. "And an apology for yesterday."

"I have to say I was beginning to worry and poor Pip was beside herself."

"You were both bloody amazing from what I can remember. And so was Paxton — he's quite a guy."

"I'd never have thought of trawling the bars in Swanage, but he said it was a man thing. Goodness knows how many he'd been in and out of before he found you."

"Only a couple. Seems he knows Swanage pretty well — said he used to go there a lot before he met you. His great-uncle was stationed there in the run-up to D-Day. He told me he first visited to buy a postcard for his gran but then he went more into the wartime history, trying to trace exactly where her brother was. But of course it's impossible. His letters home weren't allowed to mention places. It was only afterwards they found out the name of the town."

"How come? When Paxton mentioned his great-uncle to me he said he'd gone missing in France."

"One of his buddies who did make it came and told them when he got home. Said how much Corbin had loved walking on the cliffs, that he'd had a girl here and everything … Mum?"

The icy glass slides out of my hand but thankfully lands upright on the bar, foamy cream flecking the pile of black and yellow beermats.

Somehow I find a smile for Jude. "Glass is wet, that's all. Need to give it a wipe. Don't want to waste any — it's lovely." And I busy myself with the bar towel. "Like I said, Paxton did tell me about his great-uncle but he couldn't have mentioned his name."

Jude is frowning. "His name? Why … oh, yes, of course — Corbin, Gran's GI. Well what are the chances? I suppose I should have realised but things were getting a little hazy by then. I'm not going to be drinking lager for a very long time. In fact, I might very well become teetotal."

Teetotal is the last thought on my mind at the end of a long day. Stephen didn't show up tonight, but Pip helped behind the bar and now she and Jude have gone to bed. Angie's probably having a fit on both counts. Perhaps she'll come around when Pip gets her grades in about ten days' time and it's clearer what they're going to do.

Maybe clearer for me, too. It's a warm night so I take the Martell and a glass outside and settle myself at one of the pub tables, facing the sea. I can't see it; the sliver of moon is too tiny to cast much light. I can't hear it; the tide has already dropped too far down the beach. But all the same I know it's there, the same as the invisible cliff looming above it. It always has been and it will be long after I'm gone. But when will that be?

I push Amy and her offer to one side for the moment to concentrate on Paxton. The evidence is pulling him closer and closer to Corbin, the thread becoming almost visible as it winds around the stem of my glass. If there was moonlight I could see it shimmering. Instead I reach to finger it but of course there is nothing there. If I break the thread with Paxton, would Corbin disappear too? Would it all … end? *Please, please, I want it to end.* I tug the lid off the Martell and take a slug, scalding my throat and making me cough.

No, no, no, Marie. Stop. You don't want to fall up the stairs past Jude's room with Pip in there. How embarrassed would he be? And you need to keep your wits about you too — because there's something drumming at your brain, begging to be let in, only you can't quite grasp it. Stop drinking, go to bed, and think about it in the morning.

I pick up the bottle and glass and make my way back across the road to the pub, locking the front door behind me. For a moment as I turn, there is a shadow at a square, scrubbed table. A shadow as deep as the sea and a whisper — less than a whisper — of my name. I close my eyes, count to ten, and when I open them he has gone.

I put the brandy back on the shelf in the bar, nestling it half behind the Kahlua, rinse my glass and leave it on a towel to dry. Perhaps I should have spoken. Perhaps I should have asked and as I climb the stairs I curse myself. But how can you ask your imagination?

Jude has left the light on in the kitchen. Something glints in the middle of the table — the seahorse necklace. Perhaps he took it out to show Pip. Perhaps he didn't. Perhaps I'll find Paxton waiting in my bed.

Right now that's the last thing I want. I close my eyes and wrap my arms around my ribs, holding myself together before I fall apart. Get a grip, Marie. Get a grip. As I return the seahorse to my jewellery box, my eyes fall on my wedding ring. I pick it up and roll it around in my fingers, lost in thought. What I couldn't quite grasp in the pub garden is becoming clearer and with it the realisation that maybe there's one part of this mess I can put right after all.

There's a text I have to send and it's long overdue. I perch on the edge of the table and type. His reply comes as I am brushing my hair before I get into bed. It's warm and generous and makes me feel bold. My fingers skate over the keyboard again.

Is it too late to ask if you'll take me sailing?

CHAPTER 23

There's something else I need to do, but this time it wouldn't be right to send a text. I'm nervous — I've never finished with anyone before — but at least Paxton agreed to meet me tonight and his Capri is already in the lay-by just outside Wool. As I turn my headlamps off his oh-so-familiar shape emerges from the driver's door. I steel myself and I beckon him to join me in my car.

The glow of the courtesy light drains the colour from his face. Beneath his eyes are smudges of black, stubble straying untidily down his neck.

"Hey, what's up?"

"It's Grandma — she's not at all well. There was a message from my dad when I got back on Sunday night and I've spent the last forty-eight hours trying to get leave. It's a nightmare."

"Why, what's the problem?"

"Bovington say Fort Riley need to sign it off and Fort Riley say it's Bovington. Yards and yards of military red tape and all I want to do is get home."

"Oh, Paxton." I reach over and take his hand from his lap to squeeze it. He lifts mine to his lips to kiss.

"I gotta see her. Dad says it's cool but he wouldn't have called if that was really the case. What if ... what if it's the end and I don't get to say goodbye?"

"They'll sort it out — I'm sure they will. I bet you'll be on a plane by this time tomorrow."

"Gee, I hope you're right. It's not even about me; whatever I've done, Grandma doesn't deserve this."

"You've done nothing but be the best grandson you could be."

"Oh God, if only…" His breath is hot on my hand where he's holding it close to his lips. I pull our entwined fingers towards me and kiss the tips of each of his. He leans forward and folds me into his arms, the taste of his mouth melting into my own. Tonight, more than ever, he needs to forget and I figure I owe him this one last time.

We make our way between the trees, following the bouncing beam from the small torch Paxton carries. We duck under branches and dip our heads to avoid brambles and before long we are in a clearing. Crouching down he pulls a red rug from his rucksack, followed by half a dozen tealights. I hold the torch while he lights them with shaking hands.

"C'mon, Doll — let's dance. Dance ourselves happy like Grandma would."

It seems like a figure of speech but he guides me to the centre of the clearing and puts his arms around my waist. He sings to me softly: Bing Crosby, Glenn Miller, Gene Kelly. He closes his eyes and we shuffle and sway over the cool grass.

We lie together on the rug until the tealights flicker and die and the birds welcome the false dawn. Once or twice I drift into sleep, only to wake to see Paxton propped on his elbow beside me. I gesture for him to lay his head on my shoulder and rest too, but he puts his finger to his lips.

We stay that way until daylight reaches us through the trees. He seems more hopeful, cheerful, even.

"You're right, Doll — something's gotta give. I'll go see the duty officer again before breakfast. Maybe something's come in from Fort Riley overnight. If it has I'll be shooting right off — mightn't even have time to say goodbye but I'll call."

"You do that — let me know how she is."

"Aw, Doll. She'd just love you, I know she would. The way you understand."

Paxton appears that evening at the kitchen door. He is wearing a mottled camouflage uniform and his face is even greyer than the fabric.

I take the fish I'm cooking from the heat and wrap my arms around him as his shoulders begin to heave. "She's gone, she's gone," he whispers and I rock this huge hulk of a man back and forth like a child. Over my shoulder I watch as Baz crosses the kitchen and reignites the gas. He motions his head upwards towards the apartment.

By the time we settle on the sofa Paxton's tears are dry and I'm able to ask him what happened.

He looks down at his hands. "Dad said she kind of just faded away. She tried to wait for me, he said, but they just took too long. She said to him … tell Paxton how proud I am… Oh God, Doll — if only she knew."

"She knew you, Paxton — she knew the man she'd raised."

"But not the coward he'd become. I tried so hard to be like him, Doll — to be like great-uncle Corbin. She told me once I was and it was the best moment…" His voice cracks and I put my arm around his shoulder.

"I'd bet you only ever had to be yourself."

"I'm not even that anymore."

He leans forwards and picks up a piece of the jigsaw. It's white chalk with a peculiar-shaped corner. He turns it in his hand and after a while slides it into the right place towards the base of Old Harry.

"Corbin went through Omaha. He went halfway across Normandy. He'd have seen men's brains smeared down the

231

sides of tanks, a hand he recognised only because of the signet ring next to a ripped open boot but yards away from the patch of blood-soaked sand where you last saw the guy. He'd have known about all that. I bet *he* slept at night."

"I bet he didn't. Men suffered then, too, and didn't speak about it either. Perhaps … perhaps … he went missing because it all became too much."

Paxton turns on me, his breath hot on my face. "He went missing because he was blown to bits. Back then they didn't bother about pretending there was enough left to fill a coffin — they just told the families they were missing. We're not allowed to lose men in the desert, Marie — we gotta pick up the pieces and put them in trash bags so at least there's something to send home under those goddamn Stars and Stripes."

His fists are clenched into hard balls and I close my hands around them. Slowly, slowly, his fingers begin to loosen and his breathing slows.

"Sorry, Doll. I'm just so sorry. I'm screwed up over this. I just wanna sleep for a week."

"Why don't you catch a few hours at least? Go up to my room and put your head down while I finish my shift."

"You will wake me…"

"No. I'll take a look in and if you're out like a light I'll settle myself down here. But if you're awake then … we'll see."

"Aw, Doll…" If he hugged me any tighter my arms would snap like breadsticks.

We serve until nine thirty and beyond, and the apartment is in darkness when I creep up the stairs. A faint light casts a line under my bedroom door and I turn the handle, hoping it won't click. Paxton is facing away from me, his body silhouetted by the bedside lamp but he turns and holds out his arms when he hears me.

I lie next to him and run my hand over the soft stubble on his head. "Did you sleep?"

"Yes. A good couple of hours I reckon. Then I kind of half heard Baz calling goodnight so I knew you wouldn't be long."

"D'you want a drink? Anything to eat?"

"No, Doll. I just want you."

Afterwards, though, I think he could have wanted anyone. But really, that's ok. Now we're both hungry and I put on my dressing gown to make us tea and peanut butter toast.

Home is all Paxton wants to talk about. It starts with how peanut butter isn't the same without jelly, and how everything's so small here it's hard to breathe. How none of the houses have proper porches you can live on in the summer. But you wouldn't want to anyway given how rubbish summer is here. Except now it's too hot. I prop myself up on my pillows and sip my tea, nodding my head from time to time, waiting for him to run out of steam.

"Why aren't you defending your country, Doll?"

I shrug. "I've never been to the States. For all I know you could be right."

He laughs. "I'm not. I'm just looking for something to punch against. And you aren't rising to the bait."

"And what would it take to stop you punching?"

He runs his finger round the rim of his mug. Round and round and round. Finally he puts it down on the bedside table. "A distraction, a real good distraction."

The breeze from the window barely stirs the curtains but I am beginning to shiver. Once again I try to tug free, but the silk Paxton has used to bind me to the bed pulls tighter around my ankles and wrists. Where the hell is Paxton? He said he had to go to the bathroom, but afterwards I heard his footsteps on the stairs.

I struggle to sit up but with my arms tied to the brass corners of the bedstead I don't get very far. I turn and look at the knot, twisted in on itself, screwed up tight. This would be hard to get out of even with a free hand.

Paxton's uniform is draped over the chair next to the window. He must still be in the apartment. Unless he's so far gone he's wandering around the village naked. Oh God, Marie — you are such a fool. I'd call his name — yell for him to set me free — but Jude is closer; Jude would come first. And I'm not that desperate. Yet.

A floorboard creaks. It's the third one from the bottom of the stairs. And now a footstep — a heavy tread. Sweat breaks from every pore — if he's left me like this, what the hell is he planning to do when he gets back? The door opens and I am on the verge of screaming for Jude, but the look of horror on Paxton's face stops me.

He drops to the floor at the bottom of the bed, fumbling at the knots, cursing his clumsy fingers. He looks around frantically until he spots my nail scissors and cuts me free, muttering apologies. I draw myself into a ball and he wraps himself around me, saying my name over and over again.

Eventually I trust myself to speak. "Why … why did you do that?"

He runs the tip of his finger down the side of my face, making me look at him. "It wasn't deliberate. I just wanted some water and when I was in the kitchen everything sort of engulfed me again. I forgot — I swear I forgot — I'd left you that way. I swear it… I swear it…" he falters.

His words sound strangely mechanical but the red rims around his eyes tell me his story's true. He looks away.

"You won't ever trust me again, will you?"

I kiss the back of his hand. "Of course I will, Paxton. Nothing's changed; everything's fine."

It's five in the morning when he leaves. I creep to the bathroom and slowly fill the tub, so as not to disturb Jude. Even so, the pipes gurgle and groan as light from the waking sky floods the room. I ease myself into the water and reach for the soap, desperate to be clean. The lavender stings the wheals on my arms and legs.

Be strong, Marie. Be strong. But how can I turn him away?

There's only so much damage foundation can hide in the heat of a kitchen, and even my long-sleeved whites ride up almost to my elbows. Not only is Stephen eagle-eyed but he recognises the marks for what they are.

"Been a naughty girl, Marie?" he whispers, brushing past me. "Someone had to tie you up?"

There's only one way out of this with any pride. "Afraid so," I breathe. "These younger guys, well … they seem to know all the tricks."

"Luckily they teach 'em to the younger women too."

I force a laugh. "Touché, Stephen, touché."

"We're a sad bloody pair," he says and disappears back to the bar, shaking his head.

CHAPTER 24

I've been so looking forward to today — even more so because I haven't heard from Paxton in a week, so I'm guessing he's gone back to the States and I'm free. Dew seeps through the gaps in my crocs as I run down the path between the trees, the cool bag knocking at my legs. As I reach the top of the steps, the *Helen* is nosing towards Redend Point, her sail hanging limply in the morning air. I wave, but Mark is fully absorbed in his task.

I leave my shoes outside the beach hut and make my way towards the water. The tide is well on its way out and wet sand oozes between my toes. I fight the urge to stop and dig them further into the coolness; I don't want to keep Mark waiting.

"Lovely morning," I call as I paddle to meet him.

"Just enough breeze, too — especially further out." He is stretched across the boat, tanned legs dangling over the side, but in one smooth movement he's upright and holding out a hand to take the cool bag so I can clamber in.

"That looks promising."

"Bacon butties. Are you hungry? They'll still be warm."

"Brilliant. I'm starved." He starts to unzip the bag.

"Where's Troy? I brought him some cold sausage."

"I've left him with Dad — thought it might be a bit crowded with him jumping around as well."

I nod. Now I'm inside her, the *Helen* does feel small; I guess if Mark and I sat at either end and stretched out our legs our toes would touch in the middle. Not that we're doing it, of course. He is perched near the tiller while I sit on the little bench closest to the mast. I pour tea from the flask and while we eat our breakfast he explains how the *Helen* sails.

It takes just a few minutes for me to become thoroughly confused. I start off thinking sheets are the sails, but actually they're the ropes. Ordinary ones which lift the sail up the mast and a bright red one which seems to connect the end of the boom to the tiller, then to various places along the bottom of the sail.

"It's so I can take her out single-handed and control the sail and the tiller from more or less the centre of the boat," Mark explains. "Then I only have to move when I come about."

"Come about?"

"Yes, that's the tricky bit. Most people think the wind blows a boat along, but actually it sucks it. Very rarely do you sail a yacht with the wind behind you, you tack in different directions to use the breeze to best advantage, and when you go from one tack to the other it's called coming about. You'll have to be really careful because the boom swings right across the boat and you can get a nasty knock if you don't watch out."

I finger my plastic mug. "I didn't think it would be that complicated."

"It isn't — not really. I'm probably making it sound much worse than it is — it's quite intuitive really — there's a lovely rhythm to it. Let's get going and you'll see."

Mark tells me the safest place to be is on the same side of the boat as him, so I settle on the bench while he reaches into the water for the anchor. As soon as we are moving I can feel the breeze and he leans over my shoulder to release more of the sail, apologising when his arm brushes mine.

Our first tack takes us beyond Redend Point towards Middle Beach. The *Helen* sits low in the water and the grassy bank in front of the café looks like an alpine pasture. Behind it the owner is unfurling bright yellow umbrellas, ready for the day's trade. The car park will be full by half past ten, but now only dog walkers dot the golden sand.

"We need to come about," Mark says. "Keep your head down on the bench until the boom's gone over you." With a firm push on the tiller the boat changes direction and Mark's thighs flash past my eyes. He nudges me. "Come on — you can get up now."

The change of viewpoint is dramatic and I find myself looking towards Bournemouth, but Bournemouth as I've never seen it before. Rather than the bird's-eye view of the tower blocks from the clifftop, this Bournemouth is nothing but distant jagged teeth glinting in the sun as they rise from the sea. It reminds me of something — the sculpture that won gold in Jude's degree show — I get it now. I understand.

"Coming about," Mark calls and I slide low along the bench again, following his single movement to the other side. "You're getting the hang of it," he nods.

The sea air is pushing so far into my lungs I can hardly breathe. "It's amazing," I whisper. "Truly amazing."

We are facing back towards Knoll Beach and the dunes, sailing parallel to the shore. While Mark explains why we're having to tack, I gaze at the shifting mounds of sand, the tufts of marram grass no more than a greyish green stubble along their fringe. I remember walking up the beach with Paxton, touching his face… I trail my fingers in the water. *Goodbye, Paxton, goodbye. And thank you.*

The sea laps my hand and foams over my wrist. Clear as anything; if the water was still I could see right to the bottom. Perhaps I could spot a seahorse.

On the next tack we face well out into the Solent, the Needles rising from the haze then disappearing again. Part of a single strata of chalk, they say — all the way from the Purbecks to Old Harry, through the Isle of Wight and on to Champagne. I look over my shoulder to see the familiar whiteness behind me, gleaming in the early morning sun.

I turn and kneel so I can get a better view. For the first time, I notice that green fringes the bottom of the cliff as well as the top: a seaweed-coloured stain like a grubby ring around a bath. An enormous bath with sheer enamel sides, a bath you'd never climb out of. A prison of a bath. No — not a prison; I know where that is now. Not The Smugglers with its mullions, not the cliffs guarding the bay. Somewhere much closer to home and I didn't understand until a split second ago.

Below my trailing hand the sand is smudged with seagrass, swaying to the rhythm of the *Helen* as we slide past. The sun sparkles off our wake like a kaleidoscope and I know it's time. I push my dripping hand deep into my pocket and my fingers close over my wedding ring. Hiding it in my palm I lean further over the side before letting it drop, drop, drop, into the deepest darkest blue.

"Are you all right? Not seasick I hope?"

I join Mark on the rail, the warmth from his body radiating into my arm. "I'm fine. Honestly. It's just everything looks so different from the sea."

"In what way?"

"Well, I've lived here almost twenty-two years and I've never seen Studland from the water. It's kind of turned everything upside down. Shaken it up. But it needed shaking. Perhaps I needed shaking." I look towards the row of beach huts, nestled into the curve of the bay. "You can't even see The Smugglers from here — it's like it doesn't exist. Or the down — or the fields — or anything. Just endless, endless sea. Endless possibilities… It's so odd; now I can actually look back, the pub isn't what's holding me at all."

The sea spray has flecked Mark's glasses and the tint has darkened against the sun. But above them a deep furrow appears between his eyebrows.

"I'm sorry," I murmur. "I'm blathering on. Talking to myself, really. Just ignore me."

He pats my knee. "Then I won't be so rude as to interrupt. Coming about!"

The next tack sweeps us way out into the bay and he lets me take the tiller. The drag of the boat against the water travels up my arm and the breeze tickles my hair around my face. Mark helps me to steer a course beyond Old Harry and I could go on forever. A pod of dolphins some twenty yards or so ahead of us makes my morning complete and I squeal with delight. We need to tack, and Mark's hand joins mine on the smooth wood and we push and slide across the boat together. I lose my footing halfway and end up sprawled across the bench, staring at the sky and laughing.

Mark beams down at me. "Enjoying the sailing then?"

"Loving it. There's such freedom…" Freedom. That's it. "Mark — someone's interested in buying The Smugglers. What do you think I should do?"

He puts his head on one side. "So you're ready then, ready to make your move?"

"Yes I am."

"Do you mind me asking, is it with Paxton?"

"No. He's gone back to the States for his gran's funeral. I doubt I'll see him again."

"Oh, I thought…"

"It was never meant to last. We knew that before it started. Just a fling."

"Oh, well…"

"Do you think the worst of me for it?"

He throws back his head and laughs — that rolling, rumbling laugh I remember so well from the first time I heard it. "Marie — I am really not that buttoned up. And anyway, given what you've been through with Stephen it's hardly surprising."

"Did you, you know, when you realised Carina…"

He nods. "I can't say I'm proud of it though. Not now. It was her sister, too. Nice woman — didn't deserve it."

"As long as you gave her a good time." I wink. It's hard to tell with his tan, but I swear Mark blushes.

When I get home Jude is in the kitchen, wolfing down slices of toast and Marmite.

"How was your sail?" he asks between mouthfuls.

"Brilliant, thanks. I thought you'd have gone with Pip to get her results."

He shakes his head. "She's letting her mum take her — bit of an olive branch, really."

I reach over him to steal a slice of toast. "So are things any better between them?"

"Getting there, I think. I haven't seen her, but Uncle Greg's booked a table for four at the Haven tonight so I'll need to be on my best behaviour."

"And so will she." I stretch over his shoulder again but he slaps my hand.

"Stop it. If you're hungry I'll make some more."

It is while he has his back to me, slicing the bread, that I tell him.

"Jude, there's a company wants to buy The Smugglers — they've asked your father several times and he's always fobbed them off, but I'm not sure it wouldn't be the right thing to do.

But let's see what happens with Pip over the next few days, because at the moment it's your home as well. If she does end up having to go to Cardiff…"

"She won't. She says she'll defer."

"Well, if she has to keep living at home. You'll need a roof over your head too."

"No. She'll get a job, we'll have a place of our own whatever happens — we've decided. So you can't use me as an excuse not to do your own thing."

The grill rattles as he puts the bread under it and he turns and folds his arms.

"Perhaps you're right, Jude — perhaps it is an excuse. I just feel so out of my depth with it all financially. I don't know what a good price for the business is, whether there's a separate price for the property and I don't want to get ripped off. There's a massive mortgage to repay and if I walk away, I want to walk away with something. I can't see your dad selling Swanage."

"He'll have to at least buy you out."

"Of what? It's all in his name."

Jude sits down with a thump. "You're kidding me."

"No — he pulled a real fast one there and I'm so bloody naïve I'd never have even known if it wasn't for Mark."

"There's your answer, Mum. Mark."

"My answer?"

"Someone who can help you with the financial side. I bet he knows about how to value stuff."

"I did mention it to him in passing but… Jude — the toast!"

He rescues it just before it starts to burn, tipping it onto a chopping board and slathering it with butter.

"But what?" he says over his shoulder. "What did he say?"

"He seemed more interested in whether I was going away with Paxton."

"There — I knew it. I said to Pip…" He can't hide the note of triumph in his voice.

"What?"

"He fancies you."

"Oh, don't be ridiculous."

I am saved from further embarrassment by Jude's phone ringing. Pip. She's got three As. We dance around and around the kitchen until we are dizzy with happiness. And as I pick up my phone to text Mark the good news I find myself pausing. Ridiculous? Really?

"What time do you call this?"

Stephen's got a bloody nerve, given how late he normally is. I cut the chilli in half along its length and scrape the seeds into a bowl to dry.

"I said, what time do you call this?"

I look at the clock above the hotplate. "Can you not turn your neck, or is it your eyesight that's dodgy?"

He leans on the other side of the prep table, so close I can smell the coffee on his breath. "Oh, very funny. I'm your boss. And you were late."

I slam the knife down. "You are not my boss, Stephen. You never have been and you never will be." I take a deep breath. "I want to sell the pub. And while we're at it, I want a divorce as well."

Over Stephen's shoulder I see Baz's head jerk up from the colander of broccoli he's rinsing. Oh God — I'm going to affect so many lives. My mouth feels drier than the sand in the dunes.

The colour is rising up Stephen's neck. "You don't mean that."

I nod, but my words come out as a whisper. "I do."

"Oh, don't be so bloody stupid. Where would you live? What would you do?"

"None of your business," I snap.

For all his increasing bulk he can still move fast, and he is around the table in a flash. "It's your Yank, isn't it? You want to run away with your bloody Yank!"

"No. This is nothing to do with Paxton."

"What rubbish. I've seen you — you're all over him — it's obscene — he's almost as young as Jude…"

He raises his hand and I cower against the hotplate, but Baz's arm appears around his chest and he drags him to the floor. It's all so slow as the pair of them drop away from me, closer and closer to the point where they land on the tiles, a writhing mass of arms and legs. The vegetable knife glints as the table topples away from them and I reach out to try to stop it.

The crash brings Jude running from the bar and together we pull them apart. As I help Baz to his feet he shakes like an enormous jelly, asking again and again if I'm all right as I clutch my arm. The mark of Stephen's fist is on his cheekbone.

Stephen remains on the floor, head between his knees. Jude crouches next to him.

"Dad — what happened?"

"He was about to hit your mother, that's what happened," growls Baz.

The bell rings in the bar. "Service!" a voice calls. "Is anyone around?"

Stephen scrambles to his feet. "I'll go. Jude — help Baz put this kitchen straight."

As soon as he disappears, the adrenalin drains from my body and I start to tremble from top to toe. I balance the kettle on the hob and make three mugs of hot sweet tea and a coffee for Stephen. Jude and Baz lift the table and Baz sweeps the broken china and bits of chilli off the floor. Jude puts his arm around my shoulder.

"All right?"

"Yes. The table just caught my wrist as it fell but it's fine, really."

"What kicked it all off?"

"I told him I wanted a divorce. Not the best timing, probably. Look, you'd better get back behind the bar — leave the walking wounded to get on with it in here."

"You're sure you're ok?"

"Thanks to Baz, yes." But as soon as he's gone, I rush out to the yard and throw up in the drain. *What the hell happens now?*

The answer is nothing. Not until the next day, when Stephen arrives early with a bunch of red roses and an apology. I don't want to give him the satisfaction of seeing me arrange them in a vase, but all the same they are beautiful and it isn't their fault he's such a shit. I compromise by unwrapping them and putting them in a bucket of fresh water in the pantry.

All the time, Stephen is watching me. As I fold the cellophane into the bin he asks me if I meant it, if I really want to sell.

I lean against the sink. "I'd like to at least explore the possibility. Talk to that Amy and see how much they're prepared to give us."

Stephen snorts. "As little as possible, I'd guess."

"But there must be a right price for the place ... for the bricks and mortar at least ... and for the business. It's not on its knees — we'd be ok if it wasn't for the money you're spending on Ulwell Road and those big mortgage repayments. The pub itself is doing fine."

"And how come you're such a financial expert all of a sudden?" He turns and walks into the bar but I follow him.

"I've been taking lessons."

"Who from? Not your thick Yank, I take it."

I can't rise to him. "No — from George's son. He runs his own business."

"What, the dork with the dog?"

"Stephen — don't be like that. Why are you so angry all the time? You left me, remember?"

He stares at his thumbnail, pushes back the cuticle. "You didn't accept my apology."

"No. And I don't think I will." I watch as Stephen walks to the coffee machine and switches it on. "Stephen?"

"Yes?"

"Make us both one and bring it upstairs — I want to talk to you properly and Baz will be here any minute."

I wait for him at the kitchen table, but he doesn't sit down, just leans against the work surface, ready for a quick getaway.

"Well?"

"I've been thinking about it a lot. It's the right time to do this; Jude's looking for a flat with Pip — he'll be gone within the month. We need to talk seriously about sorting ourselves out. It's not the nicest of conversations to be having, but if we can do it amicably we'll save a fortune in lawyers' fees."

He puts his mug down behind him. "What will you do?"

"I don't know. But I can't carry on like this; I can't take the financial uncertainty and I hate the way we snipe at each other most of the time."

Now Stephen does pull out a chair. "It's hard to imagine The Smugglers without you."

"So you'd want to stay, buy me out?"

"What with?"

"Then we have to sell."

He clasps his hands, bending and straightening his fingers. "Unless…"

"Unless what?"

"You'd be willing to try again?"

"What? Us?" My eyes must be out on stalks.

"All right, all right. It would have been convenient, that's all."

I stand up. "Stephen. I don't want convenient. Not anymore. Now we can either do this together in a civilised fashion or fight each other to the bitter end. It's up to you."

"This is, well, a bit of a shock. I need some time to think." He's still flexing his fingers, gazing at them as though they are the most fascinating things on God's earth.

I go back downstairs and leave him to his contemplation.

CHAPTER 25

Mark opens the door wearing his sailing shorts and a polo shirt. Which leaves me feeling distinctly overdressed for the weather in a long-sleeved blouse — but needs must. I don't want any awkward questions about how I got a bruise the size of a small courgette on my arm.

The moment he hears my voice Troy rushes down the hall. I drop to my knees and fondle his ears.

"He knows what's in that cool bag," I laugh, but Mark shakes his head.

"No — he remembers the kind lady who found him in a hole and lay next to him until we could get him out. He's not entirely motivated by his stomach — unlike me."

"Well, there's chilli, lamb tagine, cod and prawn pie for your freezer."

Mark groans. "Don't make me hungry — it's hours until supper time."

"I also brought some chocolate brownies to tide you over. But this time I'll make the tea."

"No, you will not. This time I'll do it properly while you sit in the garden. I even went to Homebase this morning to buy some outdoor furniture."

"I'm suitably honoured."

"So you should be. That place is a bloody nightmare on a Saturday."

Mark's trip has yielded an attractive cast iron table topped with mosaic tiles, a pair of matching chairs and an enormous canvas umbrella. Troy follows me outside and slumps next to its base, panting. The patch of lawn has been freshly mown, but the narrow border is empty and the fences are free from any adornment.

"You're not much into gardening?" I ask as Mark puts two mugs of tea on the table then drops the ice cream tub containing the brownies from under his arm.

He shrugs. "I don't have the time."

"Your dad says you only come here to sleep."

"Pretty much. If I'm not working I'm outside and if I'm not outside I'm working."

I turn my mug in my hand. "I wonder what I'll do once we've sold the pub. I'll have to find a job, I know that, but it's hard to see…"

"So you've made up your mind?"

"Yes, and I've told Stephen. But whether he's going to be civilised about it or not he hasn't decided."

Mark raises his eyebrows. "Better if he will be, that goes without saying. And knowing how the male ego works, it might be easier for him now Paxton's not on the scene."

I take the lid off the brownies and offer him one. He bites into it then grins at me. "God, they're delicious. You can come any time if you bring some of these."

"*Only* if I bring brownies?"

"Well, I can think of other circumstances…"

"Fish pie, chilli…"

He laughs as he balances his brownie on the edge of the box. "You said you wanted to pick my brains so I guess I'm singing for my supper."

"Look on them as a bribe. Like I said on the boat, someone's keen to buy The Smugglers, but I don't know what a good price is. I don't even know how it works, whether there's one price for the building and another for the business itself. And so far Stephen isn't exactly being helpful."

Mark looks thoughtful. "Well, under the circumstances, I don't think you can rely on him to be. And anyway, I've been there, remember. I know the ropes."

"George said … when you got divorced you almost lost everything."

"Almost. But luckily not Clear Water, although I did have to have the business valued so I know how that works. I'd already given Carina the house but she wanted blood, too. Still, the upside is I can recommend a good lawyer."

I pick up my tea. "I can't afford a lawyer." *God, this is scary. What the hell have I started?*

"You can't afford not to have one. You'll need an accountant, too, because I suspect Stephen will use the firm who look after the pub."

"I don't even know them — it's one of his cronies in Swanage. I just get a tax form to sign every year."

"So, is the pub a company or a partnership?"

"What's the difference?"

"Oh, come on, Marie, surely you at least know that?"

"It's all right for you — you're educated, you understand these things. I'm just a stupid chef." I thump my mug down on the table.

"There's no need to take it out on me."

I take a deep breath. "Sorry. I feel so out of my depth, that's all."

He closes his eyes. "I'm sorry, too. Sorry you have to go through this. Look, why don't we meet my accountant next week — she'll do it as a favour and she can explain how selling a business works and the values and all that. Then if you like her — and I can't think of anyone who doesn't like Kerrie — she'll get all the information she needs from Stephen's people and you'll know where you are."

I smile at him. "Apart from providing you with more homemade food than you could possibly eat, I don't know how I'll ever be able to thank you for all this."

"Just look after yourself, ok?"

I tug my sleeve over my hand. "I'm not sure what you mean."

"Nothing... It was nothing." He looks down at his cup, and then at the umbrella above us. "Oh, look, Marie — there is something. I wasn't going to mention it but... Look, this is going to sound a bit strange, but are you sure Paxton isn't coming back?"

"I assume not, but I can't be certain."

"Right." He stands up and disappears into the flat.

Oh Lord. What's coming? Is Jude right? Is Mark carrying a torch for me? Is that why he's suddenly asking about Paxton? I should have made it clear to him it's over between us. There's a nagging voice in the back of my mind telling me I probably should have made it clear to Paxton too.

When Mark comes back he's carrying his laptop and a notebook. "Look, I wouldn't want you to think I was snooping around your boyfriend, but Dad told me how upset you were and what had been happening with Corbin. It struck me I might be able to find out a bit more about him so I did a few searches."

"You didn't just think … I was some kind of mad woman?"

"No. To be honest there was something bothering Dad, too, and I wanted to get to the bottom of it. So I did a bit of hunting around. You told Dad Corbin was from Kentucky, so that helped." He flicks through his notebook, the pages covered in slanting capitals. "First thing, I found a date and place of birth, but no record of his death. He was born 18th September 1916 in London Kentucky…"

251

"But that's right — he said he was born in London — because I was, too." But how could he have said? "Mark — where did you find this out?"

"On the internet."

"Could we ... could we look for someone else? I want to check if he had a sister."

"Sure. I bookmarked the page."

As he opens his browser my heart feels as though it's blocking my throat. I pick up my tea to try to wash it back to where it should be. Sunshine glints off the patio doors.

"There's a Ruby Summerhayes, born 29th April 1919?"

"I suppose ... that could be Paxton's gran."

"No death record either, but it says she married Henry Taylor on the 4th June 1941."

"Wow..."

"What is it, Marie? You're white as the proverbial sheet."

"It seemed ... too much of a coincidence. But Corbin really was Paxton's great-uncle."

"Paxton. Yes." He takes a deep breath. "When I was searching the web for Corbin, I found Paxton. Like I said, Summerhayes is an unusual name..."

"But Paxton's name is Taylor."

"Paxton Summerhayes Taylor. Look — you'd better read it for yourself."

PS. Paxo Stuffing. Paxton Summerhayes. Mark opens a new page on his browser, then stands and picks up the mugs. "I'll make some more tea."

I angle the screen away from the sun. On it is a news report from somewhere called Manhattan in Kansas. Paxton Summerhayes Taylor, Sergeant First Class, convicted in his absence of an assault against a woman he'd met in a bar and gone home with. He pleaded guilty to attacking her in the middle of the night. The army had already demoted him two grades and sent him overseas. The civilian court gave him a suspended sentence.

Someone nearby is mowing their lawn. Troy sighs in his sleep, his nose twitching. Through the patio doors, I can see Mark waiting for the kettle to boil. He is facing away from me, leaning against the breakfast bar, seemingly studying his deck shoes. I read the article again.

Mark is reaching into the fridge for the milk when I step into the cool of the room. I raise my hand to touch his shoulder, tell him it's ok, and my sleeve drops back up my wrist.

His eyes lock onto my arm as he says, "Oh, it is, is it?"

"No, really. Paxton didn't tell me what had happened, but it's a situation he's gone out of his way to avoid with me. It's all right, really."

"Then which one of those bastards did that to you? Paxton or Stephen?"

"Mark, no, it wasn't like that — it's all right, really…"

The fridge door smacks shut. "You keep saying it's all right but it's not. It's not all right to be around men who hurt you. How can it be?"

"No … really… Stephen's never actually hit me and neither has Paxton…"

"It's not just a case of being hit — it's … it's … Stephen spitting in your face when he's yelling at you; it's putting you under so much pressure you get a migraine every five minutes; it's one of them giving you just about the biggest bruise I've ever seen. Apparently without hitting you." His voice drips sarcasm.

"Oh, come on, Mark, it's just what happens in relationships…"

"It's never happened in mine, Marie; it's abuse, pure and simple. You're just so used to it you think it's normal. It terrifies me it will all boil over and you'll get badly hurt. And now it's not just Stephen I have to worry about — it's Paxton as well."

My chest is heaving so hard I can barely speak. "No, you don't — it's none of your business. Who are you to tell me what's wrong with my life? You're not so perfect…"

"I never said I was. I'm clearly so imperfect I'm not even worth listening to." He turns away, tea splashing on the tiles as he pours it down the sink. "Just go, Marie — ok? Just go."

Slamming the door won't make me feel any better but I do it anyway.

All weekend the newspapers scream 'heatwave' and we're run off our feet, so by the end of lunchtime service on Monday I could swear some joker has lined my crocs with lead. I'm tempted to leave them in the lobby but in the end decide to drag them upstairs, one enormous step at a time. When I get to the top, I'm going to reward myself with a pint of water — and a double brandy.

Pip is in the kitchen with the pub laptop open in front of her.

"I thought you'd be on the beach."

"No — I'm flat hunting. Mum's cut up a bit rough again now I've actually got my place at Southampton, so I'm better off doing it here. You don't mind do you?"

"Of course not. Makes sense, anyway. If you find somewhere you like you can show Jude in his break."

I run the tap until the water is icy and fill my glass. "Would you like anything to drink?"

"No, I'm fine." She pushes the laptop towards me. "What do you think of this one? It's quite near the university but it looks a bit poky. Jude's going to need room for his work."

I sit down next to her. "I don't think you can tell until you've seen it — it might be ok." I scroll down the page. "How about this? It's got a bay window, so there'd be plenty of light. As long as you don't mind your living room smelling of turps."

She grins at me. "I'd love it. It's just so … Jude. Oh, Auntie Marie, I'm so excited. I can study and he can paint and it's going to be wonderful."

"And you're going to be washing his boxer shorts and he's going to be cleaning the toilet and you're both going to get stressed about stuff … and you'll need to deal with it when those rose-tinted spectacles wear off."

She squeezes my hand. "I know. Nothing worth having's ever easy, is it? But we love each other so much — we'll be all right."

"I'm sure you will." My faces stretches into a smile but I'm tired beyond tired. I scroll down further, one set of details merging into another. I'll be doing this for myself soon.

I tell Pip I'm going to put my feet up on the sofa for a while. The abandoned jigsaw looks a little more complete than it did when Paxton was fiddling with it the other week, and I guess Jude's had a go between shifts. I reach under the sofa for my bottle and pour an inch or so of brandy into the bottom of my glass.

The room is airless, so I open the windows and the burble and chatter from the pub garden rises to meet me. Old Harry and the cliffs glint in the sun, my constant companions for over twenty years. What will it feel like to wake up somewhere else? It's all very well planning my escape but having enough energy to actually do it? That's a different thing entirely.

I've had a call from Kerrie, Mark's accountant. After the way things ended when I saw him I was surprised, but she sounded so friendly I couldn't help but agree to meet her on Friday. Perhaps being a woman she'll be more understanding. I pick up my phone. I should text Mark to thank him. But I remember the rigid set of his shoulders as he told me to go. He meant it, all right. He thinks I'm an idiot. Perhaps I am.

I sort the remaining jigsaw pieces into colours. Fingers of green protrude down the chalk where the cliffs are less steep and the brambles have been able to colonise. I work my way from right to left, but the closer I get to Old Harry the more relentlessly white the pieces become as the cliffs rise sheer from the Mediterranean blue of the bay. I run my finger along the grassy line where Corbin's bench should be.

The only pieces I have left are almost completely white, so I'll have to finish the picture by shape. There are only about twenty of them but something's not right. I look again and realise what it is; there are going to be some missing.

Jude comes in as I am turning the box inside out and upside down to search for them. He stands back and looks at the picture.

"That's really odd, Mum — the missing bits are all together."

"I think it's so mean of whoever put it into the jumble sale; obviously it's deliberate — they're in two straight lines."

Jude calculates the gap with his fingers, measuring the pieces above. "Yep — seven in one row and five below. But you counted them, Mum, I remember — I saw them piled up on the table in little stacks."

I shake my head. "Couldn't have done. It must have been the Brownsea Island puzzle."

"Guess so." He shrugs.

The afternoon sun creeps into the pub yard and around to the kitchen windows. The tiniest of breezes from the heath whispers through the long grass in the graveyard, but has died by the time it reaches the door. I think it's even hotter than yesterday. Baz mops his brow about every five minutes, sweat darkening the back of his whites. Jude brings him a pint of iced coke, which he downs in a single gulp.

Jude puts his hand on my shoulder. "George is out there, Mum. Just arrived. He'd like a ham sandwich and a chat if you've got time at the end of service."

My hair feels glued to my head inside its chignon. "I'll need to clean up first."

"I'll tell him."

I take off my whites in the bathroom and run the shower cold. I want to stay here forever, but George is waiting for me.

The pub garden may be packed, but apart from three people waiting to be served the bar is relatively quiet. George has forsaken his usual table for one of the sofas next to the empty fireplace and is reading the *Purbeck Gazette*.

"Sorry," I say as I flop down next to him. "I just had to get clean — it's been like a furnace in the kitchen today."

"Don't worry, Marie — I'm retired, remember — nothing to do with my time. Except poke my nose into other people's business." He winks. "Mark mentioned he saw you at the weekend. And that it didn't end well."

I bite my lip. "Oh."

"He didn't tell me exactly what happened, but I gather he rather upset you."

"Yes, he was a bit cross with me … well, we were cross with each other…" I pick an invisible thread from my skirt. "I suppose … really … after all he's done I should have apologised. I did almost text him but Jude came in — he and

Pip are flat hunting and they wanted me to look at somewhere they'd seen on the internet."

"Hmph. That internet's got a lot to answer for."

How much has Mark told him? I smooth my sleeves down over my arms.

George clears his throat. "Mark said that Corbin was Paxton's great-uncle."

"I know — incredible, isn't it? I suppose there was a family resemblance…"

"Was there, Marie? How much of one?"

I glance towards the bar. "When I first met Paxton, I thought he was Corbin — but I'd just hit my head — I was literally seeing stars… I soon realised he wasn't. Paxton's got a beard for a start. Well, not really a beard, more designer stubble … and he keeps himself out of the sun — his mother died of skin cancer — and Corbin, he was a farmer, been outdoors all his life so he was more tanned. Always wore sunglasses too…"

How the hell did I not work it out before? It's so damn obvious. I grip the edge of the table and look George in the eye. "Mark's right. I have been monumentally stupid. But not in the way he thinks."

"You're talking in riddles."

"Paxton took me to a dance at Bovington. I found a pair of vintage Aviators under his bed. I never saw Corbin without his Aviators."

"So you think Paxton was Corbin all along? If that's the case, it's seriously worrying behaviour."

I shake my head. "Not in context. You've seen combat, George, and perhaps some people handle it better than others, but it damaged Paxton. And he worshipped Corbin — he said it was his proudest moment when his gran told him he was like him. Perhaps … pretending to be Corbin was some sort of escape? All of a sudden it seems much more likely than Corbin being a ghost."

The habitual softness has gone from George's eyes. "Where's Paxton now, Marie?"

"He went back to the States. It was all but over between us anyway, George. To be honest he'd been making me feel a bit uneasy so I was going to finish it, but when his grandmother got ill I didn't have the heart."

"Uneasy? In what way?"

There's nothing I can say. I shake my head. George reaches over and pats my hand. "It's ok — you don't have to tell me. I'm just very glad he's gone home."

CHAPTER 26

I don't recognise the person in the mirror this morning. She's dressed in tailored trousers and a crisp striped shirt with button-down cuffs. Her hair is kept from her face by a wide velvet Alice band; she looks poised and confident. Then she starts to shake as I fumble with the catch of the seahorse necklace and stab myself with my mascara.

Despite the fashionable Sandbanks café Kerrie chooses for breakfast, she is refreshingly down to earth. Over strong black coffee and pancakes with bacon and maple syrup she asks me about the running of the pub, what Stephen and I both do, the other members of staff. She wants to know about the takings and I show her the spreadsheet. I guess the numbers make much more sense to her and I feel stupid and small.

"Mark told me he took a look at your books and the pub's making a profit," she says. "Mind you, in that location and with your amazing food you'd be hard pushed not to."

"Mark's been very helpful."

She scoops a piece of pancake into her mouth. "He is just such a lovely man — quite fanciable too, don't you think?" My eyebrows shoot almost to my hairline and she laughs. "Well, ok, I'd have to be twenty years older but even so… I guess the real appeal is he hasn't a clue, bless him."

"I don't think he's much interested; he's so engrossed in his business."

"Yes, you're probably right. Clear Water and that dog are his life."

"And I think once you've been through the mill, single is a good place to be. At least it looks pretty appealing from where I'm sitting, anyway."

"Have you any idea what you'll do? Workwise, I mean."

I pick up the cafetière and half fill my cup. "It depends on how much money I get. I don't suppose you can hazard a guess?"

"Not without the accounts. But if you'd like me to act for you, I can ask for copies from Stephen's advisers and get to work."

"You have to realise … until we sell I won't be able to pay you. Money's very tight. Stephen extended our mortgage to buy a place in Swanage to turn into holiday flats and it's taking all the spare cash and more. We haven't paid Jude — that's our son — for weeks. And I'm not sure I can live on fresh air much longer."

"Would you want to stay in the pub trade?"

I shrug my shoulders. "All I can do is cook. But I've not been to a job interview since I was a teenager…"

"Would you think about working for yourself? Buying another business? I only ask because I've got a client who's retiring at the end of the year. It's a basic café at the moment but it could be anything."

"Where is it?"

"Salterns Marina — where Mark keeps his boat."

I whistle. "I'd have to make a bomb on the pub to be able to afford a place there."

When we leave the café we shake hands and I watch her walk fifty yards along the road and climb into a soft-top Saab. What wouldn't I give to be rich and ten years younger? What wouldn't I be able to do with a café in a smart marina? I turn and walk towards the ferry, past the swanky flats behind their automatic ten-foot-high gates, past the entrance to the Haven Hotel with its uniformed bellboy. And I know what I wouldn't give: Jude, that's what. Without Stephen there wouldn't have been Jude, and that single precious thing alone is what's made it all worthwhile.

My heart leaps into my mouth when I get a text from Paxton: *I'm waiting at the beach hut.*

I put my phone back on the counter. It's been a lunchtime of ploughman's and sandwiches with a roaring trade in ice creams. The sky is bearing down on us all and Baz is literally dripping with sweat as he washes the pans. I open the freezer door to move some crabmeat into the fridge and I'm strangely reluctant to close it.

I'm about to go upstairs to change when my phone beeps again. *Where are you, Doll?*

Walking out the door. I dart into the lobby for the keys but they've already gone.

The shock of seeing Paxton wearing Aviators stops me in my tracks. At the top of the steps to the beach, gripping the rail for support, a barrage of questions ricocheting around my mind. He looks up and raises his hand in greeting, so I have to walk on. Thirty seconds or so — that's all I have to find my voice.

"Hey — I've not seen you in those before." He is clean-shaven as well, two unwashed smears of blood on his neck where he's cut himself with his razor.

I reach up to take the glasses off. His eyes are raw with deep black bruises beneath. "Oh, Paxton — what happened?"

"You know — you know what happened."

"When did you last sleep?"

262

"I … I can't remember. I was relieved of duties this morning. Meant to be seeing the doc but I came here instead."

"You don't think you should've…"

"What the fuck do you know about it?" he snarls, pulling away.

A woman with two young children, sitting yards in front of us, turns around and glares at him.

"Sorry … sorry, ma'am," he stutters. "C'mon, Doll — let's go for a walk — there's too many people around here."

He waits at the end of the decking while I close the hut doors and slip the keys into my pocket. We make our way along the beach towards the cliffs, Paxton ahead of me, following the ridge of seaweed and shingle at the high tide mark like a drunk on a white line. "I hate sand," he mutters.

The closer we get to the path to the cliffs the pebblier the beach becomes. Paxton slows, takes my hand, kisses it. "Sorry, Doll." Thunder rumbles in the distance.

"That's ok. It's tough. When I didn't hear I thought you'd gone home for the funeral."

"What's the point? I didn't even put in for it." He shrugs and climbs the steps to the grass ledge where the path begins.

Sunlight dapples the earth between the trees but the birds are silent and still in the branches. The cooler air dries the sweat under my armpits, and now we are in the shade I undo the top button of my whites. I could stay forever in this relative haven and I call to Paxton to stop.

"How about we find someplace just off the path to sit and talk for a while? No one much uses this way to the cliff and it's out of the sun."

"Hmmm — you really thinking of talking, Doll, or of something else?"

"Talking, Paxton. You need to talk and I want to listen. I want to hear all about your gran — the happy times with your family; your dad, your sister, your grandfather, your great-uncle Corbin…"

He's looking down the slope at me, arms folded against his chest. "Why him? I never even met him."

God, I could kick myself… I try to keep my voice level. "Because I know how much he means to you. And he was here, wasn't he? You told Jude. You said he was stationed in Swanage, liked walking on the cliffs. Probably these cliffs."

"D'you know what, Doll? I've never walked up there. Never. Never got to tell Gran about the place he loved. It was the least I could have done, but no, I got distracted. Too distracted."

The waves wash the shingle below us, mixed with the shouts of children playing on the shore.

I hold out my hand to him. "I thought distraction was a good thing."

He shakes his head. "I'm sorry … just so sorry … so tired." He stumbles as he turns, but then he seems to gather himself and strides up the slope ahead of me with all the energy of his thirty-one years.

He waits at the point the path meets the chalk bridleway. As we emerge into the light the sky is heavy, dark clouds chasing in from the west. The Aviators are superfluous but he keeps them on and there's something in his stance, the angle of his head… He's lying — he must be lying. But perhaps, now we're here, we'll sit on our old familiar bench and he'll tell me the truth.

When the path opens onto the down we walk side by side, kicking up puffs of earth along the track. Paxton entwines his fingers with mine and our hands swing rhythmically between us. Bournemouth opposite is bathed in sunlight but the clouds have already rolled in across the bay, the breeze picking up and urging them on. I cast a glance over the fields; the sky towards Swanage is blacker than black.

He walks straight past the bench.

"You don't want to … rest for a while?"

"I gotta see these cliffs, Doll. Walk them before I go."

"I thought you said you weren't —"

"Did I? I told you I was only here for a short while — you knew that."

Oh my God, he's all over the place. I tug his hand. "Come on — it's going to rain any minute — let's get back to the beach hut."

"I like rain. Gran liked rain. Saved her having to water the flowers on the porch."

"What else did she like? Paxton, tell me."

And he does. Mint tea and fried chicken and cross-stitch. Ginger Rogers and Danny Kaye. We follow the edge of the cliff almost to the point where open downland gives way to the shrub-lined path when the first huge drops splatter in front of us. Paxton holds his hand out flat and laughs.

"Hey, Doll — we can sing in the rain. Sing ourselves happy. Like Grandma said. Always do what Grandma said. C'mon…"

He wraps his arm around my waist and, humming the tune, cross steps back along the down, just like Gene Kelly does in the film, taking me with him.

"C'mon, Doll — can't you hear the music?" Gradually his stepping turns into a waltz, and he swings me into an old-fashioned hold with our interlaced hands out in front of us. He laughs again, and looks up to the sky, Aviators specked with water.

His gran taught him to dance so well. He even incorporates a few tap moves which I stumble over, upping the pace as we whirl around. It's strange and surreal and almost frightening, but he's humming and smiling and I guess the happy memories are doing him good.

"Hey, Doll — you're something special, you know," he murmurs, and slows to a smooch, pulling my soaking body tight against his. My hair is sticking to my head and he pulls a strand away to curl around his fingers. "I want to remember this — remember this moment, for when I'm gone. Will you remember it too?"

"Forever."

He kisses me, tucking my hair behind my ear before caressing my neck under the collar of my whites and rolling the chain of my necklace between his fingers. He pulls away a little, tracing it along its length and scooping the silver seahorse from between my breasts.

He grips the charm, lips set into a hard line. "What the fuck are you doing with my grandma's necklace?"

"W-what?"

"You heard me." He yanks the chain upwards, tight across my throat.

"Someone … someone gave it to me."

"Who?" His face is inches from mine, my horror reflected in those terrible glasses. Corbin's glasses.

"You did, Paxton — you did. The first day we met."

"You stole it from her — you must have done. You thieving little bitch." The force of his push rips the chain from my neck and I stagger backwards, my only thought to run, but before I can recover myself he is onto me again, pinioning my arms to my sides as I kick and scream.

"Let me go — Paxton — let me go!"

"You must be fucking joking, Doll. For this — for your fucking, thieving lies — I'm taking you with me." And he starts to drag me backwards towards the cliff, words spilling out. "I thought about… I thought about it anyway … dancing with you … right to the edge … so you couldn't say … couldn't tell 'em … you know too much … too fucking much…"

"Paxton … please… You gave me the necklace. Don't you remember?"

My crocs can get no purchase and our slide over the wet grass is relentless. I try to drop to my knees to escape him but he hauls me up and off my feet, my slithering, shin-kicking weight a feather in his hands.

"Paxton — for God's sake — think of your gran — she wouldn't want this. For her sake — you have to let me go."

"No, I don't."

We are feet away from the gorse and brambles lining the cliff edge. Just feet. Then nothing. I remember — back in the spring — sitting on the bench and wanting to fly. Will I remember everything when the moment comes? I'll fall and fall and fall … the cliffs looked so high from Mark's boat. Oh Christ … oh Christ … help me.

Thunder crashes over us and lightning splits the sky above Old Harry in two, flashing off the chalk like the beginnings of a migraine. Paxton throws me to the ground, covering his head with his hands. My face thuds into the grass, but my right arm is free and I reach out and grab a stem of gorse. Paxton moans and I wriggle some more. The thunder explodes above us and his body convulses — just enough for me to wrap both hands around the bush.

Inch by inch, I edge from under him, praying the storm will last. Lightning races across the bay and I can hear the waves crashing on the cliffs below. Paxton is curled into a ball beside me, but I am shaking too much to get to my feet and run. I have to. I have to. I struggle to my knees but his hand is around my ankle and I make a lunge for the bush again, clawing at its slender trunk where it disappears into the earth.

Flat to the ground, Paxton is edging backwards towards the drop, his hands grasping my ankles. I kick for all I'm worth, but his grip is vice-like, burning my wet skin. My body turns through the grasping stems of the brambles, but my fingers are wound so tightly around the gorse I wonder they don't break. How long can its roots hold in the shallow soil?

Thunder and lightning roar across the cliffs in an almighty crack and the grip on my ankles vanishes. It takes an eternity for the scream to reach me through the howling gale.

The rain runs down my back and into the waistband of my whites. It seems as though an infinite amount of time passes before I have the strength to raise myself onto all fours, and then to sit back on my knees. I can breathe. I can breathe. One great gulp after another.

The clouds are so low they cover the clifftop, but through the murk a figure walks towards me and I scramble to my feet, shaking from head to toe. *Aviators. Grade one haircut. Tanned skin. White T-shirt — completely dry.*

He inclines his head. "Good afternoon, Marie."

"Corbin?" I whisper.

"Go home, my English rose. It's over. We can both go home."

My throat is too tight to speak, too tight to swallow. I reach out to touch him, but at that moment he bends to pick something up.

Smiling and shaking his head, he drops the seahorse into my hand. "Go. Quickly. Before the storm passes."

I don't need to be told twice. My legs have found their strength and I pelt across the grass, then make my slippery descent of the chalk path to the village. The rain is coming down in sheets and the lights are on in The Smugglers but I run straight past; the keys are still in my pocket, thank the Lord, and I throw myself into my car.

I'll never feel safe in Studland again.

I park in one of the visitor spaces and gaze across the battered flower beds. There's a glow from George's living room and my knees tremble with relief.

The rain has eased to a gentle drizzle, but I keep my head down as I make my way along the path to George's door. He's there almost instantly, ushering me in and shutting out the world behind me. I feel… I feel … nothing. I put out my hand and steady myself against the wall.

"Marie — what's happened? Are you all right?"

"Paxton. He … he's thrown himself off the cliffs. He tried to … he tried to…" I can't say it. Will I ever be able to say it?

George shakes his head. "You can tell me once you're warm and dry. Come on, I'll run you a bath."

He grips the bannister and makes his way up the stairs, one tread at a time. At the top is the bathroom and I drip on the lino while he turns on the taps and pours in a generous amount of bubble bath.

As I slide under the pine-scented foam I hear him shuffle along the landing. His mind's so sharp it's easy to forget he's old. I probably shouldn't be putting him to all this trouble but he's the only one who'll understand.

My skin begins to tingle as the water does its work, waking me up to the scratches that cover my arms and legs. I raise them out of the layer of bubbles to inspect the damage —

nothing a good dose of Savlon and a week of long sleeves won't put right.

Outside the bathroom door George clears his throat. "Marie, I think you'll have to make do with a pair of my pyjamas while your clothes dry. It's the best I can do. I've put them just outside the door with my dressing gown."

"Thanks, George." It's almost a whisper.

"Take your time. I'll go and put the kettle on."

I listen to the creak of the stairs as he makes his way back down, but there is another sound: a key in the front door followed by an excited bark and Mark's voice.

"Marie's here then?"

"Yes — she's drying off in the bathroom."

"Thank God for that. I had a call from Jude — he's frantic."

Oh shit — what time is it? I cast around the room for a clock, but there is none.

"Well, don't just stand there — phone him back — tell him she's with me."

"Yes, but what's happened?"

"Mark — just do it."

Their voices disappear along the hall and the kitchen door closes. I strain to hear what they're saying, but the water pipes judder and whine as George runs the tap. I need to get out, tell Jude I'm ok, tell him… What? I close my eyes but all I see is my terrified face reflected in Paxton's Aviators. I finger my neck — is there a mark there as well?

There is a gentle knock on the bathroom door.

"Marie — Dad asks should he make the tea?"

"Yes … yes, that's fine. Did you speak to Jude?"

"Yes. He's all right now. I told him you popped over to see Dad but got a migraine. I hope that's ok?"

"Sure."

"Right — I'll leave you to it. Dad says to bring your wet things down and he'll put them in the tumble dryer."

I ease the plug chain between my toes and pull, a sharp pain rushing through my ankle. God, I'm a wreck. But I'm alive. At least I'm alive. I search the corners of my heart for joy at the thought but there's nothing.

The striped towel on the rail is warm and I wrap it around me and hop towards the toilet, where I raise my foot onto the seat. Already my ankle's puffy but I can wiggle my toes so at least it's not broken. How the hell did I run all that way on it? Perhaps I turned it on the slope, my hand closed tight around the seahorse as the sky and trees flashed past me.

Dressed in a pair of blue and white striped pyjamas and a navy towelling dressing gown, I limp downstairs. Mark is waiting at the bottom.

"D'you need a hand?"

"No — it's ok — just a twist…" Paxton's hand on my wet skin. Oh God. I can feel it now. "You spoke to Jude?"

"Yes, I told you…"

"Sorry."

He puts his hand under my elbow and guides me to the living room. George has just finished pouring the tea and Troy is settled in front of the radiator. The clock on the bookcase tells me it's not much past five thirty. I point to it.

"Is that right?"

Mark consults his watch. "Pretty much spot on. Why?"

"Then why was Jude so worried?"

"Sit down and I'll show you."

I drop into the velour folds of the sofa. Mark perches on the edge of George's chair, which means the old man has no choice but to settle himself beside me, nursing his mug of tea.

Mark leans across and hands me his phone, the screen filled with a photo. "When Jude went upstairs for his break he found this."

It's the jigsaw — but the pieces aren't missing any more. Written into the cliff-face in two neat rows are the words *Goodbye Marie.* I feel empty as an oil drum washed up on the beach, scoured by the sea of any trace of emotion.

"He meant to do it, then." I hand the phone back to Mark.

"Paxton? Dad said … he's killed himself."

"Yes."

"And you were there?"

"Yes."

I look out of the window. The rain has almost stopped but there is a steady drip from a broken gutter somewhere nearby. The whir of the tumble dryer reaches us from the kitchen.

George nudges me. "Drink your tea while it's hot."

Obediently, I pick up my mug. It's so sweet I almost gag. I can't look at Mark — his face will say it all. His face will say: "I told you he was dangerous — why in hell's name did you go up there with him?"

Actually, it doesn't. His hand hangs over the arm of the chair, resting on Troy's flank and his eyes are closed, crows' feet etched deeply into his tan. Below his fine, straight nose he is biting his lower lip and his jaw is clenched. I drop my gaze into my mug.

"Marie — do you want to tell us what happened?" It's George who breaks the silence.

"I don't think I can. Not right now. I mean… I came here because…"

Mark jumps up. "Is it me? Shall I go?"

"No. Not at all."

"I was pretty … judgmental, before. I thought, perhaps…"

"But you were right. In so many ways. Please stay."

Mark sits back down. The tumble dryer whines.

George touches my hand. "You told me Paxton had gone back to the States?"

"I thought he had. But he turned up this afternoon. He wanted to walk on the cliffs … but the storm … the thunder freaked him out. He never could take loud bangs — fireworks — that's what saved me really… He let me go. He let me go."

"You mean — he tried to take you over with him?" Mark says the words as though he can hardly believe them. I can't either, but I nod.

"Are you angry with me? For going up there with him?"

Mark stands and walks towards the window. The lights are on against the darkness of the afternoon and his reflection merges into the glass, the last of the raindrops like tears on his cheeks. "No," he says. "Just relieved. Unbelievably relieved."

George eases himself out of his chair. "I'll just see how your clothes are getting on." He shuts the living room door behind him.

Troy slinks across the carpet to sit at Mark's feet. Automatically he reaches down to scratch between his ears and Troy rests his head against Mark's thigh. Man and dog. They have each other and it's all they need.

I sink back onto the cushions and close my eyes. My ankle is beginning to throb like buggery. But the rest of me … the empty oil drum, washed up on the beach. Paxton's body, washed up on the beach. What happens when they find him?

I must have said it out loud because Mark clears his throat. "A whole load of questions, I expect. There'll be an inquest. And I'm afraid you'll be in the thick of it."

"Oh God. I can't… I…"

"Then we'll say you were with me all afternoon — you never saw him — we took the boat out for a while…"

"I can't ask you to lie for me."

He sinks onto the sofa. "Marie — right now I'm so bloody grateful you're alive you could ask me to do anything — and not even have to bribe me with food." He smiles, but there is the tiniest of tremors in his voice.

I only have to turn my head to find his lips. The merest of brushes, but he leans into me and responds. Just for a few seconds, then we pull away.

"I'm sorry." His Adam's apple bobs. "My timing…"

"No — I wanted to … I mean, if you…" I swallow hard. "But I can't, not at the moment. Not after this. My head's all over the place and it wouldn't be fair. That's all I want to ask you: will you … will you wait?" Tears are streaming down my face and he wraps me into his arms, stroking my hair.

"I was waiting anyway. Probably holding my breath, too, only I wouldn't admit it to myself. Dad saw it and we had a heart to heart last night. I was meant to phone you — we really could have been sailing this afternoon, that's the honest truth. Only I heard the weather forecast and it was just an easy excuse not to call. I was so scared you'd say no. If I'd been a bit braver I could have spared you all this."

"No," I sniff. "If I'd been a bit braver, I'd have kicked Paxton into touch weeks ago. It's my responsibility, my life."

"But…"

I put my finger on his lips.

EPILOGUE

It's been a long old winter for me, and for Mark, too. In the middle of it all George caught bronchitis. It's taken him ages to get over it, but he's on the mend now. Perhaps we all are; some days I think so, anyway. The sale of The Smugglers fell through twice, but we got there in the end. Stephen's still the manager. Jude helped in the bar over Christmas. I haven't been near the place. Troy gets his walks at Hengistbury Head these days. At least he does when I tag along.

The result of the sale is that I'm now the proud owner of the Marie's Bistro. The two enormous fridges that arrived yesterday are humming against one wall and the electric range is waiting to be wired in. I don't know how I can afford all these wonderful things, but Mark's put some money in as well so I guess I can. Or we can. No — he says it's mine — he's just an investor — a silent partner. Except he's so brim full of ideas he's never silent about it.

Silence isn't always a good thing anyway. I've learnt that. Silence was what killed Paxton: his own, and probably the army's, and maybe even mine. At the inquest the medical officer from Bovington said he hid his suffering so well it was generally thought he was getting over it. But I knew that wasn't the case, didn't I?

I tortured myself with it for months. Sitting with George as he slept or struggled for breath; walking along the beach with Mark and Troy; trying to deal with the minutiae of my own everyday life. And I suffered in silence too.

What could I have done differently? Ignorance of post-combat stress was no defence. I could have looked it up. I could have tried harder to make Paxton talk. I could have told someone who knew what to do. And when it came to it, I could have made sure he was all right after his gran died and I could have kept him off those bloody cliffs. But I didn't, because by then I was running scared. And running to Mark.

It was George, of course, who cracked my shell and listened as the tumult of words spewed out. It was just a few weeks ago, a mild day, bright with the first promise of spring, and I drove him to Branksome Beach. He was still too frail to walk very far, so we sat in the car and shared a flask of tea while on the other side of the bay Old Harry and the chalk cliffs beneath the downs glinted in the sun.

He asked me when I was going back there. I shook my head, mute. After a while he asked if I was ever going to let Mark get close. For a moment I didn't understand, but then I stretched out my hands.

"There's blood on them, George," I told him.

He shook his head. "No there's not. Paxton was killed on active service. It just took the poor man one hell of a long time to die of his wounds. And in the meantime, you gave him at least some happiness." He squeezed both his hands in mine, and I cried for the longest time.

Soon afterwards, Mark went to Greece on business and I missed him more than I would have thought possible. I kept myself busy, getting the bistro ready to open in time for Easter, but all the same there was a huge hole in my life I didn't even know was there. Now he's back I need to do something about filling it.

I put my paperwork to one side and pull on my coat. The walk to the boatyard is a short one and I spot Mark almost immediately, washing the *Helen*'s anchor rope in a bucket of water. When he sees me he stands, his smile crinkling the corners of his eyes.

"Fancy taking her for a spin?" As Mark runs his hand along the *Helen*'s rail, something stirs deep in my stomach. I watch as his fingers trace the grain and nod.

He grins at me. "Then what are we waiting for? Let's get her into the water."

The breeze is sweeping over the Purbecks, ripping the clouds to reveal tantalising patches of blue and scattering waves across Poole Harbour. We are under sail almost straight away, the snap of canvas against the mast above our heads.

"Where do you want to go?" Mark asks. "Couple of loops around Brownsea Island?"

I shake my head. There's only one place to say what I want to say. "How about we pay a call on Old Harry?"

He looks away from me to fasten a rope around a cleat. "If you like."

Outside the shelter of the harbour there is more chop to the sea. We make a long tack around the training bar and out towards the Isle of Wight.

"It'll take a while," Mark tells me. "The wind's against us. Good sailing though."

After we come about, he hands me the tiller and drops to the bottom of the boat to sort out some of the spare ropes. With Bournemouth behind me, we are heading almost for Shell Bay and the start of the dunes. Figures dot the sand: brightly coloured jumpers and anoraks, dark blurs of dogs circling their feet.

This time I gauge the tack for myself. "Coming about," I call and Mark ducks as the boom swings across and the sail fills with a satisfying crack. The spray leaps in front of us, dusting Mark's hair, curling the strands clinging to the back of his neck into unruly springs. It's all I can do not to reach out and wrap them around the ends of my fingers.

He looks over his shoulder. "Well judged, Marie. Not bad for a rookie."

For the first time I am facing the cliffs. The sun is forcing its way through the clouds and although the sea is gunmetal in hue, the chalk has a hint of sparkle about it. Up, up, up, it climbs, into the arms of grass and gorse and brambles fringing its top. I reach down and touch my ankle, but the burning has long gone and the scars have faded to nothing.

As we approach Studland Bay the breeze drops. I think of Mark, last summer, bringing the *Helen* to a slow halt off Redend Point then folding the sail before jumping ashore, Troy splashing through the shallows at his feet. That's not for today. There's something else. Something more important.

I tack again and Mark joins me, perched on the rail and together we gaze over the Solent. A distant container ship noses between us and the Needles, and the white sails of half a dozen dinghies dot the water towards Cowes. A seagull swoops low over the *Helen*'s wake, its wings glinting as the sun finds its strength.

I hand the tiller to Mark. "I'd like to go quite close in if we can. Best you steer."

"I don't know, Marie — the tide's quite low."

I look over my shoulder. At the base of the cliff the rock ledge is visible as the waves drop back. It's where Paxton landed. Broke almost every bone in his body, they said. But I understand now.

"Just one more tack?"

He shakes his head. "I don't think so. Too close … what with the tide…"

"But you're such a good sailor."

"For God's sake, Marie — just leave it."

He won't look at me, so I reach out and touch his cheek. "Mark?"

"I can't be here, ok?" he mumbles. "Can't look at that bloody cliff. I'm surprised you can."

My hand drops away. "Let's get out of here then."

We don't speak again until we are mooring the *Helen* beside Swanage pier. I sit at the stern and watch Mark take down the sail, fumbling almost every fold. For God's sake, Marie — this isn't all about you. The boat wobbles as I stand to take the ties from him and wrap them around the bulging canvas.

"I'm sorry." I put my hand over his and it stills. "I'm so sorry. Oh, Mark — I've been so selfish… I didn't think… You've been so … patient with me. So wonderful…"

"How could I not be patient? You needed me to be patient. But going back there — it brought every single bad memory right to the surface. All the times I've watched you descend into some sort of hell where I can't reach you — all the times you've fought back so bravely but you've had to do it on your own because you couldn't tell me … and I thought I could learn to live with that. But sailing in that bay… I can't forgive…"

"But, Mark," I interrupt him. "There's nothing to forgive. I understand now. All winter I've been turning it around and around, worrying at it, trying to make sense… Paxton may have actually been killed on the cliffs at Studland, but who he was died in Iraq — I've no doubt about it."

Mark looks away from me, out to sea. "I wasn't blaming Paxton. He was a sick, sick, man. Although I can't deny there are moments when I hate him."

I pull my hand away. "Then you're blaming me? I thought you would … right at the beginning…"

"No, Marie, no." The *Helen* lurches as he spins back towards me. "Never — not in a million years. I can't forgive myself."

"But what for?"

Marks grips the bundle of sail so tightly his knuckles turn white. "For being too much of a coward to phone you that morning; for not saying, 'Let's go sailing today — let's start again.'"

"And I'd have said no." I promised myself there'd be no more lies between us, but this is the only way to release him. After spending all winter blaming myself — for not doing enough, for doing too much, for even being there. Now I understand. It would have happened anyway. Paxton almost said as much the day we went swimming: that he wouldn't die back in the US or in the desert — he couldn't go back there.

Mark breaks into my thoughts. "You'd have said no?"

I shrug. "It was coming up to August Bank Holiday — we were flat out — I would have asked if we could go another time."

"Really? And you'd have meant it?" Mark takes off his glasses and polishes them on his sleeve.

"Yes, really. God, Mark, I was halfway to being in love with you, even then. You're everything I never knew I wanted. And today… I had some silly romantic notion … the bay would be a good place to tell you … well … it's all behind me now and I'm … you know … ready… I mean, as long as you are…" I'm twisting the last of the ties around and around in my hand.

Finally I look Mark in the eye. "I've really messed it up, haven't I?"

The *Helen* rocks as the waves lap her hull. Mark reaches out, his fingers gentle as they cup my face.

"It's not too late, you know… I'm all ears…" He is steadying his voice, trying to smile. Oh my God — this dear, dear man. And I have no words. Instead I stand on tiptoe and taste the salt on his lips and the warmth inside his mouth. His arms around my back are firm, and as he pulls me to him I slide my hands under his fleece and meet the smoothness of flesh. The gulls split the silence overhead. The sun warms our shoulders. And I know — it's just the beginning.

HISTORICAL NOTES

All through the Second World War the Studland peninsular in Dorset was used for military experimentation. Although close to Bournemouth and Poole it was easy to restrict civilian access to the area after the ferry from Sandbanks ceased early in the war and the residents were given special passes to allow them to come and go.

In late 1943 American troops began to arrive in the area, a large number of them stationed at Swanage, the next bay along the coast. They were there to prepare for the invasion of Hitler's Fortress Europe, but in the main it was a time of boredom and waiting.

Studland bears certain geographical similarities to Normandy, with low dunes at one end and high cliffs at the other and it was partly this which led to it being chosen for major live ammunition practices in the run up to D-Day. There were many technical uncertainties which needed resolving, even at this late stage, including the creeping barrage, amphibious tanks and Hobart's Funnies — tanks specially adapted for landing on well defended beaches.

On 4th April 1944 Exercise Smash began with a tragedy. Amphibious Valentine tanks were launched in unusually choppy conditions for Studland, almost three miles from the beach. Seven of them were lost and six men from the 4/7th Royal Dragoon Guards died. This was a top secret exercise and their families didn't know the truth until almost sixty years later. The remains of the tanks are still underwater in in Studland Bay and were listed as part of the commemorations for the 75th anniversary of D-Day. A memorial to the men was unveiled on 4th April 2004 and an annual service is now held there.

On 18th April 1944 a live ammunition set piece battle was performed for the benefit of King George VI, Winston Churchill and high ranking British and American generals. They watched from Fort Henry, an enormous concrete bunker built for the purpose by Canadian military engineers. This time there were no casualties.

Exercise Smash lasted until mid May 1944, filling Studland with noise, smoke and cordite for five days a week as the dunes were pummelled with artillery. Firing stopped at five o'clock on a Friday, not because of some peculiar Britishness, but because the unexploded ammunition needed to be cleared.

The legacy of Smash was that the lessons learned — mainly by the British — saved many lives on D-Day itself. The amphibious tanks were launched much closer to the beaches and Hobart's Funnies were used to great effect to climb dunes and to detect mines. Somehow the lessons didn't get through to the Americans in the same way; the tanks at Omaha were launched too far out and only three out of the thirty-two made it ashore. It's probable that far fewer men — including many who had been stationed at Swanage — would have died if they had had their protection.

In the sixty years between D-Day and 2004 when *Another You* is set warfare changed greatly. The major conflicts involving American and British troops of the modern era were still fought on sand, but this time deserts rather than beaches. In the Iraq War American technicians like Paxton could find themselves in front line operations with very little training. The tragic and far-reaching psychological effects of combat on soldiers and those close to them was still not well understood, and its existence not acknowledged in the more macho units.

Thankfully in the last fifteen years we have come on leaps and bounds in our understanding of the mental effects of combat on soldiers and PTSD is treated not as weakness but as the illness it is. There are a number of charities helping injured military personnel but the one I support is Words for the Wounded, set up and run by author Margaret Graham. Find out more about their work at **www.wordsforthewounded.co.uk**.

A NOTE TO THE READER

The greatest pleasure for a writer is when someone reads and appreciates your book. Clearly, dear reader, you have made it this far, so I hope that means you've enjoyed *Another You* and I thank you for investing some of your valuable time in Marie's story.

I have a passion for history, in particular how the past reaches forwards and affects the present. I also have an open mind about the many ways this could happen, because I firmly believe if we think we know everything about our world and the way the human mind interprets it then we are being particularly arrogant.

Sacrifice in times of war takes many forms, some less obvious than others. For example my mother gave up her dreams of becoming a teacher to leave grammar school at fourteen to work collating details of casualties in the merchant navy. In *Another You*, George's wife Eileen lost her hearing in a bomb blast. Many other invisible losses are carried by those touched by warfare for the rest of their lives.

Another You was a rather different story until a friend arranged for me to meet a former paratrooper to talk about his experiences in Afghanistan and Iraq. He was open and frank about the mental effects of combat on men who were unprepared for it, in a system which didn't always help them, fighting wars that many people 'back home' thought of as unjust. The hour or so we spent together in a supermarket café just outside Guildford shaped Paxton, and therefore the book.

Reviews are important to authors. It's not about basking in five star glory (although that is rather nice), it's also about learning how to improve our work. Reviews don't have to be lengthy or erudite — a few words will do — but rest assured they are all appreciated and for this book I will be making a donation to 'Words for the Wounded' for each one posted on Amazon.

If you have any questions about *Another You* or would like to consider it for your book club, please contact me via **Twitter: @JaneCable**, **Facebook: Jane Cable, Author**, or **my website**. There is more background information about *Another You* and my other books there.

Jane Cable

janecable.com

Sapere Books is an exciting new publisher of brilliant fiction and popular history.

To find out more about our latest releases and our monthly bargain books visit our website:
saperebooks.com

Printed in Great
Britain
by Amazon